INTRODUCTION
Dark Love Stories from Cleveland

Ateenaged girl pimps out her more alluring classmate as sexual bait to steal possessions from the homes of wealthy Bratenahl men. A dirty cop in East Cleveland receives his just desserts for framing residents to cover up his own crimes. A reporter discovers that he can talk with the murdered and missing girls of Cleveland's past. These noir short stories are told in the language of Cleveland, a city like no other.

We have assembled a stellar cast of Cleveland writers to plumb the city's darker soul. Paula McLain, best-selling author of *The Paris Wife* and most recently *When the Stars Grow Dark*, and Mary Grimm, author of two volumes of fiction whose work has also appeared in the *New Yorker*, both weigh in with stories whose atmosphere and mood could only take place in this city. Shaker native Jill Bialosky, an executive editor at W.W. Norton, as well as a poet, novelist, and essayist, gives us a Shaker Heights noir in verse.

Edgar Award winner and Cleveland Heights native Daniel Stashower has written a period piece about a bygone era in Coventry's heyday. Abby L. Vandiver gives us a gritty piece about East Cleveland and dirty cops—she's not writing cozy this time.

We also asked local favorites to contribute. Susan Petrone, author of three novels and a contributor to ESPN, writes about Cleveland baseball from a unique and unexpected vantage. Horror writers D.M. Pulley and Dana Mc-Swain delve into what often feels like Cleveland's haunted history in Tremont and Little Italy.

Whatever your literary taste—literary fiction, horror, poetry, classic detective stories, mystery, etc.—as long as you like it dark, we have something you will love. These stories are as diverse as the city itself, so much so that Cleveland is really the central character of this book. They traverse it from the eastern suburbs to the western suburbs, from downtown and the Flats to Hough and East Cleveland—filled with murder and arson and kidnapping. Some stories are peopled by grifters, socialites, and sociopaths, but more often they center around "normal" people, individuals in the middle of the spectrum: a church's bookkeeper, a gay teenager in Parma, a software designer.

With flawed protagonists, fast plots, and snappy dialogue, classic noir often entertains with stories of besotted and debauched private detectives, and femmes fatales who drive men to their inevitable doom—or the reverse. In modern noir, the women are just as bad as the men. To paraphrase Otto Penzler, editor of mystery fiction and proprietor of the Mysterious Bookshop in Manhattan, noir is about sex and money and revenge, but mostly sex and money. There are no heroes in noir and no happy endings.

Cleveland is a working-class town, though its great institutions were founded by twentieth-century robber barons and magnates such as John D. Rockefeller, Howard Hanna, Joseph Eaton, Samuel Mather, and Louis Severance, who built conglomerates like Standard Oil and Republic Steel and grew their companies' wealth around the Cuyahoga River until the fish died and the water burned. Their tactics, employed to crush competitors, would have made a great noir story.

CLEVELAND NOIR

EDITED BY
MICHAEL RUHLMAN
&
MIESHA WILSON HEADEN

BROOKLYN, NEW YORK

Published by Akashic Books
©2023 Akashic Books
Copyright to the individual stories is retained by the authors.

Series concept by Tim McLoughlin and Johnny Temple
Map of Cleveland by Sohrab Habibion

Paperback ISBN: 978-1-63614-099-5
Hardcover ISBN: 978-1-63614-118-3
Library of Congress Control Number: 2022947073

Akashic Books
Brooklyn, New York
Instagram, Twitter, Facebook: AkashicBooks
E-mail: info@akashicbooks.com
Website: www.akashicbooks.com

For Dorothy and Thomas Wilson

ALSO IN THE AKASHIC NOIR SERIES

MIAMI NOIR, edited by LES STANDIFORD

MIAMI NOIR: THE CLASSICS,
edited by LES STANDIFORD

MILWAUKEE NOIR, edited by TIM HENNESSY

MISSISSIPPI NOIR, edited by TOM FRANKLIN

MONTANA NOIR, edited by JAMES GRADY
& KEIR GRAFF

MONTREAL NOIR (CANADA), edited by JOHN
McFETRIDGE & JACQUES FILIPPI

MOSCOW NOIR (RUSSIA),
edited by NATALIA SMIRNOVA & JULIA GOUMEN

MUMBAI NOIR (INDIA), edited by ALTAF TYREWALA

NAIROBI NOIR (KENYA), edited by PETER KIMANI

NEW HAVEN NOIR, edited by AMY BLOOM

NEW JERSEY NOIR, edited by JOYCE CAROL OATES

NEW ORLEANS NOIR, edited by JULIE SMITH

NEW ORLEANS NOIR: THE CLASSICS,
edited by JULIE SMITH

OAKLAND NOIR, edited by JERRY THOMPSON
& EDDIE MULLER

ORANGE COUNTY NOIR, edited by GARY PHILLIPS

PALM SPRINGS NOIR, edited by
BARBARA DeMARCO-BARRETT

PARIS NOIR (FRANCE), edited by AURÉLIEN MASSON

PARIS NOIR: THE SUBURBS, edited by HERVÉ
DELOUCHE

PHILADELPHIA NOIR, edited by CARLIN ROMANO

PHOENIX NOIR, edited by PATRICK MILLIKIN

PITTSBURGH NOIR, edited by KATHLEEN GEORGE

PORTLAND NOIR, edited by KEVIN SAMPSELL

PRAGUE NOIR (CZECH REPUBLIC),
edited by PAVEL MANDYS

PRISON NOIR, edited by JOYCE CAROL OATES

PROVIDENCE NOIR, edited by ANN HOOD

QUEENS NOIR, edited by ROBERT KNIGHTLY

RICHMOND NOIR, edited by ANDREW BLOSSOM,
BRIAN CASTLEBERRY & TOM DE HAVEN

RIO NOIR (BRAZIL), edited by TONY BELLOTTO

ROME NOIR (ITALY), edited by CHIARA STANGALINO
& MAXIM JAKUBOWSKI

SAN DIEGO NOIR, edited by MARYELIZABETH HART

SAN FRANCISCO NOIR, edited by PETER MARAVELIS

SAN FRANCISCO NOIR 2: THE CLASSICS,
edited by PETER MARAVELIS

SAN JUAN NOIR (PUERTO RICO),
edited by MAYRA SANTOS-FEBRES

SANTA CRUZ NOIR, edited by SUSIE BRIGHT

SANTA FE NOIR, edited by ARIEL GORE

SÃO PAULO NOIR (BRAZIL),
edited by TONY BELLOTTO

SEATTLE NOIR, edited by CURT COLBERT

SINGAPORE NOIR, edited by CHERYL LU-LIEN TAN

SOUTH CENTRAL NOIR, edited by GARY PHILLIPS

STATEN ISLAND NOIR, edited by PATRICIA SMITH

ST. LOUIS NOIR, edited by SCOTT PHILLIPS

STOCKHOLM NOIR (SWEDEN), edited by
NATHAN LARSON & CARL-MICHAEL EDENBORG

ST. PETERSBURG NOIR (RUSSIA), edited by
NATALIA SMIRNOVA & JULIA GOUMEN

SYDNEY NOIR (AUSTRALIA), edited by JOHN DALE

TAMPA BAY NOIR, edited by COLETTE BANCROFT

TEHRAN NOIR (IRAN), edited by SALAR ABDOH

TEL AVIV NOIR (ISRAEL), edited by ETGAR KERET
& ASSAF GAVRON

TORONTO NOIR (CANADA), edited by JANINE ARMIN
& NATHANIEL G. MOORE

TRINIDAD NOIR (TRINIDAD & TOBAGO), edited by LISA
ALLEN-AGOSTINI & JEANNE MASON

TRINIDAD NOIR: THE CLASSICS
(TRINIDAD & TOBAGO), edited by EARL LOVELACE
& ROBERT ANTONI

TWIN CITIES NOIR, edited by JULIE SCHAPER
& STEVEN HORWITZ

USA NOIR, edited by JOHNNY TEMPLE

VANCOUVER NOIR (CANADA), edited by SAM WIEBE

VENICE NOIR (ITALY), edited by MAXIM JAKUBOWSKI

WALL STREET NOIR, edited by PETER SPIEGELMAN

ZAGREB NOIR (CROATIA), edited by IVAN SRŠEN

FORTHCOMING

HAMBURG NOIR (GERMANY), edited by JAN KARSTEN

HONOLULU NOIR, edited by CHRIS McKINNEY

JERUSALEM NOIR (EAST),
edited by RAWYA BURBARA

JERUSALEM NOIR (WEST), edited by MAAYAN EITAN

NATIVE NOIR, edited by DAVID HESKA WANBLI WEIDEN

SACRAMENTO NOIR, edited by JOHN FREEMAN

VIRGIN ISLANDS NOIR, edited by TIPHANIE YANIQUE
& RICHARD GEORGES

CLEVELAND

LAKE ERIE

DOWNTOWN

SETTLER'S LANDING

THE FLATS

GORDON SQUARE

LAKEWOOD

TREMONT

90

71

METROPARKS ZOO

HOLY CROSS CEMETERY

PARMA

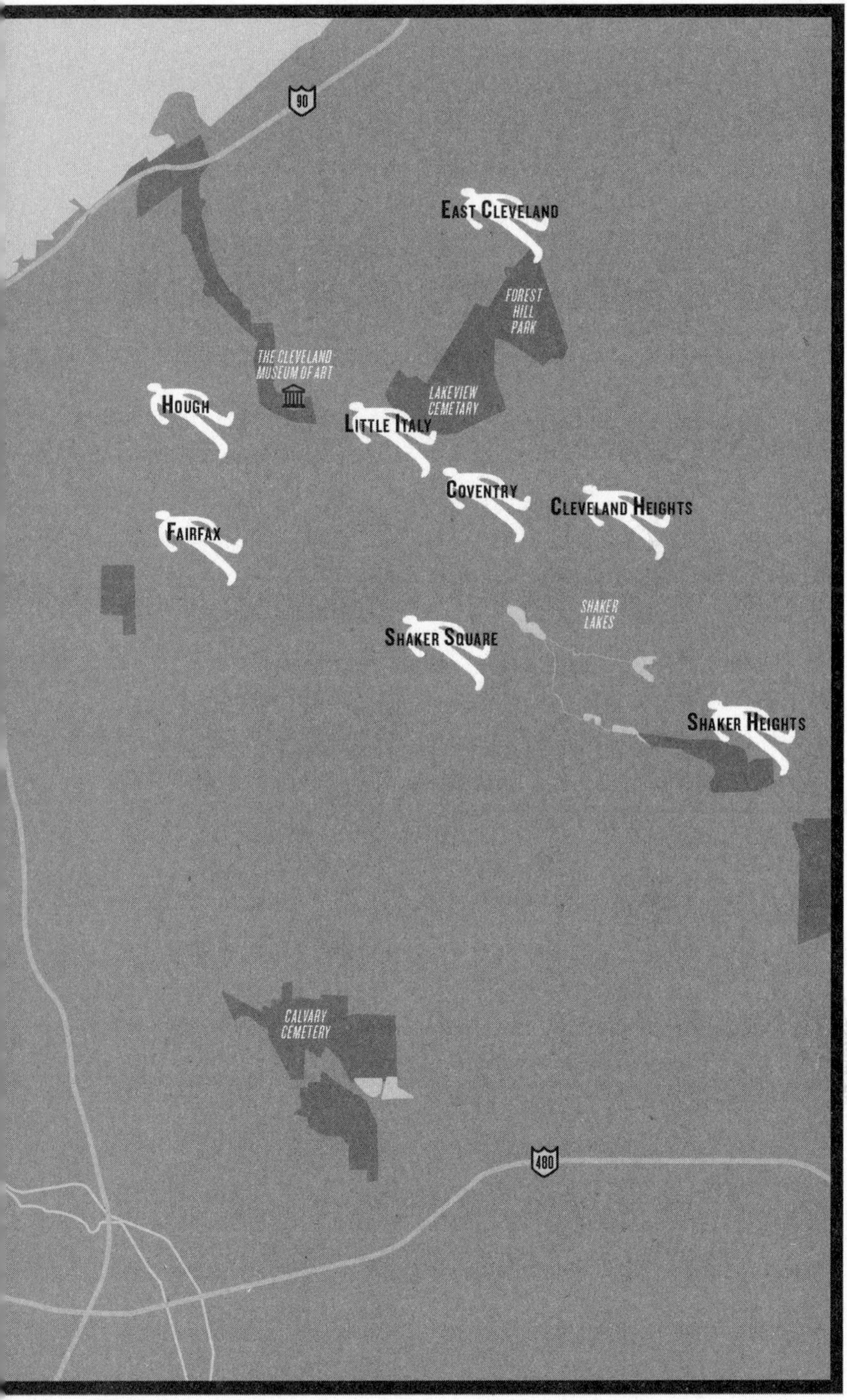
90
East Cleveland
Forest Hill Park
The Cleveland Museum of Art
Lakeview Cemetary
Hough
Little Italy
Coventry
Cleveland Heights
Fairfax
Shaker Lakes
Shaker Square
Shaker Heights
Calvary Cemetery
480

TABLE OF CONTENTS

PART III: THE TRENDY

PART IV: THE HEIGHTS

It's this mix of the wealthy and the working class that makes the city—an urban center of brick and girders surrounded by verdant suburbs—a perfect backdrop for lawlessness. Cleveland has certainly seen its share of high-profile crime. Eliot Ness, Cleveland's director of public safety in the 1930s, hunted unsuccessfully for the "torso murderer" who killed and dismembered twelve people in Kingsbury Run, the area now known as the Flats, then populated by bars, brothels, flophouses, and gambling dens. The famous disappearance of Beverly Potts in the early 1950s on Cleveland's west side made national headlines. The sensational murder of Marilyn Sheppard in Bay Village and the imprisonment and eventual acquittal of her husband, the surgeon Sam Sheppard, became the basis for a popular television drama, *The Fugitive*. And, of course, the mass murderer Anthony Sowell, who choked eleven Black women to death and disposed of their bodies around his home, and Ariel Castro, who held three young women as sex slaves, are stories all too fresh in our memory.

The noir stories in this volume hit all these same notes, and their geographies reflect the history of the city and its politics, its laws, poverty, alienation, racism, crime, and violence.

We love Cleveland. And in many ways, this is what *Cleveland Noir* is really about: love. As the great James M. Cain, author of such classic noirs as *Double Indemnity* and *The Postman Always Rings Twice*, once told the *Paris Review*, "I write love stories."

These stories are no different. The plots of virtually every one teeter explicitly on this fulcrum: erotic love, romantic love, love of a brother, love of a son or daughter or a mother, love of baseball, love of the church.

So, welcome to this collection of dark love stories from the great city of Cleveland.

Michael Ruhlman & Miesha Wilson Headen
April 2023

PART I

City Center

LOVE ALWAYS

by Paula McLain
Settler's Landing

After Gwen's body was found in Settler's Landing Park, I crawled out of my bedroom window and onto the fire escape, letting the icy metal brand my ass and my backbone while I stared at the moon. It looked about as cold and remote as I felt, like a frosted, misshapen eyeball watching me to see why I hadn't cried yet.

That was two years ago. Long enough for me to have plenty of time to think about the ways I messed up, and all the things that might be wrong with me. But I did love Gwen. We had important things in common. Things you would have had to look way past our faces and bodies to know, through to the sadness in her that matched up with mine. The ladders of hidden scars. The compulsive loneliness that made us crave things we couldn't have.

Gwen was actually almost too beautiful for her own good. She had a black Irish mother and a Colombian father, a genetic mash-up that gave her creamy skin and enormous sea-blue eyes. Her hair was black and so shiny, it didn't seem real. Most of the time she wore it up in a knot the size of a Cinnabon, which opened the view to her shoulders. They were narrow and delicate, and her clavicle stood out with hollows that looked fragile but also hot in the just-shredded-enough Henleys she wore with snug vintage jeans. She was like a Hollister ad, but bruised where you couldn't see, which made her irresistible to pretty much anyone with a pulse, male or female, animal or otherwise.

I'm not sure Gwen really knew how beautiful she was or how much power she had at her disposal. If she did know, it was only for seconds at a time, before doubt crept in. If someone complimented her, the praise seemed to graze over the surface of her just briefly before blowing away, like an eyelash Gwen could make a wish on, but never for herself.

She fooled most people into thinking she had life figured out, but not me. When she showed up at Promise Academy, the alternative high school I'd been at since I was fourteen, after being deemed too emotionally disruptive for the standard route, she seemed too smart and sensitive to be there with the burnouts and baby hoodlums and pregnant girls. She told me she'd flunked out of her regular high school in Brecksville, before her mom moved downtown, but I had a feeling she was lying.

I was right about that, as it turns out. But the thing about Gwen that surprised me most was how malleable she was, eager to have things decided for her. She was also needy in a way she tried to hide, the way I had been when I first moved to the Flats, back in middle school. I could sense she had to have a lot of attention directed at her, and since I didn't have a girlfriend at the time, I took all of that energy and gave it to Gwen, zooming in on her, and listening while she told me things, so that she felt like a worthwhile person, at least when we were together.

We met in October and by Halloween were hanging out after school most days, either down on my side of the river, or at her apartment, which was on Superior near the viaduct, only a ten-minute walk or so from where I lived with my mom, Beverly, on 10th Street.

Gwen and I were both only children of single mothers but the similarity ended there. Mine was housebound and mildly schizophrenic, addicted to Web MD, tin foil, and the deep past. If Beverly wasn't chatting with strangers online about mysterious rashes and migrating symptoms, she was having elaborately involved conversations in her mind with people she hadn't seen or heard from in twenty years.

For her, I was still six-year-old Ally in a pink leotard, doing backbends and handstands on the lawn of a house that had been foreclosed on a lifetime ago, my blond ponytail like a whip swinging upside down and sideways. When the real me would walk in the door after school, Beverly would look confused. Also sad. Also disappointed. She would shake her head, thinking, *What happened to you?* Or, *You used to be so pretty.* It wasn't hard to read her mind from the expression on her face, because enough of the time, she would say these things out loud.

Gwen's mom Audrey was a bartender at the Flat Iron, the oldest Irish pub in Cleveland. Before AA and God straightened her ass out, Audrey used to be a terrible drunk. A bar didn't seem like the likeliest place for an ex-drunk to stay sober to me, but Gwen said that being around liquor bottles made Audrey feel safe, like standing in a lion's mouth surrounded by familiar sets of teeth. It was one of the first times I realized how smart Gwen could be about people.

"Plus, it keeps chaos in her life," she said. "Drunks love drama. Particularly dry drunks."

"What's a dry drunk?"

"Someone who hasn't dealt with all the shit that caused them to drink in the first place. So the booze is basically beside the point."

"Well, I think your mom is cool."

"Yeah, I do too."

Gwen's room wasn't bigger or that much nicer than mine, but for some reason I liked myself better there, and felt a lot more like a seventeen-year-old than I did at home. We would talk on her bed, eating veggie hot pockets and drinking vodka from little Western-themed shot glasses Audrey had a whole collection of. I would refill my tiny cup until I felt both slippery and solid, slow and accelerated, while Gwen would sit tucked into the corner where her twin bed met the wall, surrounded by pillows, looking like a ballerina in a plush music box.

One day when we were hanging out there, she told me how her dad had left her mom before she was two. Lots of people have holes inside them for no reason, but I could see that Gwen's started with him taking off on them.

"Where is he now?" I asked.

She shrugged in a hollow way. "I haven't seen him since I was eight. Not since he left me alone in his apartment overnight and my mom revoked his visitation rights."

"That sucks. I'm really sorry."

Later I learned that her dad had been addicted to painkillers, and often neglected her to score fentanyl, or whatever he could get his hands on. Gwen never sounded like she hated her dad for letting her down, though. Instead of being an actual person, one who had disappointed Gwen time and again, he was more of a symbol for her. An emptiness at the center of a pit of longing.

I was starting to figure out that even though Gwen was fucking gorgeous, she was also perforated and leaking from a hundred different places. Wherever she went, she left a trail that certain people could pick up subliminally. Most were middle-aged men, dad types who sensed that missing piece in her without knowing what it was. They just had a feeling that they could have her. I don't know how to explain it better than to say that Gwen gave off the vibe of a hitchhiker ready to go wherever you were going. You didn't even have to tell her. You could just drive.

It didn't seem to be an accident that Gwen had turned up when she did, and that life had bashed us around in ways that lined up so meaningfully. Gwen needed a manager, someone to harness the powerful magnet she had, and keep her out of trouble. I happened to be specifically equipped to be that person.

If you've never been to the Flat Iron, I'm not sure I can completely explain how a place that's so old and clearly haunted can also feel somehow perfect. The St. Patrick's Day–green carpet is ancient and sticky, and the main room is cut up into different levels, with pipes that hang from the low ceiling. You get the feeling that things have happened here. It's not a Chili's in a strip mall, in other words. One of the best stories is about a woman named Irene who was killed in a fire as she slept upstairs, sometime in the early 1900s. I was always hoping she would show up for us, particularly on quiet nights, but she never did. Other lucky things happened at the bar, though. Like the night we met Candace.

It was February, maybe four months after Gwen and I had started hanging out, and we had gone down there to watch *Jeopardy!* and see if we could beg a sandwich out of the cook. It was snowing hard outside, thick wet flakes that painted the corners of the windows and frosted the tops of the cars on the street. Besides a few regulars and us, the place was mostly empty except for an overdressed fiftysomething woman who had been drinking martinis the whole time we were there.

She clearly didn't belong in a joint like the Flat Iron, but we didn't really pay much attention to her until she slid off her stool onto the floor.

"I guess she's feeling no pain," Gwen said, as Audrey squatted over the woman, trying to bring her back around.

"Except the pain that brought her here," Audrey said, sounding like the Obi-Wan Kenobi of recovery. She patted the woman's face, which was puttied and powdered over with expensive makeup, and the woman came to, blinking like a baby in her pearls, wide-eyed and surprised to be alive.

There wasn't a smudge on her Chanel jacket or crocodile-print loafers. Somehow her mascara wasn't even smeared as the three of us worked to get her up off the floor.

"You're so nice," she slurred as she found her feet.

"Is there someone I can call?" Audrey asked, prompting the woman to pat herself down in an exaggerated way, looking for a cell phone that seemed to have gone missing.

"I'm sorry," she said, and seemed about to cry.

Another sort of bartender would have called a cab or an Uber, even though everything about the woman screamed, *Take advantage of me!* Audrey had a different idea. Gwen and I would drive her home in her own car, and then Audrey would swing by and pick us up in an hour when she closed the bar. Together, we managed to find the key fob to her white Benz SUV, thankfully parked just outside, and her driver's license. Her name was Candace Rankine, and she lived at One Bratenahl Place, an address that was well-known by Cleveland standards, because it was right on the lake. It also meant money.

We took St. Clair east on Audrey's advice, because the snow was heavy and I-90 would be a mess. Candace was out cold in the back, sprawled across the seat, and Gwen was on the passenger side, swallowed up by good leather, and letting out little expletives as she found all of the controls. The steering wheel was heated and felt squishy under my quickly warming hands. The mirrors cleared themselves, releasing slush like dirty lace as we inched along in time with the traffic lights, through Asiatown and into Glenville, past ugly mini-marts and ravaged-looking salons.

"What does *No Copper* mean?" Gwen asked, meaning the message we'd seen spray-painted on half a dozen crumbling houses.

I thought she was kidding, but then remembered she'd come from Brecksville. "Copper is worth money. Crack hounds will bust through drywall with nothing but their own hands or maybe a butter knife."

"Shit, that's dark."

"Makes our piece of Cleveland look pretty fucking tops, right?"

Candace's body juddered in the backseat as we hit one last pothole, and then passed under the elevated train tracks that separated the wasteland of 105th Street from Bratenahl Village. Instantly there were full-growth trees, glazed white from the storm. Where had the fucking elfin forest come from? And the tennis courts next to the police station? Even the snow was cleaner here, as if crews regularly tidied the sludge before they could offend the mansion owners we glided past, each palace unnecessarily large behind elaborate gates and wrought-iron bars.

"To keep out the riffraff?" Gwen threw out.

"We're here anyway." I laughed. "And we have a key card."

Candace lived alone, we soon learned, in one of the two high-rise condo buildings that stood side by side, jutting straight up from a park that was gated off to guarantee further security. Getting inside the gate and front door weren't a problem since we had her key card, but upstairs was another story. She was like Silly Putty in the elevator, flopping between Gwen and me as we tried to wake her up enough to do her own walking. Meanwhile, I had to keep my eyes in my head once we got inside her condo unit.

The floor was glassy-looking marble tile. Along one wall, a gigantic framed mirror made the room go double. A sectional the size of my whole apartment was covered with tasseled pillows and shearling throws, all of it plush as fuck. Heavy coasters and art books on the end tables. A bar with cut crystal. And all of it for this one person, who wouldn't remember anything tomorrow, certainly not that she had brought it all on herself.

We wrestled Candace into the likeliest direction for the master bedroom, taking a few wrong turns along the way. When we got there and flipped on the lights, Gwen shot me a *What the hell?* look. The room was like an *Elegant Living* magazine cover, with a bed on a raised platform, textured bedding, and legions of coordinated accent pillows. Deep white pile rugs everywhere. A chaise longue nearby in case she ever needed to stop and lie down midway to the bathroom. Why did Candace get to have so much? It didn't even seem to be making her happy. Not the way she had been drinking, using gin like novocaine.

We sat her on the side of the bed as best we could, took off her shoes and jacket, and then rolled her beneath the duvet like a little burrito. Only then did Candace rouse a little.

"You're being too nice to me," she said without opening her eyes. Not *so* nice, but too nice—which was an interesting way to put it. "I've been awfully tired lately," she went on, slurring gloomily. "You know what I mean?"

"Life is hard," I said. Then I turned out the bedside light and met Gwen's eyes. A little ripple passed between us as she read my mind, and then questioned me silently. An entire conversation flared up mutely, in micromovements and code. *I'm driving*, I told her with my thoughts. *Just get in.*

Gwen had never stolen anything beyond nail polish and candy bars, I could tell as she trailed me into Candace's closet. She couldn't stop touching the clothes, rows of silk blouses on padded hangers, all in shades of white and off-white and beige and tan. It did calm the mind just to look at them, I had to admit, but we only had about fifteen minutes before Audrey would be downstairs to pick us up. While Gwen petted cashmere sweaters, I rifled through the drawers of the built-in and Candace's vanity table, and found a monogrammed case full of jewelry. There was a Rolex I quickly pocketed, along with an emerald cocktail ring, two sets of pearl earrings, and a diamond tennis bracelet that was so thin it trembled like mercury. As I held it up to Gwen, I noticed two sapphires near the clasp, where almost no one would even notice them.

That's when I knew I wasn't going to feel bad later. We had accidentally landed on a planet where the air was too thin for guilt to populate. How could all of this wealth sit in such close proximity to houses needing to advertise *No Copper*? It was almost obscene. Even Candace had said we were being too nice to her, as if she realized the unfairness. Maybe she *wanted* us to pull a Robin Hood maneuver to even things out? Coiling the bracelet around my index finger like the world's tiniest jeweled python, I pushed it into the front pocket of Gwen's sprayed-on jeans, and waited to see if she was going to push back. But all she did was close her eyes for a minute and lean sideways, just long enough to press her face into a bolero jacket made of rabbit fur.

I never got over that night at Candace's, in a way. It was like standing at the top of a mountain and realizing, for the first time, just how much better things were on the other side. When I brought up the idea to Gwen that we could set up a kind of business, doing what we did to Candace, she said she couldn't imagine ever feeling okay about robbing someone.

"What if it was a scumbag who sort of deserved it?" I suggested. Stealing from women would be a waste of our assets—namely Gwen. It made so much more sense to put her magnet to good use. As I saw it, if some rich middle-aged asshole was going to be disgusting enough to hit on a sixteen-year-old, wasn't he asking for what he got?

"We could use the date-rape drug on them," I continued, solidifying my plan. "Wouldn't that be hilarious? We'd be like vigilantes."

"Except we'd be fishing for *them*." Gwen seemed uncomfortable. "Plus, how would we get our hands on roofies?"

"There's a kid named Nate who drifted through Promise last year. I hear he sells street drugs now. He might give us a deal. Also, some of those pawnshops down on Lorraine probably wouldn't give a shit what we were trying to offload, let alone where we found it. First we have to get you a really legit-looking fake ID, though."

"If we're using bars to look for men, we can't go to the Flat Iron."

"Why would we need to?" I threw back. "We wouldn't even need to hit the same place twice. The Flats has the highest concentration of bars in the Midwest. Go, Cleveland."

Gwen flicked her eyes at me. "And the roofies are so we can get them back to their car or house or whatever without them remembering?"

"Or punching us, yeah."

"You've got this all worked out then, don't you, Al?"

"That's my job." I smiled at her. "That's why I'm here. You just have to look pretty."

The first time we tried it, everything went off so perfectly I started thinking we should have gotten wise to our opportunities a long time ago. It was a Thursday night, just after nine thirty, when Gwen went into Shooters in a belly-baring turtleneck, tiny skirt, and thigh-high boots. I'd prepped her to look for the right sort of guy, a little older but clean, business-y, in a suit or nice slacks that looked expensive. She should pay attention to shoes and watches, and avoid anyone too big or edgy looking.

Once she found her target, she let him buy her a drink and pretended to get tipsy fast. Also touchy, flirtatious. Once he was responsive, giving off all the signs that he thought he had a sure thing on his hands, she doctored his drink when he went to the bathroom. I was waiting outside for Gwen's text that they would be coming out soon. The whole fishing expedition took an hour and a half, tops. When I saw her exiting with the perfect-looking mark, already staggering and draped over her shoulder, I felt like a proud mother bird.

I followed the two of them through the parking lot behind the bar, hanging back as they reached his massive black Lexus. Within five minutes, she flashed his headlights, the signal for *all clear*. By the time I reached the passenger side, Gwen was already stepping out with his wallet, a chunky platinum watch, and a gold signet ring. Through the darkened glass, the guy was passed out over the steering wheel, hugging it like a life preserver.

It was like taking candy from a baby, as they say. All the way home, we couldn't stop laughing.

We fell into a routine after that, as February turned to March, sticking to weeknights, when the kind of men we sought were more likely to be out, and alone rather than with buddies. Occasionally the dosing got tricky. Either Gwen slipped him too much and he passed out at the bar, or she gave him too little and he didn't go down when they reached his car. Or didn't seem fazed at all.

The first time we struck out like this, Gwen had no choice but to give the guy head before she crawled out of the car, looking defeated.

"Listen," I told her when we got back to my house, "maybe the R-2 was weak or something. I'll talk to Nate."

"I just want a shower."

While she cleaned up, I made her hot chocolate, microwaving the cup until the undissolved powder began to smell like burnt-chocolate lava, the way she liked. I stayed over with her that night, though I knew Beverly might think the aliens had finally gotten me. It was the right thing to do, since Gwen was so rattled.

I stripped down to my T-shirt and boxer shorts and laid next to her in bed while she stared at the ceiling. I assumed she was trying to rewrite the events of the night in her head, but after a while she surprised me by saying, "You never told me about your dad, Al. Who was he?"

"All I know is that his name was Ross. Not much to go on. He sounds like an accountant, maybe. Or a cable guy."

She turned toward me on the pillow, and something squeezed shut in my chest. A fist or a flower. "The Missing Fathers Club," she said without irony. "Maybe that's why we're such good friends."

I couldn't have told you why I was so *full*, suddenly. That was the only word for the feeling that came over me. "I guess so."

Then she said, "I thought I was going to vomit before."

I knew she meant in the car with the guy, and waited to hear if she was going to say more, but she didn't. "When shit happens that I don't know what to do with," I finally offered, "I just decide that the person who did those things isn't me. I'm only watching. The real me, I mean."

Gwen let out a breath I didn't know she'd been holding, and said, "I do that too. Sometimes it doesn't work so well, though."

"Yeah," was all I could say. Then she turned her back so she could scoot up against my body like we were litter mates, out in the cold. And we were, I guess, or that's what I was thinking as we both fell asleep in her tiny bed.

March turned to April, and everything started to run smoothly for us again. The weather improved, making things less unpleasant for Gwen in her tiny top and skirt, and she started getting consistent about estimating body weight in terms of the dosing, and so made fewer mistakes. We began feeling bolder and decided to experiment with driving a guy home, the way we had with Candace, to see if our take might improve. Our trial run happened in the middle of April, with a guy Gwen had picked up at the Alley Cat. He was a little stocky for my comfort, but everything went smoothly. With Mr. Wonderful laid out in the passenger seat of his Rover and Gwen in the back reading me directions from her phone, we ended up along the lake, about a mile away from our old friend Candace's house, this time at the Shoreby Club.

After clicking the gate opener attached to his visor, I pulled into his spotless garage, and we left him motionless in the passenger seat while we went through the house. Thankfully, it wasn't alarmed. I'm not sure what we would have done then, but as it was, we felt safe going room to room, pausing longest in the den, where a collection of vintage baseball cards were housed in a glass case, like a small terrarium. The cards alone were enough of a jackpot, but he was a watch collector too, it turned out, with a dozen or more fancy timepieces perched on velvet holders. While I stuffed everything into my backpack, Gwen wandered into the master bathroom. When I ducked my head in there, she was marveling at the shower, which had no door. It was the whole room, with all sorts of nozzles and heads, and a control box. She pushed buttons until several of the nozzles began to hiss and pop, and then steam rose in wet clouds. Gwen pushed up the sleeve of her sweater, and swept her arm back and forth through the mist like a ballerina. She looked beautiful, surrounded by veils of fog, even with a bruise on her forearm where some other guy had recently grabbed her a little too hard. It glowed like a dark plum in the mist.

Afterward, we left the keys on the dining room table and went out through the front door. Spring was coming. You could smell it in the air, distant but rising, like a bulb pushing up from below. Along Shoreby Drive, strings of posh condos were connected at the back by a landing—empty for now— where the residents' summer boats would dock. Ready for sunset cruises and Sunday get-togethers. In the distance, we could see a stone clubhouse that looked like a castle. Putting off the cab ride home, Gwen and I walked toward it and up the circular drive to get a better look. We were ten or fifteen yards from the front entrance when I caught the beam of a moving flashlight. It was the night watchman, standing just inside the door. Before we could even properly startle, the man lifted his chin at us, as if saying, *Hello, how do you do?*

Without a word, we walked past him and down the other side of the circle, hardly believing that we'd just passed as the daughters of one of these rich families. It wasn't until we were outside the gates and Gwen was pulling up Uber on her phone that we let ourselves have a laugh about it.

"What if this really was our neighborhood?" Gwen asked, her face alight in the glow of her iPhone.

"Right? That would be something."

"Do you think it's like a roll of the dice or something? Why certain people get all the luck?"

"Seems that way sometimes."

"Yeah," she agreed, all of her humor having faded. "It really does."

Maybe a month after that, Gwen started to act distracted and antsy. I thought it was about the school year ending soon. Gwen would be getting her GED, while I would stay stuck at Promise Academy for at least another semester if not a full year. Secretly I'd been thinking about not going back at all. Things were going so well for us. Who cared about a piece of paper if I could get by without it?

Then one afternoon, when we were about to head over to the casino to meet up with a guy at the loading dock who'd started buying the credit cards we brought him, Gwen wanted to stop at a store for cigarettes. She came out with rounded shoulders. Her eyes seemed to flit past me. "I bought a bus ticket," she finally said.

"What? Just now?"

"A few weeks ago." She thumbed her lighter, still not

meeting my gaze. "I have an aunt in Bozeman who says I can come live with her."

"Why would you want to do that?"

"To stay out of trouble. I don't know. You probably think I'm stupid."

"And Audrey's okay with that?"

"It was her idea."

I felt disoriented and naked, and not in an abstract way. She'd just taken everything that had been covering me up, including my skin, and ripped it off like a gum wrapper before wadding it up in a ball. Suddenly I couldn't see my options. "What if I came with you?" I was trying to sound neutral, though I already knew it would be hard to play that line for long. That at some point I might stoop to begging.

Gwen said, "You'd hate Bozeman, Al. It's too small for you. We wouldn't be doing stuff like this."

"Then we can pick someplace else. Wherever you want. I don't even care."

She drew in hard on her cigarette, holding the smoke before directing it at the sky. "I want to be different."

"What does that mean? Everyone wants to be different."

"No, I mean I *have* to." Her voice vibrated like a harp string, but didn't waver. Didn't break. "When I'm with the guys we pick up, I don't feel bad, really. I'm not sure I feel anything. It's like I'm not in my body half the time."

I stared at the center of her face, trying to understand how the ground had shifted between us. She didn't seem to be talking about the sex that sometimes had to happen for her to get away from someone safely, but about all of it. Our whole arrangement. At the edge of my periphery, I glimpsed a tiny flash, a pop in the air as if a blood vessel had burst somewhere over the river. "What are you saying, Gwen?"

"I'm not sure."

I held incredibly still, wondering if she was finally going to tell me why she'd gotten kicked out of Brecksville. And she did.

I listened—leaning in to *show* her I was still listening—as she relayed the details. A parked car and her AP history teacher. He was married, with a baby, and had been fired. But there'd been rumors of others too, which she didn't want to talk about, and so they'd moved. Gwen tugged at the strings of her snug hoodie as she finished explaining herself, her eyes huge and dim. Over her shoulder, the river was so dark it seemed to represent negative space. A crooked ribbon of nothing, going nowhere.

I didn't know what to say. Even *I'm sorry* would have come out wrong, because I also wanted to tell Gwen that she had everything backward. People didn't need to *want* change, let alone chase it all the way to Bozeman. Change just *happened*, and no one had any choice about it. I had been a tumbler once, I could have pointed out if I'd needed any backup evidence. A pretty chatterbox doing roundoffs in the living room and making my grandma smile. My mom too. That was before Beverly experienced a breakdown that lasted several years. Lasted all the way to Cleveland, in fact, where my grandparents didn't even have our address. I wasn't allowed to call them, and wouldn't have anyway. Because I'd stopped being Ally.

All through middle school, I had grown and spread, my middle bulging. My thighs pressing out against my jeans. I was like dough expanding in a bowl, left under a towel overnight, in a place that didn't know me, or care if I used to be cute and pretty. I couldn't stop the process or even slow it down. Pustules of acne erupted, and my hair grew lank. Soon

I didn't recognize a single element of the old me, and I knew there would never be any going back to the cartwheels, or the white chenille bedspread in my room, or the sugar bowl in the kitchen smelling of Sanka crystals. I had spilled over the edges of myself, past where Green Bay could touch me. Of course I'd been emotionally disruptive at school during that time. My whole life had been snatched away and wasn't coming back.

On the curb, as I spun inward, Gwen looked at me, those enormous eyes now like magnifying lenses. "I wasn't ever going to just run off without telling you. I wouldn't do that."

"I know," I said, though I didn't.

"Maybe I won't even go," she said.

"You have a bus ticket."

"I've done that before." She sighed and dropped her cigarette, grinding it under the toe of her platform Nike. "I'm just *tired*."

The word chimed in my inner ear, and there was Candace, called up like a genie, or our first ghost. I considered being a bitch and telling Gwen that life was hard. But I didn't need to say it. Life *was* fucking hard, and we were only sixteen and seventeen.

"We'll just do tonight, then? One last push?" I offered, not sure if she'd agree or spit at me. Walk into Cleveland's wan version of a sunset.

Gwen seemed to hover for a moment, shifting in several directions without moving at all. As if trying to recalibrate, or balance the unbalanceable factors of us. Finally, she pocketed her cigarettes, shoved her hands deeply into her jacket. "Sure, Al. I know this isn't what you bargained for."

"It's okay," I said vaguely, feeling sorry for myself. How had things flipped so that she was doing me a favor instead of the other way around? "I'll see you later."

* * *

"What does it feel like?" I asked Gwen one time, back at the beginning. "To have people want you?" As soon as I said the words, I felt idiotic and wished I'd kept my mouth shut.

She had only shrugged. Even then, she'd been lost. Ransomed away to some dark place, but trying to fight her way back.

I didn't see Gwen for our last hurrah that night, or ever again. A little after seven o'clock on May 20, two hours before we were supposed to meet up, Gwen was cutting through Settler's Landing Park, probably headed to the Flat Iron to get something to eat, when she ran into the guy from Shoreby Drive, the stocky one with the baseball card collection that had turned out to be a windfall, netting us nine hundred dollars. It was probably worth ten times that, at least.

There were few witnesses, and no one could say for sure whether he meant to hurt her or just scare her. She had tried to run, it seemed, before he backed her against a ledge at the border of the park where the grass stopped. The drop to the concrete landing below was only four feet. She'd tripped, one witness said. Another said he'd pushed her. Either way, she'd cracked her skull in the fall and died before the ambulance came, sprawled out like a broken doll just a few feet from the river.

His name was Jeffrey Ostrom, I was reminded by the newspapers, once he was arrested and awaiting trial for Gwen's death. Beverly had started watching the papers like a hawk. She's the one who spotted the interview he gave some reporter at the *Plain Dealer*, saying that Gwen was a prostitute who had robbed him of almost thirty thousand dollars worth of memorabilia, but that he hadn't meant to kill her.

I'd been questioned, like a lot of kids from Promise. I

showed up at Gwen's vigil at Settler's Landing Park too, the day Jeffrey Ostrom was convicted. By then, I didn't know if he was a murderer who deserved the twenty-five years he had been sentenced, or a victim who had inadvertently crossed our paths. Either way, he would never return to his palace with a steam shower and night watchman. Either way, Gwen was gone forever.

At the spot on the landing where she'd died, people who didn't know her began leaving Gwen candles and flowers and teddy bears. More candles arrived the night of the vigil, carried there and held while Raquel G., a girl we barely knew from Promise, read a poem she'd written, and Manny from my life-skills class sang a rap song about Gwen that actually could have been about anyone. I didn't say a word, just thought about her face. Her wide eyes, shaped like a cat's. The freckle at the tapered end of her left eyebrow, like a perfectly placed but mysterious bit of punctuation. I thought about how amazing she was, and I waited to cry, wondering why I hadn't yet. If I was too messed up inside to grieve for her. If the damage had been done, maybe, long before she was ever in the picture.

There were lots of little things that made Gwen specifically her. You could only see moons on the cuticles of her thumbnails, not the other fingers. She'd eaten pigeon once, in a fancy restaurant, and liked it. But then went home and ate mushroom-flavored ramen, which she liked just as much. Her left foot was longer than her right by a centimeter. Her first dog's name was Bean, a Cavalier King Charles spaniel with bulging eyes and velvety ears.

And this too: she had almost made it to Bozeman, to another life.

No one gets to stay the same. I realize that more than anyone, probably, but now I can see that the changes in Gwen had been happening on the inside, where they wouldn't show. Maybe the whole time we were together. I could have been some sort of tipping point for her, even. The last straw that made her realize she had to get away. Weighing that possibility was one of the hardest things of all. Because Gwen had been a catalyst for me too, only in the other direction. Which maybe she knew, and maybe she didn't. I had no idea, actually.

There was one night in particular I would come to replay in my mind for a long time. Maybe it will be with me forever. We were down at Edgewater Beach in the middle of the school week, sometime in January, before we'd even met Candace or gotten tangled up in that mess. I don't even remember why we ended up there, but Gwen had the idea to take a walk after we drank all the beer we'd brought in my car. I'd never been down at the shore in winter. It was a different place without any food trucks or dogs or kids running in and out of the water in sagging diapers. Empty and cold and strange like that, the beach could have been an alien landscape or a parallel universe that had nothing to do with Cleveland. Gwen took off her yellow puffer and used it as a pillow so she could look at the stars. The sand was so hard it felt like cement.

"You're nuts," I told her.

She laughed. "Just listen to the waves. They're like a lullaby."

I stretched out beside her in my parka and listened for a while, and she was right.

You can say what you want, I guess, about what love means to you. For me, that night felt like the two of us had been dropped out of the sky to land side by side. Maybe we'd been linked a long time ago, even. Maybe her mom and my grandma sang the same lullaby once, at the same moment, in different states. Somehow, we knew to recognize each other and collide when we did, tangled up and looped together like wires.

At a certain point as we lay on the beach, I realized that Gwen was talking to me, saying stuff I couldn't hear because the wind was blowing too hard. I had the idea right then that I could probably say anything back to her and it would be erased by the night and the weather. So I said, "I love you," and I was right. Nothing happened.

I looked up at the clamped-down stars, still buzzed from the beer, and felt so good. I was new, somehow, though that seemed impossible after all the things I'd been through in my life.

Gwen rolled over close to me. Her face was right there, like the shape of a heart. "Are you crying?"

"No," I said, though I was crying like a baby. That's how happy I was.

THE SILENT PARTNER

BY SUSAN PETRONE

Downtown

I'm going to tell you a story about a ball and a skull.

It starts with a baseball diamond. Most good stories do. Of course, I'm biased. I wrote for the *Cleveland Press* for nearly twenty years—Indians beat writer for nine and covered the Browns too, but my schtick was baseball history. It started with a little piece on the anniversary of former Indian Big Ed Delahanty's was-he-pushed-or-did-he-jump-off-a-train-over-Niagara-Falls death and grew from there. People liked it, and bringing something different to the table meant I didn't have to do all the traveling that came with the daily baseball beat. The traveling was nice for a while, but I'd rather do my drinking closer to home.

Some events in history loom larger than others. The fiftieth anniversary of Cleveland player Ray Chapman taking a pitch to the head in 1920 and dying from it was worth a two-thousand-word Sunday feature. Chapman played his entire career in Cleveland at shortstop and was, from all accounts, a great guy. It's the kind of story they coined the word "tragedy" for. The pitch came from Carl Mays of the New York Yankees. As a journalist, you're supposed to be impartial, unless you're a sports writer. In Cleveland, hating the Yankees is practically a city-wide hobby. A lot of that has to do with Chapman. I had written about it before—how could you not? For the fiftieth anniversary, my editor, Gary Blinkman, asked me to do something different.

"Different how?" I asked. "Mays threw. Chapman died. That hasn't changed." We were sitting in Blinkman's horrifically clean office on a Thursday afternoon at the end of July for our de facto weekly meeting.

Blinkman took a sip of coffee. He drank coffee all day and claimed he never slipped any booze in it and never had trouble sleeping. He was probably a damn liar. "Talk to somebody who was there," he said.

"Carl Mays is close to eighty and lives in California. Is the *Press* gonna pay to fly me out to talk to him?"

"You ever hear of a telephone interview, Einstein?"

"Already tried. Got a woman who was either a nurse or a second wife who said Mr. Mays doesn't give interviews. He's talked about Chapman on the record twice."

"That's all?"

"All they had at the Cleveland Public Library. He talked to *Baseball Magazine* a few months after it happened and did a longer interview in 1940 with some journalist from Podunk, Kentucky, but I haven't been able to find an actual copy. I have a lead on the writer though."

Blinkman ripped a page off the steno pad on his desk and handed it to me. There was a name, *Jocko Pruitt*, and a local phone number written on it. "Don't say I never did you any favors."

"Who's this?"

"Some old guy in the nursing home where my neighbor's cousin works. Supposedly spent part of the 1920 season with the Yankees."

"You don't say? I'll talk to him."

"See? You can always find a new angle," he said like I was some kid fresh out of journalism school. I wanted to say there wasn't anything new to find but kept my mouth shut. Sometimes you just have to let the boss have the last word.

There were old-time ballplayers scattered across the Great Lakes and Midwest, so it wasn't a surprise to find someone like Jocko Pruitt. It *was* a surprise to find someone who had been on the field the day Chapman got killed. Or at least in the dugout.

St. Augustine Manor was a nursing home situated on Detroit Avenue just west of downtown. It was doing its best to offer a dignified, peaceful environment for its residents; unfortunately, some of the residents hadn't gotten that memo. Pruitt was one of them. Somewhere during his nearly eighty years on this earth he had lost his right foot to diabetes and, it seemed, some of his senses. A kindly nun named Sister Lareto led me down a wide hallway with residents' rooms on either side. I couldn't resist glancing into all the open doors. Some rooms were empty, others held a brief snapshot of old folks reading books or knitting or staring off into space or, in a few cases, yelling at people who weren't there. Guess which one Jocko Pruitt was?

Sister Lareto knocked on the door and said in an overly cheery voice, "Mr. Pruitt? You have a visitor."

"I don't have a visitor," he declared. He was sitting in a wheelchair staring out the lone window of his room.

"You do today. This is the nice man from the *Cleveland Press* I told you about. He writes about sports."

"Sports?" Pruitt turned his wheelchair around to face Sister Lareto and me. "Did you know I was once a professional baseball player, Sister?"

"I *had* heard that. It sounds fascinating. This gentleman would like to talk to you about baseball. Won't that be nice?" She started backing out of the room as she spoke. To me she murmured, "Don't be alarmed if he starts yelling. It's a lot of sound and fury."

"Signifying nothing?" I said.

She gave me an approving smile. "He does have some . . ." she searched for the right word, "colorful stories. Let me know if you need anything."

I thanked her and sat down on the cushioned chair next to Pruitt's bed as she left the room. "She's a nice lady, that Sister Lareto," Pruitt said.

"I agree."

He gave me a once-over like a concerned father checking out his teenaged daughter's prom date. "You write sports?"

"Yep, been with the *Cleveland Press* for eighteen years. I used to be the Indians' beat writer."

Pruitt nodded like I had passed his test. "I played baseball. In the majors."

I scooted my chair a little closer to his wheelchair and said, "Wow, that's impressive." I figured he had some kind of dementia, one of those old men who could tell you everything that happened fifty years ago but couldn't remember what happened five minutes ago. "What position?"

"Utility man. Mostly outfield. Boy, I had a rocket for an arm . . . You should have seen me."

"I wish I had," I said with a smile.

Pruitt proceeded to tell me how he grew up in Cleveland, then played in the Pennsylvania Industrial League and the Pacific Coast League. He got picked up by the White Sox after the Black Sox scandal and spent nearly two seasons in the majors. He had a motormouth to go with that rocket arm.

I let him ramble for about twenty minutes, then said, "I heard you played for the Yankees in 1920."

"Yeah, yeah . . . I did well for them. Three homers in

two months. And that was deadball. But they didn't like me. They cut me. Ended my career."

"That's too bad."

"That's baseball."

"I understand you were there the day Ray Chapman got hit," I said gently.

Immediately, Pruitt's expression changed. He suddenly looked angry, even a little scared. The subject clearly hit a nerve. "I'm not supposed to talk about that," he said.

"I'm sorry," I backtracked, "I didn't mean to upset you."

He lowered his voice: "It doesn't upset me. It upsets *them*."

"Who? The nuns?" I asked with a smile. Maybe Sister Lareto didn't like gruesome baseball tragedies.

"No," he said, and paused for a moment, like he was trying to decide what he could tell me. "The owners," he whispered. "Not Mr. Huston or Mr. Ruppert. The other one. The quiet one."

I had no idea what Pruitt was talking about. "What was his name?"

Pruitt clenched his jaw then worked it side to side. "You know, the tall one. Looked like the grim reaper."

"Okay . . . Do you remember his name?"

"I won't say!" Pruitt yelled. I tried not to react, hoping he'd calm down. We sat there looking at each other for a moment, then he asked me in a low voice, "You ever wonder if maybe Mays threw at Chapman on purpose?"

One of the things that had always bothered me about the Chapman incident was that Mays seemed unremorseful. He kept his distance after he threw the ball—never left the mound, never went to the hospital or spoke to Chapman's widow. "Sometimes," I replied.

"You ever wonder if maybe somebody told him to do it?"

"Why would they do that?"

"Some people do dark things. They offer up a sacrifice to get what they want."

"You're saying Chapman was a . . . sacrifice?"

Pruitt nodded slowly.

Despite thinking he was off his rocker, I asked, "Why?"

"To make them win. To be unbeatable."

When Sister Lareto warned me about Pruitt's colorful stories, I hadn't expected dark magic blood sacrifices in exchange for baseball supremacy to be among them. She said colorful, not crazy. The interview was a bust. I stayed and talked to Pruitt awhile longer before making a polite exit.

I was one of a handful of people who lived in downtown Cleveland, in an apartment building called the Chesterfield. It was supposed to provide sophisticated downtown living, even though you could roll a bowling ball down Euclid Avenue after six p.m. and not hit anything. I liked it because I could walk to the ballpark and the downtown branch of the Cleveland Public Library, which was as big and imposing as a library ought to be. It was also the source of most of my research.

I went to plan B. The last person to get an interview with Mays, at least that I could find, was a fellow named Robert Duncan. He got it into his head that Carl Mays would talk to him because they were both from the same small town. He drove cross-country in 1940 to interview Mays. Robert Duncan must have been pretty persuasive because Mays spoke to him at length about the pitch. I had managed to track down a phone number for Duncan and was surprised when his widow, Gladys, invited me to come down and look through his notes. People are awfully trusting.

That was how I found myself driving three hours from

Cleveland to Mt. Vernon, Ohio, to meet with the widow of a baseball writer I'd never met. She invited me into her neat little bungalow and we made polite small talk about the weather and baseball writing. There was a faded black-and-white wedding portrait on the mantle, sandwiched between photos of people I presumed to be her grown children and grandchildren. She'd been a dish. Robert was kind of a schlub, so I'm guessing he'd been persuasive in a lot of ways.

Gladys noticed me looking. "Robert's been gone nearly thirty years. Can you believe it?" she said as though I had known him too.

"Wow, that's a long time," I replied. What else are you supposed to say to that?

"It was right after he published the interview. He was driving back from a meeting with some people in Cincinnati and had a heart attack driving over a bridge. They said he was dead before the car crashed into the guardrail." Even after so many years, you could see it still pained her to speak of her late husband. None of the women I've been with would recall me so fondly thirty years down the line. Probably why I've never been married.

I removed the lid from the banker's box of clippings and legal pads and scraps of paper sitting on the coffee table in front of us. It was far more than I needed to write a Sunday feature. Near the top of the jumble was a battered yellow legal pad with Carl Mays's name and the date, *June 15, 1940*, written at the top, followed by a list of questions. I realized it had to be Duncan's handwritten notes from the interview, which Gladys confirmed. I started paging through the legal pad, skimming the quotes from Mays. This was turning out to be worth the drive. I grabbed my own notebook, which goes everywhere I go, and started to copy down a quote from Mays about knowing he wasn't popular with his teammates. Hell, even Ty Cobb hated him, and everybody hated Ty Cobb.

I realized I was ignoring my hostess and looked up. "I'm sorry, I guess I'm getting lost in all this. It's really great stuff. Do you mind if I spend a little time with it, take some notes?"

"Actually, I was hoping you'd take it with you," Gladys said in a voice that sounded like she was talking to an exterminator about a dead rat.

"Excuse me? Take what? The legal pad?"

"All of it. Please take the entire box."

"Are you sure?"

"Yes, why don't you bring it out to your car now?" she said, standing up. I hadn't been there more than twenty minutes, but apparently our visit was over.

I carried the box to the little vestibule inside her front door and stood there feeling awkward. "Thank you again for your time and hospitality," I said. "And for passing on Robert's notes. That's very kind of you."

She paused, then said, "You may not think I'm so kind once you've seen what's in it."

At first I thought she was making a joke. Probably half the box was junk. Why else would she hand it over to a stranger? But her face wasn't the pleasant, cheerful retiree I'd been talking to. She was dead serious. "Is there something you're trying to tell me?" I asked.

"You seem like a good man. Be careful with whatever you find in that box."

"Of course. Are you . . . sure you want to give it to me? I won't be offended if you're having second thoughts about parting with it. After all, this was part of your husband's legacy and work."

"I've debated what to do with it for a long time. I want

you to take it. After all, Chapman's widow didn't keep the ball that hit him either."

With that, she sent me on my way. I tried to decipher what she said on the drive back to Cleveland. It was so late when I got home that I didn't want to do anything but sleep.

A couple days later, I devoted my entire day off to going through the whole thing and slamming out my two thousand words for the Sunday feature.

In addition to the legal pad, there was a stack of brittle yellowed clippings from Cleveland and New York newspapers, mostly from the late teens or early 1920s. Mrs. Duncan had rattled me, but there didn't seem to be anything explosive there, just handwritten notes, clippings, and photographs. Pretty standard research material. I couldn't quite reconcile what she'd said by her front door with what I found in the box. I was surprised to see that the focus of Duncan's research wasn't Ray Chapman. Just about every clipping mentioned one or both of the owners of the New York Yankees at that time—Jacob Ruppert and the illustriously named Tillinghast L'Hommedieu Huston. Photographs in newspapers were few and far between at that time, but there were some. Three of the clippings had shots of the Yankee owners, and there were some faded black-and-white stills of the two owners with their names printed neatly on the back in what I had learned to recognize as Duncan's handwriting. In each photograph, there was a circle drawn in red pencil around the face of a third man; he was tall and gaunt with slicked-down black hair.

The photos were obviously taken at different times, in different locations, and frequently had other people in them, but the three constants were always Ruppert, Huston, and the gaunt man. On one of the stills, Duncan had written *Wilmington?* on the white border near the gaunt man's picture. I wasn't sure if that was supposed to be his name or the place the photo was taken. With the exception of the actual notes from the Mays interview, just about all the clippings and notes were about the Yankees's ownership.

Near the bottom were some folded newspaper pages from the Cleveland papers about Chapman. At the very bottom of the box, I came across another legal pad, this one with *June 16, 1940* written at the top of the first page. It kind of seemed like Duncan hadn't wanted this one to be easily found. The second legal pad was practically new, he had only filled a few pages. The only thing I had ever heard Mays say about Chapman was that he "regretted" the pitch. He essentially said the same thing to Duncan, who had written, *"regret my role in the whole affair."* Quotation marks his.

In one of his notes, Duncan had written *Huston & Wilmington said no talk to Mrs. Chap. Too pain.* So that explained part of it—one of the owners told him not to speak to her. Farther down the same page Duncan wrote, *Wilm thanked. Said everything complete,* but no mention of what *everything* was.

Duncan had written the name *Wilmington* at the top of the next page but it was blank, as though the conversation had stopped there.

The box also held a copy of the interview Duncan had published in the small *Liberty Herald,* which I read with Duncan's notes alongside. One of the direct quotes from Mays read, *"Mr. Huston told me not to talk to Mrs. Chapman as it would be too painful for her."* No mention of Wilmington. In fact, Wilmington was mentioned six times in the direct quotes from Mays in the notes but his name wasn't mentioned once in the actual interview. It was as though he didn't exist, but Jocko Pruitt was starting to seem like less of a crazy old coot.

I stood up and stretched. Sitting hunched over the box was wreaking havoc on my back. While I was up, it seemed like a good idea to have another drink, and that took up the rest of the afternoon.

I went to work the next day still pondering everything I'd found in the box. I may have been employed by the *Cleveland Press*, but my real office was Cleveland Municipal Stadium, that concrete colossus perched on the edge of Lake Erie. Between covering the Indians and Browns, I spent a large portion of my adult life there. The media entrance was by Gate B along the left field line, which was kind of pointless because you had to double back along the concourse in order to get to the press box. Most of my colleagues went in Gate B. I typically sweet-talked my way past the ushers at Gate A. The stadium was built in 1932 and only had one elevator. I always walked up the concrete ramps. From different spots on the ramp you could look down into the box seats or out onto downtown Cleveland, the city they use to illustrate the word *gritty* in the dictionary.

Up in the press box I found the usual suspects—my friend and rival George Kowalsky from the *Plain Dealer*, Buddy Barnes from the *Lorain Chronicle*, Tom O'Rourke from the *Lake County New Herald*, some assorted radio guys, and the beat writers for the visiting team, which happened to be the Yankees. Like I said, I wasn't the Indians beat writer anymore, but there's a method to my madness.

"Evening, gentlemen and Mr. Kowalsky," I said.

"Ah, the man mothers warn their daughters about," Kowalsky replied. "How's it hanging?"

"Low and inside," I said, and set up camp in my usual spot next to him.

One of the Yankee beat writers was new, a kid really. He looked lost.

"How's it going?" I said to him.

"Okay."

"Who're you with?"

"*Daily Post*. Tommy Franks is on vacation. My name's Dave."

"You old enough to travel by yourself, Dave?" Kowalsky asked.

"Oh yeah. I graduated from Columbia two years ago."

"He graduated from *Columbia*, Kowalsky," O'Rourke said, and you just knew they were going to give the kid a hard time.

"I stand corrected."

Dave gave a nervous little laugh. "This is a nice ballpark," he said like he was trying to change the subject.

We all laughed like drunken hyenas, which we sometimes were. "You don't need to be polite," I said. "It's a hole. Stay out of the public bathrooms unless you like pissing in a trough."

"Okay . . . Speaking of holes, what's with all the holes in the wall?" He half gestured to the wooden wall behind us. By this point in the season, it probably had twenty or thirty pockmarks on it.

"Foul balls," Barnes said. "Stay alert."

"Why don't you close the windows?"

"You want to close the windows, be my guest," Kowalsky said. "Don't come running to me when the window breaks and you're picking glass out of your skull."

O'Rourke snorted. "Like that bald guy from UPI?" He

and Barnes and Kowalsky laughed it up, so did most of the other guys.

I looked over at young Dave and said, "Yes, that really happened, and yes, it was funny."

"It's always funny as long as it's not your head," O'Rourke said.

Over the years, my profession had earned a reputation as a haven for heavy drinkers who couldn't write about anything besides sports. I always did my best to earn my reputation. In 1970, drinking on the job wasn't necessarily condoned, but nobody cared if you grabbed a little nip here or there as long as you filed your story on time. I always made my deadlines. I may or may not have had a flask with me at the ballpark to give my Coca-Cola a little kick.

It was a Tuesday night in early August with ten thousand people in a stadium built for seventy-two thousand. Those ten thousand fans got a treat because the Indians actually took the lead early and never gave it up.

Around the fourth inning, Dave asked, "Is the stadium always this empty?"

"No, sometimes there's only five thousand people," Kowalsky responded.

"This is Cleveland," I said. "We don't have a big payroll, we don't have a good record, and we get ten thousand people on a Tuesday night."

"And your river caught on fire last summer . . ." one of the other New York writers said.

I ignored him. "Dave, you're an educated young man . . . Let me pose a theory. I'm writing a feature on the fiftieth anniversary of the death of Ray Chapman. You know who he was?"

Everybody within earshot in the press box looked at poor green Dave.

"Didn't he get hit by a pitch?" the young man said.

"Killed, actually. In 1920. I talked to an old ballplayer the other day who pointed out something fascinating. How many World Series have the Yankees won since 1920?"

"Um, lemme see . . . Eighteen?" Dave said.

"Twenty, actually. Cleveland's won two. Ever since 1920, the Yankees have kicked our asses."

"Everybody's asses," Kowalsky added.

"What's your point?" Dave looked like he was worried we were going to steal his lunch money after recess.

"My point is that ever since Ray Chapman got killed, the Yankees have pretty much been unbeatable."

"Wow, that's a crazy coincidence." Dave kind of chuckled, so did some of the other guys.

One of the visiting beat writers started waving his arms and saying, "Woooo . . . it's a conspiracy!"

"I'm just remarking on the succession of events, not implying causation." I took another swig of Coke and Jim Beam and wrote a couple paragraphs. Sometimes you can tell the outcome of a game before it even ends. I didn't say much else for the rest of the evening.

The next day, I made a late-afternoon phone call. I had tried getting a quote from Carl Mays before and been rebuffed. This time I had a different question.

I dialed the number I had for Mays. After about six rings, a woman answered. I was pretty sure it was the same woman who had told me he didn't do interviews a few weeks earlier. I introduced myself as being with the *Cleveland Press*, but before she could say anything, I blurted out, "I'd like to talk to him about Mr. Wilmington."

There was dead silence on the other end. I counted to

ten, wondering if the woman had hung up. Finally she said, "What was your name again?" I gave it to her, along with my home and office numbers. I didn't spend much time at the *Press* offices but at least it gave me some credibility.

That long silence made me believe Jocko Pruitt wasn't as crazy as he appeared, and maybe Gladys Duncan wasn't either. I started writing my feature. It took longer than usual to pound out two thousand words because every time I started a new paragraph I looked back on what I had written and thought I must be turning into a crazy old coot too. The idea of a blood sacrifice in order to fuel a team's ascendency was ludicrous. Maybe I just wanted some explanation for why the Indians were so bad, why they seemed destined to lose. At least that's what I said to Blinkman when I handed him a draft of the feature article the next day.

It was our regular Thursday meeting, and he seemed pleasantly surprised to see the article finished ahead of deadline. Then he started reading it.

I watched his face and knew exactly when he got to the part about the pitch being deliberate and when he got to the part of about it being part of a larger plot. That's when he laughed and put down the pages.

"Oh brother, you had me going there for a minute. Maybe we can use this on April Fool's Day. Where's the real feature?"

"That is the real feature," I said.

"Ray Chapman was a blood sacrifice? Are you nuts? I can't print this."

"It's true." I told him my sources, how everything fit together.

"This is the wackiest thing I've ever heard. I won't run it. I can't."

"I'll publish it somewhere else. I'm sure the *Sporting News* would be interested."

"Go right ahead, but don't blame me when you get sued for libel."

"I won't."

"If you want the Sunday feature, give me two thousand words that aren't bullshit."

"Fine. But you'll regret not running this."

"No, I won't."

I left Blinkman's office and went to my desk in the corner of the sports newsroom. I figured if I had to rewrite a vanilla version of the feature, there was no time like the present. I had just settled in at my typewriter when the phone on my desk rang.

"Sports desk." That was my standard greeting because you never knew if it was going to be the operator or a source or some irate reader. I had found it was always safer to be anonymous. It didn't seem to throw this caller off his game.

"Hello," a deep baritone voice said. "I understand you reached out to Carl Mays yesterday regarding Mr. Wilmington." The guy didn't waste any time on niceties.

"I did," I replied. "Thank you for getting back to me so quickly. May I ask who I'm speaking with?"

"I'm a representative of Mr. Wilmington."

Over the years, I had learned to perfect a calm, monotone phone voice, even if the caller was confirming the existence of a mystery silent partner. This caller identified himself as Mr. Jones, which had *fake name* written all over it. Sometimes folks don't want to use their real names when talking to reporters, at least not at first. Mr. Jones was in Cleveland on business and said he was in a position to answer some of my questions. He made it sound as though Wilmington might still be alive, except he'd be ancient. We arranged to meet later that evening at the Barrister's Club, a small bar on West 3rd near the Justice Center. I knew it because I know all the watering holes between my apartment building and the stadium.

When I walked into the Barrister's Club at seven thirty, it was semicrowded and I wondered how I was supposed to recognize the guy. I found a spot at the bar, ordered a whiskey sour, and glanced around at the lawyer types. Slightly more than half the tables and booths were occupied with pairs or small groups of men and women. It looked like I was the only person solo at the bar. I was also the only guy not wearing a tie. I figured that would make me easy to find.

For a minute I thought maybe this Jones guy had stood me up, then a man and a woman around my age got up from a booth at the far end of the room, near the back door. As they made their way toward the front door, they had to pass by me. The woman was peering right at me, long enough that I thought maybe she was flirting. Then I realized the man was looking at me too. Neither of them spoke to me as they passed.

I watched them walk out the front door. Something made me turn back to the booth they had just vacated. A broad-shouldered young guy in a gray suit was still in the booth, facing me. He half stood up and waved to me. He was younger than I was expecting.

I made my way through the steadily growing crowd in the bar. "Mr. Jones?" I said.

"That's me. Have a seat. Let me get you another drink." He waved to the cocktail waitress and held up his glass like the kind of man who's used to getting what he asks for. "So I understand you have some questions about Mr. Wilmington."

"Yeah, I'm writing a piece on the fiftieth anniversary of Ray Chapman's death and came across Wilmington's name as part of the larger story."

"What larger story?"

"That's what I'm trying to find out." I drank the last of my whiskey sour, taking my time while we sized each other up.

He gave me what some people would call a winning smile but looked more smug to me, then glanced over at the bar. "I don't know what the hell is keeping that waitress. What've you got? Whiskey sour? I'll be right back."

I didn't particularly like the guy, but I've never been averse to somebody else buying the drinks. When Jones came back, he sat down in the booth and placed another whiskey sour in front of me. He had a beer for himself.

"Thanks."

"Well, I figure we might be here awhile. Cheers." We both took a healthy drink, then he folded his arms on the tabletop and leaned toward me a bit, like he was pretending we were friends. "Why don't you tell me what you think you know, and I'll tell you if you're right."

I figured I'd take a gamble with something easy. "Was Wilmington a part owner of the Yankees back in the twenties?"

"I can confirm that. He was a silent partner. But why would that be part of a story on Ray Chapman?"

"Can you confirm whether Mr. Wilmington had something to do with Chapman's death?"

Jones tried out that broad smile again. "What do you mean by that?"

"I have reason to believe that the pitch might have been deliberate."

"You'd have to ask Carl Mays if it was deliberate."

"Or ask whoever told him to throw the ball at Chapman's head."

Jones looked incredulous, then gave a condescending chuckle. "Who do you write for, the *National Enquirer*?" I waited. "You're serious?"

"Oddly enough, I am." I took another sip of my drink, more for emphasis than because I wanted it. I was starting to feel a little queasy, probably because I hadn't eaten any dinner.

"You okay?" Jones asked. He didn't look particularly concerned.

"Yeah. Just suddenly have a headache to beat the band."

"You wanna go outside for a minute? Get some air? Come on." He didn't wait for my answer, just stood up and pulled me out of the booth and to my feet. "Let's go out the back door. It's closer."

The back door opened onto an alley that fed back onto West 3rd. There wasn't much in that neighborhood, some office buildings and bail bondsmen, closed for the night, and parking lots and old warehouses, most of them empty.

"Maybe we should take a little walk. That might make you feel better," Jones said. He put an arm under my right shoulder and helped me walk down the alley toward the sidewalk. I hadn't even realized that my feet weren't listening to my brain.

We hadn't gone far when I noticed two other people walking alongside us. One of them, the man who'd looked at me when he was leaving the bar, put his arm under my left shoulder. The woman I'd seen earlier got close up to my face and said, "How're you doing?"

"Been better," I said. It occurred to me that something wasn't right, but at that moment I couldn't really figure out what it was.

"You really shouldn't let a stranger run your drinks, cowboy," she said.

The four of us walked down West 3rd toward the stadium, toward the lake. I could smell the water, except that everything seemed very far away at the moment.

"You know, you were close," Jones said as he half hoisted me down the sidewalk. I really couldn't feel my feet anymore. "The pitch was deliberate. But it wasn't Mays."

"It was Wilmington," I said. I knew that much, even if it was getting difficult to speak. I kind of wished we'd stop walking and maybe sit down on a bench somewhere and take a nap.

"Correct. It's my job to keep that knowledge private," he responded.

"I already wrote the story . . ." I managed. It seemed like it was taking the words a long time to get from my brain to my mouth.

"Did your editor like it?" Jones was still half carrying me down the street. At that point, if he stopped holding me up, I'd fall.

"No," I said. Normally I wouldn't have told him this but I found I couldn't control much anymore.

"Of course not. I'm not worried about your editor, just you." We were near the lake, behind the stadium. I could smell the water and the vague scent of dead fish. "You know enough to cause problems," Jones continued. "Sorry to say, but you aren't going to be with us much longer. I'll give you a choice: the Delahanty way or the Chapman way."

The world was getting blurry, but I could understand enough that I didn't like either option. "Doesn't the Delahanty way require a train?" I gasped.

"You know, you're right," Jones said, and pulled a baseball out of his jacket pocket. "Looks like it's the Chapman method."

A baseball in a swinging fist feels like a set of brass knuckles when it collides with your skull. Another fun fact: baseballs float—it's that cork in the center. Bodies don't, especially not if somebody loads up your pockets with rocks. Someone might find the ball sometime, floating gently on Lake Erie.

UNDER THE HILL

BY MARY GRIMM

The Flats

When I got almost to the bottom of the hill, my car died, and no key jiggling or accelerator pumping would start it up. It was ten days before Halloween, still hot enough for summer. The sky ran with bands of clouds, gray and hard, a steel shine on them where the light hit. I left the car with the hood propped up.

I had an address written on half an index card from the bartender at the Greenwood. "Persis don't like to give it out to just anybody," he'd said.

"She'll be glad to see me," I said. "She'll want to hear about Aunt Ida and the kids."

If I had an Aunt Ida, I wouldn't know a thing about her, or care. And I didn't want to tell Persis anything. I wanted her to tell me—what she'd done to me, what she thought she was doing.

"She don't like strangers," the bartender said. The old men at the bar had laughed, dry and choking, and then had to raise their beers to wash out the dust.

Now I was walking, still half drunk, in the reaches of the Flats on the west side of the river, *under the hill*, as people here called it. I walked toward the dark that gathers before sunset, the reach of shadow from the bluff behind me.

I could always put one foot in front of the other, no matter how drunk I was. Persis. What kind of name was that anyway? If she wasn't there, I'd wait. Or I'd make them tell me where she was. If there was a man, I'd hit him. I clenched my fist to test its readiness.

Some way past the top of Jennings Hill, I found the street. Number 135 was a yellow house, built long ago for mill workers, two narrow stories and an attic, a rickety fire escape clinging to the side. The yard was full of tomato plants that had survived into late October. Clumps of dead flowers fell across the broken sidewalk.

I stepped onto the porch and knocked, using the side of my fist. I grabbed the knob to shake it, and it turned, the door sliding open so that I fell inside. The last of the sun was coming in low, lighting up the room. A couch with lace draped across the back. A lamp dripping crystals. An armchair with a stack of books beside it. There was a playpen in the corner, beyond the reach of the light.

I pushed the door to the kitchen open. It was as quiet as the bottom of a well, the light dim and greenish. I opened the cupboards and refrigerator, as if I'd find something among the cereal boxes or the vegetable bin. I wasn't as drunk as I'd been when I left the bar, but I slumped against the table and slid into a chair.

"Hey."

I half stood, swiveling to search out the direction of the voice.

"Hey, you."

I rose, clenching my fists. Here, I reasoned, was the mystery behind Persis. I pushed the door by the sink open so that it smacked against the wall.

There was a bed, with a man in it. He had the look of someone who'd been asleep, lids heavy, face creased from the pillow. He had long hair, and it was tangled and knotted.

He'd raised himself up on his elbows to look at me. "Who are you?"

"Ray Dacey. Who the hell are you?"

"Selden. Can you get me a drink of water?"

I looked at him as if to say, *What the fuck?* And he looked back at me as if to say—well, nothing. There was nothing in his look to be angry at. I found myself getting an old jelly glass in the kitchen, filling it, and bringing it back to him. "Where's Persis?"

He drained it to the bottom, watching me. His skin was as white as the sheets.

"No one's here." He turned his head toward the window.

"You know who I mean, right?" He didn't turn his head back to look at me, and I went on: "Persis? Hot. Long black hair." I made a twirly motion with my finger. "Thinks she's the shit."

"Did she do you an injury?"

Had she? I didn't know. I looked around the room. The bed, a chair beside it, a dresser. No rug, no curtains at the window, no mirror over the dresser. The bed had only one blanket, thin and lacy with moth holes.

Selden turned back to me, his eyes pinned on mine. I looked down at the scarred wood floor and then to the window he'd been so fascinated by a minute ago. I could see more plants outside, green and shadowy, whispering as the air moved them.

"She comes by to visit. And to see Mayliss into bed some nights."

"Who's Mayliss?" I asked, my anger starting to rise.

"See," he said. "Only see." His voice was growing fainter. "I saw when I was sleeping in the bowl of the Flats, spilling the river into the lake. The people coming one by one, specks among the throng of the trees. They didn't know to live up high and they sickened and died. It was a hard place then. The river went where it would, leaving a swamp behind. Children died by the score."

"What the hell are you talking about?" It was darker outside, and the room was dim, the white sheets the only brightness other than the brilliant slits of Selden's eyes.

"They ought to be back soon," he said.

"Who? Persis?"

His eyes closed all the way, and I saw that he'd fallen asleep or unconscious. *Or dead*, a voice in my head intoned. Alone in this creepy house with a dead guy, the giant tomato plants rustling outside. I backed out. In the front room the light seemed to flit, gleaming on the surface of a mug or the frame of a picture. I could hear a sound outside, a rhythmic squeaking or wheezing, getting gradually louder.

I was almost sober. I put my shoulders back and opened the front door. Someone was coming up the walk. The wheezing squeak was louder.

"Who's there?" someone said. A round gray head, covered with a scarf. Knobby fingers. A face seamed and furrowed, lips pursed tight.

"Who're you?" I asked.

"That's information I don't give out to any and all." She came up the steps and put her hand on a switch. At once, mosquitoes flew into the cone of gold around us. She was pulling a baby carriage, complete with baby. "I ain't letting you in unless you name yourself."

"Ray Dacey. And I've been in."

"Have you?" She looked at the baby, as if to ask something. Then she laughed, a raspy cackle. "Come in, if the damage is already done."

She pushed the carriage past me. Besides the baby it held two loaves of bread, a bag of apples, and something wrapped in newspaper. "Come in, boy. Do you think I'm going to hex you?"

"Course not," I said, feeling foolish.

"Not that I can't, but so far you're a guest, ain't you? Take him out and put him on the rug." She gestured toward the baby. "Go on, he won't hex you neither."

The baby stared at me as I set him on the floor.

"He likes you." The old woman had brought a plate with kolacky on it, snowy with powdered sugar, and a glass.

"How can you tell?"

"Is that the question you want to ask? I ain't going to answer a great line of them. And he's no business of yours." She sat in a rocking chair and began to rock.

"Where is Persis?" I felt as if I'd been in the house for hours, or as if I'd been there long ago and never forgotten it. I knew what the rooms upstairs looked like, the feel of the curtains, the thump of the pillows, the drip of the leaking faucet.

"What kind of question is that?" She looked at the baby and shook her head. "That ain't worth our time."

"What the fuck?" I glanced at the baby, and it was watching my mouth, as if memorizing the bad word. "All I want to know is where Persis is."

"You could've asked the neighbors. They can manage answering a question like that."

"I'm asking *you*."

The old woman took the scarf from her head, folded it, and offered it to the baby to play with. She pointed to the kolacky. "If it's to be conversation, take a bite and a sip."

I picked up the glass and sniffed it.

"Only tea," she said. "Where did you say you're from? And your parents—from the Irish, are they?"

I took a sip of the tea, as sweet as syrup, and hot. "What?"

"The garden's nice, ain't it? I don't do it all myself, of course, not anymore." She pointed to the kolacky with a stern look.

A cloud of sugar clogged my throat and I started to cough.

"Persis," she said, just as I started to lose patience. "She ain't an inhabitant."

I began to speak, but she held up a finger. "She comes by now and then, works in the garden a bit. She does for May-liss," she nodded to the baby, "to give me time to myself. If you want to see her, she'll be at the Silence Bar three nights from now. No point in looking before that."

The baby had crept across the carpet so that it was almost under my feet. The room was brightly lit now, and the light seemed to fill every inch, pressing against the windows to keep out the dark. I opened the screen door and went out onto the porch.

"When you come back," the old woman said, "bring a little something for the baby."

I let the door slam. The baby looked up and smiled at me. I could see the spaces between its little teeth.

It was Sunday, no work to do. I went out back and leaned on the chain link. When my great grandfather had built here, on Revere Court, the valley had been wild, before the zoo moved from the east side. There had been a decent yard then, but the edge kept crumbling away, and now there was only five feet between the house and the cliff.

You could get down if you wanted to. The paths had been worn by dozens of kids, getting out before someone made them do chores or homework. You could sneak into the zoo that way. I'd made friends with the elephants by the time

I was eight. I thought I spoke their language, that I knew magic words to make them obey me. Later, in high school, I'd sneaked girls down the cliff. There were good places to fuck as long as it wasn't too cold.

It was bright October, warm. The houses across the zoo valley clung to their cliff, crowded to the edge, just like this one. The train tracks snaked under the bridges. I could see the elephants out in their yard, standing in the sun. It was hard to believe that I'd done what I had last night, hanging out after a woman. I must have been crazy, I told myself. She'd done something to me, who knows what.

My sister Grace came out and leaned against the fence. I offered her a cigarette.

"Where did you go last night?" she said.

"The Greenwood on Broadview."

"I thought you hated that place."

"I was looking for someone." I waited for her to ask me who, and I'd tell her, make it into a funny story, and it would turn small and stupid, the house and the old woman and the baby. But she didn't ask, and I knew there was no way to make Persis small. If I closed my eyes I could see her. I could feel her hands on my skin. It felt like I'd known her since we were kids, like we'd played tag and doctor together, walked to school, swapped lunches, hanging out under the Rhodes High School stadium. That's how it felt, years of Persis instead of weeks.

She'd been tending bar at the Greenwood when I went in with Kevin and some guys from work, celebrating being laid off. Her hair was as black as mine, long and wavy, but her eyelashes and eyebrows were pale. Later I'd see she had freckles, so faint they only showed in a strong light. She was standing on a case of bourbon when we came in, reaching for something on a shelf. One of the regulars called to her and she turned and started to fall, so I hopped over the bar to catch her. But by the time I got there she was on her feet, laughing, as if she'd floated down. I was looking into her eyes, at her fair skin and her pink fingernails. I felt a buzz beginning in my head, like the highest part of a good drunk, although I'd only had a couple of beers. I took her arm as if to be helpful, but really because I wanted to touch her.

"Thanks," she said.

"I didn't do anything."

She went to the tap and pulled down a glass. "On the house, for the thought."

"Blake won't like that," one of the regulars said. Blake was the owner, and a mean bastard.

"He'll be amenable." She turned to me. "I love a man who's amenable."

Kevin and the guys were waiting for me, ready to razz me as soon as we settled in a booth. "I'll be over there." I pointed with my glass.

"I think I'll be able to find you."

I had lost all my ability to come up with a smooth line, so I went to join the guys and put up with their jokes.

I thought about this while Grace and I leaned over the fence, smoking. I knew she was thinking about her ex. Grace was someone who held on to things. She held on to me, her only family since our parents died. But that same thing made her hold on when it was useless or stupid. She'd go on thinking about him and wondering if she should have done this or that. Her holding on to things went on almost long enough to kill her once, and I didn't want to see that again.

"Where's your car?" she said.

"It broke down."

"You should have Kevin look at it."

Across the valley I could see someone making their way down a path through rows of plants. Some Vietnamese lived on one of the streets off Archwood Avenue, and they gardened precariously on the cliff. I liked our side better, its wildness, the possibility of escape, of going down and away from everything, even though I wasn't a wild teenager anymore. But it was pretty over there, the layers and pattern of greens.

When Grace left for work, I got my bike out. Not having a car wouldn't matter for work, since I could ride with Kevin when I had a shift again. If I really needed one, I could borrow Grace's. It had belonged to the geezer she did for, a big boat twenty years old or more. He'd given it to her when she started doing his errands and driving him around. She kept it parked at his house.

The day had turned gray. I lay on the couch, clicked on the TV, searching for something that wouldn't kill me with boredom. If Grace were here, she'd give me a list of things that needed to be fixed or painted. So I was glad to be alone, even though the house was gray and dim, the light from the TV bouncing and flashing in a way that made me queasy.

I used to have a habit of falling in love, but I'd made up my mind a few years ago that I wouldn't have a permanent woman. Grace still hoped to get married, I knew. Our parents hadn't been a happy-ever-after couple, although they lived together until one of them died. They joked about it when they weren't mad at each other, shacking up for twenty years.

I wasn't worried I'd end up married to or even living with Persis, but she had planted something in my head, something that made her jiggle and dance in my mind. I wanted to fuck her again, even though it would be a bad idea. A bad idea, but I'd probably do it anyway.

Eventually I fell asleep. I dreamed, but when I woke up, hair plastered with sweat, I couldn't remember anything except falling. Not the kind that jerks you out of sleep. More like the fall from a plane. It was dark, which made me glad, because the day was over. I could hear Grace in the kitchen opening the fridge, then the whoosh of the gas stove lighting.

Three nights from now, the old lady had said, which pissed me off all over again. As if Persis only existed three days ahead, as if she weren't someplace right now.

I got up, swiping my hair back. I needed a shower and something to eat. And then maybe I should go out and look around. Fuck the old lady and her advice. I wasn't waiting.

When I stepped outside, it was as if all the sadness and guilt built up in the house sloughed right off me. I took a breath of the dark air, cool, like a swallow of water. I'd decided I'd borrow Kevin's other car, if I could do it without telling him what for.

When I got to Kevin's, music and light spilled from the front door, the hard thump of the bass rattling the neighbors' windows, but his truck wasn't in the driveway.

I saw a flash of pink. Kevin's kid, Holly, standing in the street with another kid. She was wearing her Halloween costume over her clothes. "Ray," she yelled, "we need to call animal control!" She pointed to something in the gutter. A cat, its ear half torn off.

"A car hitted him," the other kid said.

I thought I ought to touch the cat, figure out if it was dead, but I couldn't bring myself to do it. "Probably we can't do anything for the cat," I said. "It's probably—" I cast around for a way to say *dead* without saying it. The other kid started to cry.

I peered down at the cat. It moved a little. Not dead. But it looked terrible. The kid was petting it, probably too hard for a cat that was all but gone. "Animal control is for catching animals. They don't fix them up."

"We can take her in the house," Holly said. "She needs to be warm."

I could see something white where the ear was torn that could have been its skull. I looked around for help. Tonight was garbage night, and there was a cardboard box in Kevin's neighbor's trash.

I put the flattened box next to the cat. It bared its teeth at me, but probably felt too shitty to bite, so I scooted it onto the box. Its body felt limp, boneless, as I carried it, Holly and the kid following.

I didn't think Kevin would appreciate having a dying cat in his house, but it was his fault, wasn't it, because if he was here, he could be dealing with it.

Holly fussed around, trying to give it some cheese, and then water from a baby-doll bottle. She covered it with a dish towel.

"Maybe we should call the vet," I said, although God knows who would pay for that.

"No," Holly responded. "The witches. Call the witches. They can fix Candy."

"Honey, I don't know any witches." I opened Kevin's refrigerator and took out a beer, which I figured was the least he owed me.

Holly was standing there with her arms crossed, a miniature woman ready to give me hell. "Kevin said you were hanging out with a witch."

"Kevin was just kidding. And even if there were witches, and even if I knew how to call one, I don't know if they do magic on cats."

The other kid started crying again.

"She has black hair. You were kissing her."

I'd had Persis at my house once. We'd been doing more than kissing, which I hoped she hadn't seen. "Why do you think she was a witch?"

"Kevin said. Besides, I could tell."

I heard Kevin's truck in the driveway, thank God. I drained the rest of the beer and prepared to give him hell. But when he came in, he seemed to take the whole thing in with a glance—the crying kid, the bleeding cat, Holly's defiance. I sometimes thought Kevin wasn't much of a father, yet I could see now that he had his moments.

He called the little boy's mother, made Holly wash her hands, taking time to twit me for my squeamishness. In ten minutes, he was supervising the removal of the cat. He had his arm around the boy's mother, all but feeling her up. "I know someone who'll come and stitch up the ear," he was telling her.

"I can't afford that," she said.

"He's a good friend of mine. We served together in Kabul," Kevin said, with a noble, soulful look on his face. "We can work something out." When he saw me watching, he winked at me. "You come along too, Holly. I know you'll want to make sure the kitty is okay."

He ushered them out, carrying the cat, mouthing silently, *Don't wait up.*

I got on the bike and peddled down the street to the old geezer's house. His car was in the driveway, the key on a nail under the eaves, handy for Grace.

The house was dark, except for a weak light over the kitchen sink. I imagined the old man shuffling to the kitchen for a glass of water, standing like a ghost on the rug his wife had hooked. I had no plans to get that old.

I put the car in neutral and let it slide down the slope of the driveway. When I was in the street, I started it, bracing myself for the noise. But it was smooth, one of those big engines they didn't make any more. I adjusted the seat and drove, feeling as if the car was taking me instead of the other way around.

The Silence Bar was at the bottom of Jennings Hill, on one of the streets that led down into the Flats from Tremont. I drove through the maze of streets, an old steelworkers' neighborhood. Both my grandparents had grown up here, a block away from one another. Played together, married out of high school. They had one of the lives it was impossible to live anymore, as extinct as the dinosaurs. Gramps worked in the mills rolling steel for forty years, Grams stayed home, cooking and sewing and cleaning away the black soot on the curtains.

At the top of the hill, the dark bowl of the Flats opened up in front of me, sparked with lights here and there, but mostly blank and dead. If it was daytime, I would have seen the old loading docks, the freight barns, the ancient brick buildings that housed companies that made widgets and gadgets, the piles of gravel and sand behind chain-link fences, waiting for construction to boom again.

The Silence Bar was in an old house at the bottom of Literary Avenue in Tremont, a boardinghouse once, I'd heard. Gabled roof, front porch, shutters on the windows upstairs hanging askew and banging when the wind blew.

The parking lot was rutted dirt, cars parked every which

way. I found a spot down the road, near the river, and snugged under a tree. When I got out, I could hear water lapping against the bank below me and, far away, traffic going into downtown. I could see the lights of the tall buildings from here, random windows lit up as if they were stars in the sky.

The entrance was on the far side with a neon light glowing above it, *OPEN*, with a tipped martini glass beside it, orange and pink. The noise of voices and a jukebox hit me, swelling into the night with the smoky light. I stood by the door to get my bearings. I didn't see Persis, which made me feel angry, as if she'd broken a promise. Angry at her, or at the old lady for getting my hopes up—I didn't know which.

The bar ran along the back wall, and there were tables and booths. Up toward the front I saw some couches that looked as if they'd been picked from tree lawns, overstuffed and saggy.

I ordered a beer, took a stool where I could see the room. It was dim—some lights over the bar, and a few by the tables. The jukebox glowed like a rainbow. An ancient pole lamp with a fringed shade hung over the couches. The people sitting there were shapes only, but I was sure none of them were Persis. I turned my back to the room, but kept my eyes on the mirror behind the rows of beer steins.

I couldn't think of anything clever to do. I felt stupid. I knew bars, I knew how to act in bars. You drank, you shot some pool, you waited until a woman caught your eye, and you zeroed in. It was as familiar to me as sitting in my living room and watching TV.

But the Silence Bar didn't feel like home. It didn't have the buzz that bars have, the beer-and-smoke-scented air that said anything could happen. The lights were too gray, the music from the jukebox too thin, as if it had stretched and tightened as it came from the speakers. Whatever was playing sounded as if it had been recorded a hundred years ago by people long dead, in horrible ways.

I ordered another beer. When the bartender put it down, I asked him about Persis. A woman, so high, long hair, with feathers braided into it, or ribbons. She wore a long dress with boots sometimes, I said. She had a leather jacket with fringes on the sleeves. My words seemed to drain of meaning even as I said them, to have nothing to do with anyone real.

"She's not here tonight." He was old, white hair falling in his face, a once-broken nose. "Why do you want to know?"

"Is that your business?"

He wiped his hands down his filthy apron. "I don't care. But she's a nice girl."

"I know she is," I said, although I wasn't sure I did know that. "We're friends." Although I wasn't sure we were.

"Friends are good." He laughed. "Everybody should have one or two."

I saw someone coming up behind me in the mirror. Before I could turn, an arm snaked around my shoulders.

"TomTom, who's this?"

"Persis's friend." The bartender nodded. "It's good to have friends, now and on the day of our death, amen."

"I'm Morrison." He took my hand as if to shake it, but then slid his grip up my arm so that he was holding my elbow. "It's always better to drink in company, don't you think?"

"I'm not here to drink with anyone."

Morrison looked me up and down. "Persis can be hard to find." He exchanged a look with the bartender. "I might be able to help you out."

"He needs help," the bartender said. "Anyone can see that."

"What do you know about Persis?"

Morrison peered at the bartender, and then at the ceiling. "I'm the kind of person who knows things, isn't that right, TomTom? Strangers whisper things to me in passing. Young girls reveal their pure little secrets. Strong men," he tapped one of my clenched fists, "tell me their hearts' desires."

"I'm not telling you anything."

"I know Persis. We're by way of being related."

For some reason, I thought of the old lady. She had sent me here. Maybe she and this Morrison were in it together, whatever *it* was. He wanted something from me, that was clear, but I couldn't imagine what. I should have brought Kevin with me. I needed someone to watch my back.

"I'm out of here," I said.

The door was past one last godforsaken couch, an enormous one, high-backed and old-fashioned. Someone was lying on it, and as I pushed past, he reached out to grab me.

I snarled and pulled him up by his shirt collar.

"In those days," the man said, "the people looked to the skies and the skies rained down upon them. Each man looked into his heart and found that it was a garden of dead things. Children dreamed of love as unobtainable. The color blue was abandoned. The sky was named Oblivion."

It was Selden. He hung from my hand like a rag, his arms and legs limp. "What the hell are you doing here?"

He smiled, his face in the darkness a pale mask. "Witnessing."

I glanced over my shoulder. A fight had broken out by the bar, and the crowd was roiling in knots around it. I saw Morrison watching, a smile on his face.

"Do you need a ride?" I asked.

"I have everything I need," Selden said.

"Do you ever give a straight answer?"

"You should leave. Is that straight enough for you?"

The fight was on the floor now, people gathered around in a circle. Selden turned to watch, his head propped up on his elbow.

I pushed the door open. The boards of the porch sagged and squeaked under my boots. Behind me the noise swelled, and someone screamed. I ran around the building, toward the river. My lungs strained to take in the night air and I started to cough, as if my body was trying to push something out. I fell onto my hands and knees and hacked, spit hanging from my mouth.

When I could, I got up and started walking, breathing carefully. The stars were out, I saw, with veils of cloud across them. The lights strung at the edges of the parking lot were dark, the streetlights also. When I got to the car, I had to feel for the door handle. I pulled it open and fell inside, sucking air.

"Ray."

I turned my head. Someone was sitting in the passenger seat.

"Forgot me so soon? My feelings are hurt."

It was Persis. Her head was turned toward me, though I couldn't see her eyes. I put my hands on the wheel, breathing hard and deliberate.

"You were looking for me."

"Are you some kind of witch?" I said, feeling stupid. I looked at the moving dark of the water laced and netted by the darker branches of the tree.

"That's a funny word." She sounded like she was smiling.

"When you say *witch*, I hear *intelligent and dangerous woman*." Her voice was light and sweet, as if nothing in the world could be wrong.

All the frustration of the last three days—my stupid idea that I'd wanted to see her again, had to see her again, Grace's sorrow, the old woman and Selden, the sliminess of Morrison—it was a wave that bowled me over. I was drowning in it, pictures in my head rushing at me, the coy smile of the baby Mayliss, Kevin's mocking face, Grace bent over crying when she thought no one would see.

I let go of the steering wheel and maybe I meant to shake Persis, but instead I took hold of her hands. Her hair was plastered against her forehead as if it was wet. Her hands were cold. I could feel the bones in her small wrists. I was still breathing hard, as if I had run up a hill, but I was here, with Persis looking at me.

"I heard you met them," she said. "Mrs. W., and Mayliss. Selden." She clenched her hand in a fist. I thought she might hit me and I braced for it, but she stroked my chin with her knuckles, let them slide down my neck, down my chest.

I reached for her then. The bench seat in the old man's car was as good as a bed. I moved over her, kissing her wherever I could reach. My hands were under her, lifting her up a little. She was lying in my arms, feeling not so much like flesh but like a body made of water or a tree come alive. She made a sound, and I pulled back to ask if I was too heavy, but she put her hand on my mouth.

She opened the door and I watched, numb. She stood outside under the tree, looking in at me. While I watched, she pulled her dress off her shoulders. She was wearing a man's sleeveless undershirt. She took that off too, and her underwear. "Ray," she said, "come out." She turned, her body silver-white in the darkness under the tree, and walked toward the river.

I was thinking it was a bad idea, but I took off my shirt. I kicked off my boots, stepped out of my jeans, and followed her.

The moon was half showing through the clouds and it glinted off the water. The tree leaned over a low bluff, the grass hanging off the edge like a woman's hair. I trailed her, going down, half sliding, thinking how stupid this was, wandering around in the dark nearly naked. But if she'd walked into the water, I'd have followed her.

She was standing on a narrow bit of sand. The tree hung over us like a tent, its scant leaves rustling. Persis reached for my hand and we stood there between the river and the bluff. I was still wearing my boxers and she pointed at them. "Modest, Ray?"

The blood was humming in my body, I thought I could hear it running, like the water in the river. I took hold of her, one hand on her shoulder, the other at her hip, and pulled her against me, taking us down on the sand.

There are a lot of things you learn to say to a woman, to turn her up sweet, to make her see things your way. But all of them had gone out of my head. I put my mouth on her throat and then her breast. I rolled her under me, waiting to see if she would pull away. I put my hand between her legs. She dragged my boxers down, and I knelt above her, pushing inside her, the sand gritty and cold against my knees.

I had no room for thought, but all of the last days were running through my head, like it's supposed to happen when you're dying—the strangeness of the city, Holly and the half-dead cat, Grace's sad face, the horrible mystery of the Silence Bar. All of them, and me too, wanting something that we couldn't have, or if we could, it would poison us. The river was loud in my head. Persis pushed back against me, and then we were both lost, breathless, as if the water had risen over us, drowning us, as if the bluff had fallen and buried us where we lay together.

BUS STOP

BY DANA MCSWAIN

Little Italy

S he's ignoring him in favor of the blistered spray paint on the bench next to her and Calvin can't blame her. They've been meeting at a bus stop in Little Italy for fourteen years now. Two hours, once a year in the RTA shelter at the base of Mayfield Road. It's always midmorning on a late-summer day, the sky hazy over Lake View Cemetery across the street, the marquee lights above Guarino's Restaurant flickering. She never says much, but sets the tone by treating him like her high school detention teacher. Considering it was probably another medium-build, medium-brown-haired white guy who sent her to this purgatory, he can't really blame her for fidgeting her way through these appointments.

"Hey, would you like to start the clock?" he offers. She stops picking at the blistered paint and snatches the smartphone from his hands. The phone usually works. She's fascinated by it, and why wouldn't she be? Time stopped for her in 1986, and as far as she's aware, an Atari 2600 is the height of technology. She taps the start button and the countdown begins.

"Did you build that funny clock yourself?" She pulls her hair to the side and twists it. Water pours out, the tangled strands and the pavement glittering with her soap bubbles. Draped around her hips is a similarly drenched army blanket that she fidgets with from time to time. "Are you one of those RadioShack nerds?"

He hides a smile as she returns the iPhone with a reluctant hand. "Biggest nerd in my graduating class. You should see my pocket protector collection." He crosses his eyes and mimes pushing up imaginary glasses, earning the ghost of a smile. Twenty years of journalism has taught him patience, but her anniversary is always trying. Most of the dead kids he visits are cagey but ultimately guileless; it's usually just a matter of finding the right angle, waiting them out. Yet there is nothing easy about this girl; innocence and candor were luxuries she could not afford growing up as she did. Calvin taps *start* on his recording app and sets it in the space between them. It's futile, but he tries again anyway. The timer works fine here, though his iPhone won't record shit or take any pictures, yet another frustrating condition of these visits.

Two hours. His appointments with her are always exactly two hours, exactly once a year, but with the others, the time varies. Fifteen minutes, six hours, an hour and a half. Beverly's appointments each last three long days. Interrogating a ten-year-old is a sucker's bet, so he chalks his visits with little Beverly up as a lost cause, plays hopscotch with her, makes mud pies, pushes her on the swing at the retro playground, and never asks her one single question about the August evening she walked home from Halloran Park to nowhere.

Another girl's visitation, however, lasts a nauseating forty-five seconds. Forty-five seconds sounds like nothing, but it takes months for Calvin to shake the encounter. They never even get a chance to talk; all Calvin has time to do is register her expressions: confusion, realization, fear. She opens her mouth to scream, reaches for him, and *poof*, she's gone. He's scoured the backlog of Cuyahoga County Jane Does, but he just stumbled upon her last stop and has no idea who she could be. He consoles himself that whatever happened to her, mercifully, happened fast. Calvin meets all of them at their last stop or where their remains were found, and each visit only lasts as long as their final hours did. Some of them he tracks down, some he finds by chance, like a sick game of memory. What happened to Bus Stop Girl took two hours. He tries to remember that when she's difficult. Two hours can be a long time.

The first time Calvin learned he could talk to dead girls was luck, depending, of course, on your definition. He just happened to be in one of his moods, brought on by a fight with his girlfriend, Claire. *It's morbid, Calvin. This obsession.* She'd accidentally seen some of the more graphic files, his stream-of-consciousness notes. *You're choosing to do this, Calvin. It's . . . perverse.* His then-editor had rejected his piece about the anniversary of the day Beverly Potts disappeared from a neighborhood theater festival in 1951. *No one cares, Cal. She's probably buried in a basement, the pervert that killed her is drooling in his soup in a nursing home, and no one gives a rat's ass. Why don't you shake your cop pal Kelly down? See if he's got a lead on a story that's not older than my mom.*

And worst of all, his best friend, Officer Sean Kelly, his ride-or-die from third grade on, who faithfully took all of Calvin's tips, theories, and red-string hunches to his sergeant, gave him a look that Calvin suspected was pity. *Maybe you should take a break from all this, Cal. You don't want to see the things I see. Find something new to write about and leave this shit alone.*

Fuck 'em all, Calvin thought. *They just don't get it. Someone has to care. Someone has to try.* He drove to Halloran Park that evening, sat down in the grass on the same day,

August 24—and, little did he know, the same time Beverly was taken—and that's when it happened. It was like getting knocked on his ass by a wave. One minute it was 1997 and the next, there she was, wholesome as a glass of milk, all buckteeth and knobby knees. *Hey, mister, wanna push me on the swing?*

Each time, Calvin slips across the border between his world and theirs slowly, his own time and space dissolving until he arrives at the moment time stopped for them. The journey to there and then is the easy part; the return to 2010 wrecks him. He's weak and confused, trapped in a slowly lifting fog. Fortunately, most of their locations are out of the way, and Cleveland being what it is, no one notices a grown man stumbling around mumbling for a few hours. He wondered if, like Dorothy, he'd had the power all along, just click his heels in the right place, the right time, and *bam*, there he was, a temporary visitor to the other side. Of course, once he knew he *could* do it, Calvin couldn't very well *not* do it. In fifteen years, he'd never missed an appointment, no matter how many new cases he located each year, and God knows Cleveland has enough dead women and children to keep his calendar full. It was his responsibility, his job to be there for them. Most of them just wanted company. They seemed confused and lonely, trapped in both time and place in little pockets all around Cleveland. Bay Village, Shaker Heights, Ohio City, Mt. Pleasant, South Collinwood. Honestly, it was the least he could do. Almost none of them could give him anything but maddeningly useless clues. *He kept my shoelaces. He bought me ice cream. He grabbed me from behind. He drove a silver car.*

There's no sane way to maintain anything approaching a normal life with a calling like his. Calvin could draw a straight line from the day he'd discovered his ability to the moment nearly every part of his life went to shit. It wasn't like he could explain to bosses and girlfriends he was communing with dead kids all over Cleveland. Sean was the only one who seemed to understand Calvin's obsessive focus, even though he was unaware of the paranormal extent of it. *Honestly, no one else gives a shit about any of these girls, Cal. You're the only one that fucking cares. Everybody else moves on, forgets they ever existed.* But still, Sean was always there to pick him up—from the bar after a difficult visit to the other side, from the police station when he crossed a line with a detective— Sean would smooth things over, sober him up, get him back on his feet. Sean's wife, Sophie, probably would have preferred he cut ties with Calvin—the broken peg that didn't fit into their picture-perfect suburban life—but Sean never let him down. Even made him Gabby's godfather, and Calvin couldn't imagine what kind of sweet-talking that took with Sophie. But these days, Sean was more and more looking at Calvin with that pitying expression. Over the years, Calvin had debated telling Sean about his metaphysical appointments, but now? Now it was too late. Telling his best friend, a Cleveland police officer, he was visiting the dead girls in some kind of ghostly Neverland would probably be the last straw.

Bus Stop Girl is trying to unearth a clump of grass sprouting through a crack in the pavement with her toes. Calvin lets his satchel drop to the ground and settles into the corner. Water runs down her legs, mingles with the dirt in the concrete, something vulnerable in her muddy chipped toenails. Last year, she wouldn't talk to him at all and they spent the entire two hours in silence. But he's determined to find a way to make her talk to him today. Because for the first time since his visits started, Calvin has a solid hunch.

Most of the girls are unconnected, solitary victims of opportunity. One-off compulsions of relatives or neighbors, sexual assaults that went too far, wrong place, wrong time in a city busting at the seams with crime. But six months ago, Calvin pulled a thread and felt it tug on a pattern. Another girl the same age as Bus Stop Girl, just a few weeks shy of her quinceañera, found in the Lake View Cemetery Reservoir off Mayfield. He'd been visiting Cemetery Girl for ten years in four-hour increments when she confided in him that she had been waiting for the man who took her. She shut down when his questions got too close, though not before she told him it was an ambulance driver. *He said my abuela had a heart attack and he'd take me to the hospital.* How she'd tried to get out of the back of the ambulance once she realized what was happening, the sound of the sirens drowning out her screams. Calvin dug though his notebooks and found another girl, this one recovered on the beach at Mentor Headlands, who he'd met for the first time three years prior. Her appointments lasted more than ten hours.

I was waiting for him, she'd cried against his shoulder, the waves rolling over them. *He said he would take me to her, that she'd been in an accident.*

"Who was in an accident?" Calvin asked, rocking the weeping girl, her long brown hair wrapped like seaweed around his shoulders.

My mom. He said . . . he said . . .

"What did he say? Tell me!" Calvin pleaded. But their time was up. She vanished before answering, and Calvin found himself alone at Headlands Beach, soaked to the bone. He'd promised to meet Kate, the newest girlfriend struggling to put up with his bullshit, for drinks at Johnny's Little Bar that night. But he was two hours late and Kate, like Claire before her, was long gone. Calvin had stopped trying to date after that.

I was waiting for him. He said he'd take me to the hospital.
He said he was taking me to her, that she'd been in an accident.

Headlands Girl and Cemetery Girl had been found in water; any hope of usable forensics washed away by the elements. Bus Stop Girl's remains had never been found, at least not as far as he knew. But she was always soaking wet during their visits and Calvin had a hunch that whoever took her, took all three of them. Three girls, all around fifteen, long brown hair. An ambulance driver? A fireman? People rarely question or engage with someone in uniform, especially in the parts of town these girls were from. Distrust of strangers and authority runs deep in most east side Cleveland neighborhoods. Watchful eyes would slide past, grateful not to arouse any attention. Without saying exactly how he'd arrived at this suspicion, he shared his hunch with Sean the last time they'd met for beers at the Academy Tavern.

"Listen, Sean, the girls they found at the Headlands and Lake View Reservoir? And that girl that vanished from the bus stop by our old apartment on Mayfield when we were kids? I'm thinking they're connected. Might be someone impersonating an officer . . . EMS worker, something like that. Anything about that ring any bells for you?"

Sean had shot a glance at Calvin's satchel on the bar. "Not off the top of my head. You got anything solid to back your crazy up this time?"

"No, not yet. I might, soon. But Sean, here's the thing. What if they're not impersonating? You used to work EMS.

You ever sniff someone . . . I don't know. A little off? Meets the description?"

Sean groaned. "Fuck me, man. Don't do this."

"Sean, I'm serious."

Sean leaned in, jabbed a finger at Calvin's chest. "So am I. Medium-build white guy with brown hair on the force or drives an ambulance with anger-management issues? You just named half my department."

"But what if I can get something solid?"

Sean rolled his eyes, gestured for another round. "Listen, you find anything concrete, you come to me. You could put yourself on the wrong side of the blue line, man. Get yourself into the kind of trouble I can't get you out of, okay? Now shut up and drink your beer. You're not the only one talking crazy, I think Soph wants another kid. We can barely afford the one we have."

Back at the bus stop, the blanket slips as she stretches and yawns, an unguarded sequence of movements that reminds Calvin of his seven-year-old goddaughter. Her hair is long and brown, eyelashes thick and black against her olive skin. One of her front teeth is crooked, a charming quirk, and Calvin wonders what she would look like if she ever really smiled. Then he catches sight of the ligature marks on her wrist, raw and glistening under the soap bubbles sliding down her arm. He averts his eyes and studies the ceiling of the shelter where another patch of spray paint shouts, *Voinobitch*, some eighties teen's clever commentary on the local government.

"You weren't scheduled at Mama Santa's that day," he muses more to himself than to her. "And your mom's apartment is just up the hill." She casts him a sidelong glance, eyes narrowed. "Why did you decide to take the bus today?"

She slips her hands back into the blanket, hiding her wounded wrists and hugging herself. "I wasn't waiting for the *bus*." She says it as though it's too complicated to explain, or he's too dense to understand.

The small revelation feels as fragile as one of her soap bubbles.

"Who were you waiting for?" Calvin asks.

She pretends she didn't hear him, drawing her knees to her chest and the blanket around her like a winding cloth. There's nothing special about the blanket as far as he can see. You can find one just like it at any military surplus supply store. Unfinished green wool, maybe five by seven, the kind people keep in the trunk of their cars in the Midwest. She's wrapping one corner of it around her finger and Calvin can't help but think, drenched as it is, the blanket must weigh more than she did.

Calvin will record this all later, in the notebook in his satchel labeled with her name. Try to piece together some sort of narrative, study her every word for some detail he might have missed, generate better questions for the other two girls next year. His satchel is full of palm-sized spiral notebooks, one for each girl, a record of each glacially paced, gentle interrogation. If he could just solve *one* of their cases, help nail *someone* to the wall for what happened to these girls . . . maybe he could free just one of them—and possibly even himself—from this hell.

She's retreating into the opposite corner of the shelter, dragging the blanket and the delicate moment away with her. He looks down at the phone between them and has an idea. "Hey, want to look at some pictures on my phone?"

She lets the blanket fall from one shoulder, her pink T-shirt stained with algae. "What do you mean, *pictures?*"

And just like that, Calvin knows he's finally found his angle to connect with Bus Stop Girl. Calvin's not much of a photographer—most of the pictures he takes are of documents—but he has several of Headlands Beach and a few from Sean's Fourth of July barbecue. He opens his camera roll, selects a picture of the Lake Erie shoreline, and holds it out to her. For the first time in fourteen years, Calvin has her full attention. She scoots closer. Calvin shows her how to scroll through the pictures, how to enlarge them. She's a quick study.

"Where is this?"

"That's the beach. Lake Erie."

She frowns. "Is that a lighthouse?"

Calvin slides over so their shoulders touch. "Yeah, it's pretty old. I think they built it back in the twenties. Did you ever go to the beach?"

She shakes her head and whispers. "No. Too far away."

Her words twist like a knife in Calvin's chest as she continues scrolling through pictures. She spent her whole life only three miles from the coast of one of the Great Lakes and all she ever saw was a shitty apartment, a run-down high school, and a graffiti-covered bus stop. What did he say to her at that bus stop to get her into his car? How do men like that know the exact sort of attention to pay a girl starved of it to fool them so completely? He wonders why she could briefly trust a man like that and not, after all this time, Calvin. He wonders why he can't find the right questions to get her to tell him who did this to her.

In 1986, the year she was taken, he was eighteen and sharing an apartment on Mayfield with Sean. Scholarship just big enough to make the next four years at CSU possible. Sean had a brown Mercury Bobcat that got them back and forth to summer jobs at Geauga Lake, an amusement park just south of Cleveland. Calvin spent that summer running the Big Dipper, flirting with girls as he checked their lap belts. That same summer, she was fourteen going on forty, playing mother to her own mother, working as a hostess at Mama Santa's, more likely to drop out or get pregnant than finish high school. Separated only by age and a few miles, but light-years apart by any measure that meant a goddamn.

"Who's she?" She's stopped at picture of Sean's kid.

"That's my goddaughter, Gabby." Calvin reaches to enlarge the picture. Gabby is the spitting image of her mom, golden-brown skin, eyes a shade darker than molasses, tangled dark hair. "Just turned seven."

Outside the shelter, the wind rises, the power lines in the trees wrestle with it. Her knuckles are white. Calvin casts a nervous glance outside the shelter, thrown by the shift in the weather. In fourteen years of visits, nothing has ever changed here. It's always late summer, dappled shade, and gentle breeze, a wide emptiness all around.

She taps one of Gabby's ears. "I had earrings just like that. Wish Bear, you know? I bought them with my first paycheck from Mama Santa's." Calvin notices for the first time that the finger tapping the screen is missing its fingernail entirely.

The water pooling out of her has soaked his pants, his socks, is filling his shoes. She's zoomed in on Gabby's earrings, little turquoise bears, each one with a shooting star on its chest, the enamel worn and scratched under magnification.

"Care Bears, huh?" Outside the shelter, the summer sky has gone dark. "Haven't seen one of those in a long time."

"Wish Bear is my favorite." Her voice rides the wind, triggering something deep in Calvin's memories. "He brings you luck. He's supposed to make your dreams come true."

None of the descriptions from people who had seen her at the bus stop mentioned earrings. Neither had her mom, but considering the state the woman was usually in, not surprising. She's gripping the phone so tight Calvin thinks she might shatter the screen. She's trying not to cry, poised to retreat back into her silences. A quick glance at the timer tells him they've only got seventeen minutes left. Something about Gabby's earrings has reminded her of something she's trying very hard to forget. A big part of him wants to push her, to extract whatever she's not saying and record it in his notebook, yet Calvin just can't bring himself to take more from this child. And in the back of his mind, a small persistent idea has taken hold, rearranging both his memories and his red-string theories. Green Care Bear earrings. Three girls, long brown hair. Calvin doesn't believe in coincidences.

"That's enough pictures," he says softly, taking the phone from her and setting it facedown on the bench. "Let's talk about something else. Or nothing at all. Whatever you want."

She's quiet for a long moment, studying her chipped toenails before replying. "Let's just talk about nothing today, Calvin."

Calvin carefully navigates the conversation as she struggles to relax. Hair twisting, fingers drumming and pulling at her lips, hugging herself, folding and unfolding her cuffs. Adjusting and readjusting the sodden blanket, trying to rebuild the space she feels safe in. There are soap bubbles on her cheekbones and neck too, as if she came here directly from a shower without rinsing off. Something interrupted him from his ritual with her and he wasn't able to wash her body completely. Did he wash the other girls too? In person, she looks different from her missing-person poster. No harsh eyeliner, no hot-pink blush on her olive cheeks, her soaking wet hair isn't teased and shellacked; it falls in soft waves to her waist. The almost-woman beside him is still mostly a child. Another innocent kid who will never go to prom, never get her heart broken, never get married, never have kids, never get out. Never get a chance to be anything more than a girl no one really missed, a girl someone decided to throw away.

She finally settles when Calvin tells her a story he heard about a lost camera and an explorer on Everest. She tucks her knees to her chest, rests her cheek there. Her direct gaze is unsettling, a near twin of his own. He read once that only psychopaths make eye contact for more than three seconds. He can manage far longer than that. It's a tool he uses in his line of work, a useful one. Gets people talking about things they don't mean to. But it never works here. There is no balance in the hollow world these girls inhabit and he is never the one in charge.

She asks vague questions about the missing camera, but there's distance in her voice, her eyes are now looking through him, not at him. She's wrestling with something, expressions playing across her face like a film reel. He nudges her with his elbow, gently startling her from her reveries, and says it's her turn to tell him a story.

Shyly, she tells him about her old red Walkman, how she's saving up for a new one. How she doesn't think bugs are gross at all, about the way a praying mantis turning its head makes her feel, a tiny visitor from an uncanny valley. Tells him how the best part of working at Mama Santa's is all the free pizza they let her take home. It's the most she's ever shared with him and he holds each small revelation careful as a cobweb. Asks him what his favorite game at Aladdin's Castle is and his favorite roller coaster. He tells her a story about the centrifugal ride at Geauga Lake and a guy everyone called the Rotor Man, who rode the walls all day long. He just hung there, pinned to the walls by a manmade force of nature, blissed out and numbed, alone in an ever-shifting crowd of thrill seekers. But something about that story is wrong because she breaks their lingering eye contact. The wind outside the shelter stops so abruptly, Calvin's eardrums pop.

Her eyes are darting, like a child startled from deep sleep, fingers pinching her earlobes. The moment hangs in the air, vast and silent, and Calvin feels as if the shelter is suspended in one of her bubbles. She climbs to her feet, reaches for his hand with both of hers, grips it tight. And Calvin knows she's no longer wholly there with him. That something he said has pushed part of her back to where the rest of her is, the place where her soul is still tangled in her remains, and in a moment of desperation, he pulls her into his arms. She lets him, rising on tiptoes to place her cheek against his. There's a moment when his beard brushes her jaw and he worries he's scratched her. Her hair is wet against his face. He's so shocked, after all these years of her distance and silence, that it takes him a minute to understand what she's whispering in his ear.

"He said he'd take me to Geauga Lake. Said he worked there, and I could go to the front of the line on all the rides. And we could go swimming in the lake after. He picked me up right here."

"What kind of car?" Calvin squeezes her tight, trying to warm her freezing body. She begins to struggle. "Do you remember what kind of car he picked you up in?"

She jerks away. Calvin reaches to steady her, but she shakes him off. The blanket drops, heavy and wet. "It was a brown Bobcat, all right? Who cares about his stupid car! He took my earrings, Calvin. He took my Care Bear earrings!" Her screams sound as if they're coming from underwater. "Somebody help me, please! I wanna go home!"

Calvin staggers back, drops heavily to the bench. *He said he'd take me to Geauga Lake.* Mama Santa's restaurant was just down the hill from the apartment on Coventry he'd shared with Sean. *He said my abuela had a heart attack and he'd take me to the hospital.* Sean drove an ambulance downtown for years before he went into the police academy. *He said he would take me to her, that she'd been in an accident.* What was that Mister Rogers always said? Something about looking to the helpers. Across the shelter, she's gasping and choking, water pouring down her chin. Their time is almost up and this is how she always vanishes. In a deluge.

"He came in all the time for pizza. He said . . . he said I was pretty. He was older . . . said he had his own apartment over by Coventry. Asked me if I wanted to go to Geauga Lake with him. I always wanted to go to Geauga Lake, but it's so far and we never had any money for that. And I thought . . . I thought maybe it was the earrings working, you know? Wish Bear. He makes your wishes come true."

Calvin's head is in his hands, heart pounding so hard he thinks he might be having a stoke. A hazy memory of pulling his sopping-wet duffel out of the Bobcat's trunk that summer before work. *What the fuck, Sean?* Sean shrugging, saying something about the car wash, even though the Bobcat was always filthy. Calvin being too pissed about his wet uniform to pursue it. Sean had been fired from Geauga Lake right around then. A supervisor had caught him in a restricted section of the park, Sean lost his temper, and that was that. Sean bouncing from ambulance service to ambulance service over the years—city, county, private—and nestled deep inside those years, Cemetery Girl was found facedown in the reservoir only a few blocks from all of Cleveland's major hospitals. *How many more were there, Sean?*

Calvin hears her moving across the shelter to him, knows she's kneeling down in front of him, but can't bring himself to open his eyes. His memories have restrung themselves into something monstrous, something that can't possibly be true. Something that was right in front of his face. *You don't want to see the things I see.* Sean quit his job driving an ambulance out of the blue, announcing he'd decided to go to the police academy. That would have been only a few weeks after Headlands Girl was found, the same summer Sean married Sophie De Luca with her long brown hair and burnished skin. College kid, ambulance driver, cop. He'd been right. Not three different guys, but one guy. A guy he shared all his tips, leads, and red-string theories with, the one who promised to pass them up the chain of command. *You find anything concrete, you come to me. You could put yourself on the wrong side of the blue line.*

He feels her hand on his cheek, cold and damp and dead.

"I never even got to ride the Big Dipper," she whispers.

Calvin fumbles at his side for the phone, swipes past Gabby to a picture of him and Sean. He zooms in, focusing on his friend. The years have aged Calvin in a way they haven't touched Sean; a few pounds and a few lines are all that distinguish him from the guy who drove the Mercury Bobcat. In the seconds that remain of their time in the bus stop together, Calvin holds the phone up to her. She closes her eyes to the picture, greenish water coursing down her cheeks, her image wavering and refracting.

"It's so cold in the lake, Calvin. No one ever visits me there."

And then the heavy atmosphere around them crashes down, leaving Calvin alone in the shelter, gasping in the backwash as he's dragged from her time back to his own. Sitting out front of the shelter is a squad car, standing over him is Sean, holding his satchel. Sean pulls the phone from Calvin's outstretched hand and studies the screen.

"Goddamnit, Calvin, I told you to let this go." He hauls Calvin up by his arm and drags him to the squad car.

There's a voice screaming in Calvin's head to wake the fuck up, to fight, but his conscious mind is still half in her Neverland, his limbs heavy and useless. Next thing he knows, he's slumped in the passenger seat and Sean's driving him away from her bus stop in Little Italy, across town, deep into South Collinwood. And he wonders if this is what the girls felt like, ignoring the voice in their head warning them, wanting to believe they were wrong, until the moment they knew for sure he wasn't taking them to their mother or abuela, Geauga Lake or home. Thinking this couldn't be happening, that someone would surely save them, trapped exactly like he was in an inevitability.

"You never passed along anything I gave you, did you?" he says when he finally regains his voice.

Sean flicks the turn signal, waves to a passing patrol car. "Oh, I passed it along all right. *Sorry, Chief, I hate to keep bringing you this shit, but my buddy Calvin, he's obsessed with these girls. I'm worried about him, he's lost perspective, I'm afraid of what he might do.*" Sean sighs heavily, glances in the rearview mirror. "Honestly, no one will be surprised."

"She's why you got fired that summer, isn't she? That's where she is, isn't it? At the bottom of the fucking lake." Calvin's limbs are waking up now, and he fumbles for the door handle.

Sean unclips his sidearm and jams it into his ribs. Calvin's hands drop.

"The girl from Mama Santa's wasn't the first, if that's what you're asking. Just the first I took my time with."

"Where are you taking me?" They're deep into Collinwood now, warrens of burned-out houses and apartment buildings, narrowed eyes, hunched shoulders, and tight lips that will all say they didn't see a thing.

"The thing about this side of town, Cal, is that so much bad shit happens, no one cares. Hell, we find bodies in the middle of the street, barely makes the evening news. Last week, I pulled up to a burning car, two dudes shot in the back of the head. I promise you never heard about it."

Sean stops the car and the next thing Calvin knows he's being marched through an abandoned house, gun in his side, out the back door, across an overgrown yard, into another abandoned house. The house reeks of mold and piss and something sharper, something coppery and sickly sweet. Boarded-up windows like singed eyes, broken floorboards, ceiling collapsing, the remnants of a burned couch.

Sean's foot in his lower back drops Calvin to the floor before he can even try to run. A loose nail slices through the web of his thumb when he hits the ground, pain in his spine so blinding he can't even roll over. He lies there, cheek sticking to the filth on the floor, mouth filling with blood, and watches as Sean dumps his notebooks on the couch.

"Want to know what eighteen weeks in the police academy gets you? A pension and a band of brothers willing to look the other way." Sean's rummaging around under the couch and pulls out a length of pipe. "A thin blue line that you can use to frame anything you want." He crouches down and watches as Cal feebly tries to free his hand from the nail.

"How can you be this?" Calvin rips his hand free, tries to crawl away. "How can you be my *friend*, Gabby's dad, Sophie's husband, and be this thing?"

The pipe falls and shatters one of Calvin's wrists. He screams, and somewhere upstairs someone starts crying.

"Maybe this is the only way I *can* be all those things. The only way I can stand being those things. Listen, you want a confession, Cal? You want a reason I do what I do? How's this? *It's just so easy.* Easy to take them, easy for people to look the other way, easy for everyone to forget them. Just like they'll forget you." He flips Calvin over on his back with his foot, then holds him there. Above them, the crying cuts off, is replaced by frantic splashing. Calvin pictures Bus Stop Girl's ruined wrists covered in soap bubbles, Headlands Girl's long brown hair, Cemetery Girl's gentle brown eyes. Sean frowns at the ceiling, then continues talking to Calvin like they're sharing a couple beers in his backyard.

"Got a snitch couple streets over. He'll call the cops in a few hours; say he saw you come in here with some girls. CPD will respond, find a white male, medium build, medium brown hair, kicked to death in the front room. They'll find your notebooks, see what I left in the bathtub upstairs, in the bedroom down the hall."

Calvin tries to slide out from under Sean's foot but Sean leans into it, grinding his heel into his diaphragm until Calvin can't breathe.

"It'll look like the neighborhood served up some vigilante justice for those poor girls. Case closed. And it'll be easy."

The foot disappears and Calvin gasps for air, scrambling with his uninjured hand for something he can use as a weapon and finding nothing.

Sean has taken his shirt and bulletproof vest off, and

is rolling his shoulders like he's getting ready for a game of horseshoes. "They'll pin as much on you as they can and that'll be that. My childhood best friend, and I never knew. I'll be devastated, Cal. Might pull early retirement."

Calvin is still trying to crawl away when the first kick breaks his eye socket. The second catches him in the chest, and after that Sean switches back to the pipe. Then it's just easier to close his eyes and wait for it to be over. When he finally opens them again, the pain is gone and he's back at the bus stop. But it's not just her bus stop now, it's his too. Calvin realizes he'll never see Bus Stop Girl or any of them ever again, that his last stop and theirs don't intersect anymore. He understands now why they used to fidget their way through his appointments. It's because they knew something Calvin didn't. That the minutes, days, or hours granted them once a year at their last stop are a slender reprieve compared to where they spend the rest of the year. For Cemetery Girl, it's the Lake View Reservoir, for Headlands Girl the water's edge, for Bus Stop Girl the murky bottom of Geauga Lake. For Calvin, it'll be a dilapidated house in South Collinwood.

Even now he can feel the pull of it: the temperature of his lifeless body cooling, his blood settling against his spine, his soul tangled up in the mess on the floor. As the wide quietness consumes him, Calvin settles back against the shelter and waits.

PART II
The Outliers

SUGAR DADDY

BY ABBY L. VANDIVER

East Cleveland

"He stopped giving me money," said the voice on the other end of my line.

I'd been called on my "work" cell phone. The one when it would ring, I'd do the money dance because I knew something good was coming in. The one reserved for people who were paying me and for the women giving me pleasure. The girl at the other end was neither.

"Who is this?" I said, making sure my tone conveyed my impatience. I didn't like unexpected interruptions.

"What'choo talking about, *who is this?*" Her voice was fast and flip. I could tell she was young and that she was irritated. But none of that mattered to me.

"Tell me your name or I'm hanging up."

"Caro," she huffed out my first name, "this is Tianna."

"Tianna who?"

"How many Tiannas you know?"

She was right, I only knew one Tianna. Tianna Moore. Diamond's younger sister. Diamond had been my girl. I'd been her sugar daddy. But I'd believed I loved her, at least as much as a man like me could. That was until she got locked up. Now I was leaving money weekly with her grandmother, trying to help out. Play the good guy. Why not? It had been on account of me she was doing fifteen years at Marysville.

"What do you want?" I didn't like talking on the phone.

She hadn't called me before. Never even had much to say to me when she saw me. Whenever I dropped by and she was home, she'd let me into their patched-up house—steps with missing bricks, shingles falling off the roof, screen door hanging from the frame—and wave me in the direction of the kitchen where I'd find her grandmother. The house was always clean and whiffs of sweet and savory often wafted out.

Tianna seemed to have things together. Trendy dresser. Her weave and nails always done. She carried designer purses and wore high heels with her skinny jeans. Big butt. Flat stomach. Her face, except for her dark complexion, was nearly a mirror image of Diamond's, even with them having different fathers.

But I'd heard things about her. Out in the streets.

She was loud. Braggadocious. Had a fly mouth—always talking back and talking bad. And she was trouble. She liked to keep things going—what old folks around liked to call a shit starter.

So I knew whatever she was calling me about, I didn't wanna hear.

I was just getting off my shift. The day was fading, a graying tinge of sky hovering overhead as I drove down Doan Avenue. The wide concrete street was slick with ice. My tires splashed through pools of slush heading for the freeway—crossing over Hayden, down 6th to East 133rd and over to Shaw Avenue. Counting the minutes till I was under that bridge, out of the city's limits, and could get home from this disgusting place.

East Cleveland.

I worked in it, played in it, but I refused to live in it. What I didn't know then was that my life was about to be forever mired in it.

The first suburb of Cleveland, East Cleveland had gone from sugar to shit. Back in the day, mansions dotted Euclid Avenue's Millionaire Row—the showplace of America—home to industrialist giants like Andrew Carnegie, John D. Rockefeller, and Amasa Stone. Then, in the sixties, the whites took flight, my family included, ushering in a wave of middle-class Blacks. But by the time I'd come back to the city to work, street corners were filled with Valley Low and Hot Sauce Hustlers—gangbangers and wannabes. Houses along the once tree-lined streets and the huge apartment buildings that had replaced most of the mansions were missing windows and doors, hollowed out and filled with crackheads and drug dealers.

But people from East Cleveland were proud to be called amongst its ranks. Never mind the hopelessness that seeped through from Brightwood Avenue to Coit Road. Its hapless people. Blighted buildings. Failing school systems. Overlooking those in charge who were foul and egregious. The roots of all evil ran from within its boundaries like a river of fire. Bankrupt government. Corrupt city council. Crooked cops.

Crooked cops.

That made me laugh. I was one of them. East Cleveland streets were *my* streets. I ruled them. I ran them. By intimidation. By force. By whatever means necessary. Things went my way or they went sideways. And people around knew that.

"I need you here, right now." Tianna's voice wasn't strained or riled. She was calm and even.

"Here where?"

"My grandmother's house."

"I'm not coming there," I said, sucking my tongue. Who was she to think she could order me around?

I did enjoy my weekly visits to Miss Pruitt's house—always

good vibes there. A God-fearing woman who'd raised two wayward girls, Pearl Pruitt was good-hearted. Slim. Tall. Articulate. She'd babysit neighborhood kids, pile them into her car, take them to the store. Always had something sweet she'd baked to pass out to them.

And whenever I came by, she always had something for me too. Cake. Pie. My favorite—sugar cookies. Or a pot of chili to take home to help ward off a cold, keep me sharp on the streets. Always telling me, "I made this just for you." But I'd already had my weekly visit, no need to go back by.

"For what, Tianna? What you need me for?"

"I need you to help me with this body."

"Shit." I didn't even need to ask her what she meant.

I rolled down the window and a push of the brisk winter wind rushed in with a festering moan, blistering my cheeks. I sucked up the bad taste I had in my mouth—either from her news or from the chronic pain in my stomach I'd been having lately—and spat. Rolling up the glass, I took a hard left onto Hayden and left again into Windermere's RTA station. Heading back the way I'd just come. Ignoring the *Buses Only* signs, the car took a dip as I went under the Rapid Transit bridge. I came out the other end and turned left onto Euclid Avenue.

I pulled up on Marloes and parked in front of the light brick police station. But before I got out, I reached in the glove compartment, took out a handful of Tums, and popped them in my mouth.

"Sergeant Rutherford." I nodded and threw up a hand as I passed the plexiglass that the desk officer sat behind. I didn't know what I was about to get into, but I knew I didn't need anyone putting me anywhere near Tianna's location.

"Officer Nicks." He acknowledged with a smile. "Thought you'd left for the night."

"Started to," I said, the first words in crafting my alibi. "But remembered I had this paperwork to finish on that guy I brought in earlier. It would have just nagged me and I couldn't have enjoyed my evening."

"I know what you mean," he said.

Now I'd been seen. Back at work. The desk sergeant given the impression I'd be there awhile. Then I went into the locker room and put my cell phone in my locker. Cell towers would ping me in the general area, but this might work. I signed onto my computer, then I went to the bathroom and threw up.

"Man," I muttered to myself, flushing the toilet, "this crap Tianna got going is gonna be the death of me."

I headed out the back door and walked around the building to my car. Avoiding best I could all the cameras on the outside of the station meant to keep an eye on the bad guys.

My tires bumped over a ragged glut of asphalt as I turned onto Melbourne Road off Phillips. Tianna was standing at the door. Waiting.

"Hello, Caro Nicks."

"It's Officer Nicks to you."

I stepped inside and blew into cupped hands to warm them. My fingers numb and tingling, my cheeks red and raw. She stood there staring at me. Hands on her hips.

"You gonna show me?" I said. Not that I wanted to see anything she was talking about. But I was there now.

She took me through the living and dining rooms into the sunroom at the back of the house. As we moved along, I looked to my left at the kitchen. The room I usually ended up in when I came by. But we kept going into a makeshift bedroom—curtains hung over the French doors that separated it from the living space. A TV played atop a dresser. There was a chair covered with clothes. And in the middle of the room, a bed. Laid across it, a body. Presumably the one Tianna had called me about. A pillow covering the head.

"Who is it?"

She cocked her head to the side and gave me a smirk.

I walked over and lifted the pillow. "Geesh, Tianna." My heart dropped into my stomach when I saw who it was.

Mikha Ahmed. Owner of the two largest businesses in the shopping center on Euclid and Superior. He'd opened the Shoebox only two years ago. It was *the* place where everyone came to get the newest J's. An instant success, he'd had money to burn. But the money he'd used to open it had come from Ahmed's Savmor Supermarket. The place that kept East Cleveland from being a food desert and kept the drug dealers in supply. He'd started off by selling ounces of cocaine out of his meat freezer.

Mikha was my biggest cash cow. Paying me every Friday cash equivalent to my biweekly paycheck. Easy money. The opening of the shoe store was supposed to get him away from the business. He shouldn't have let me find out, though. Now he had to keep selling *my* nose candy. Guaranteed because of my badge—he had no choice if he wanted to keep his store. Stay in the country. Keep living his American Dream.

And he was, so I'd heard, Tianna's sugar daddy.

Now he was dead.

"Tianna." I ran my fingers over my crew cut. "What the f—"

"Don't even come in here swearing." She held up a finger and took two steps toward me, standing on her toes, her face in mine. She lowered her voice. "You know my grandmother don't like that kind of talk in her house."

"I don't see your grandmother. Only you and this dead

guy." I shook my head. "Good thing too, Grandma's not here. 'Cause I'm guessing she wouldn't be too pleased with your handiwork."

"Really? That's what you got to say?"

"I don't know what you want me to say."

"I didn't call you here to talk."

"I'm still not sure what you want with me."

"To. Help. Me." She spat out the words.

I wiped the spittle from my face. "Look." I spread my hands out in front of me. "Just tell me what happened."

She gave me another smirk. "I shot him." She glanced his way. "Twice."

"Twice?"

"Yep." She pursed her lips. "He wouldn't die."

"Where'd you get the gun?"

"He gave it to me." She pointed at her dead lover. "So I could protect myself." She laughed. "Guess the joke's on him."

I didn't get that there was anything funny.

"Why you put the pillow over his face?"

"His eyes were open. Felt like he kept looking at me."

"So what happened? He hit you?"

"No."

"He tried to take it?"

"Take what?"

"You. Sex. Did he try to rape you?"

She frowned. "No, he wouldn't do that. No reason to. As long as he gave me money, I gave it up."

"Okay." I scratched my head. "What did he do?"

"I told you. He wouldn't give me any money."

"Right." I circled the bed, then bent over him to get a better look. Seemed like he'd been shot at close range. No blood spatter. Burns near the entry wound. Not only were his eyes open but so was his mouth. He'd been surprised.

"What do you want me to do?" I asked.

"Help me move him. He can't stay here." She flapped at arm toward the dead guy. "I need you to fix this."

"Fix it how?"

"I don't know." She flailed her arms. Stomped her foot. "You're a cop. Don't you know what to do? Can't you make all of this go away?"

I locked eyes with her. She had to be kidding me. "That's a crime," I said.

"What's a crime? I know killing somebody is."

"No. Moving a body. That's a crime. Helping you cover up a murder. That's a crime."

"So?"

"So I'm not helping you."

"I know you not saying you don't commit no crimes."

"I'm a police officer, Tianna."

"Don't try and play me stupid. Diamond may not have told what you did, but I will."

"Tell what?" I said.

Tianna, at twenty-four, was nearly six years younger than her sister, and she hadn't been old enough to be privy to the business Diamond and I had together.

"I see that look on your face," she said, a sly smile curling up her lips. "You think I don't know. But I ain't my grandmama."

"What are you talking about?"

"My grandmother walking around with a blind eye to the world like East Cleveland still this great place to live, and her thinking you this good guy." She shook her head. "I know the truth. About you. I know them was your drugs that Diamond got caught with."

"You don't know nothing."

"Yes I do. And I got proof."

"What proof?"

"I ain't telling you. I'm telling the judge. The FBI. Or anybody that can send your sorry, no-good, dirty-cop butt to jail just like you sent my sister."

The statute of limitations had long past on any crime I'd committed with Diamond. She'd been gone seven years. But I didn't need nobody looking into me because I'd committed a whole bunch of crimes since then.

Still, I'd already decided I was going to help this girl. As much as I could. I'd do it for Diamond. I owed it to her.

She'd asked me to look out for her baby sister, and I hadn't. Hadn't even given it a second thought. Tianna had a good mother figure in her grandmother but she'd lost an older sister, all because of me. Diamond had known the streets and knew how to keep Tianna from going astray. So I'd keep my promise to Diamond, although now—I looked at Tianna standing next to the dead body—I knew it was too late.

"What's your plan?" I asked.

"I was thinking we could burn him."

"Why you wanna do that?"

"One, so they can't identify him." She was counting out on her fingers.

"Uh-huh. And two?"

"Two," she held up another finger, "so it'll look like an accident."

"Accident. Okay. So. You gonna set him on fire here?"

"No. We could put him in the trunk of his car. Drive it over to Patterson Park. Behind the tennis courts." She smiled, pleased with herself. "Then set it on fire."

"Right. To destroy evidence." Sarcasm dripping in my voice.

"I just said that." She was talking to me like I was the dumb one. She had no clue. This was evident in her killing somebody over a few measly dollars. She was good-looking. Plenty of dope boys and business owners around happy to pay her a few bucks for what she could give them.

But then she thought burning a car would stop anyone from identifying it. VIN plates don't burn. Neither do license plates. Or bones. Not in a car fire.

"Okay," I said, "let's get him in the trunk. You drive his car and I'll meet you there."

She gave me a firm nod. Ready to get her foolproof plan into action even though it was far from that. *Foolish* is what it was.

I shook my head. I'd just agreed to help this girl. Now I was an accessory after the fact to murder. Something was going to have to be done with her. Otherwise I knew she was going to keep giving me trouble.

This day couldn't get any worse.

I threw up again after we set that car ablaze. Wind whipping around my ankles, cold setting into my bones even with a roaring fire behind me. I was bent over, holding onto the chain-link fence.

"You are such a wuss," Tianna said. "How are you even a cop?"

I didn't have the strength to answer her. Or the inclination. This girl was extra.

Tianna had stopped at the gas station—dead body on board—and came back with three plastic gallon cans filled to the brim.

"One is diesel," she'd said proudly. Now she pulled them from the trunk where she'd nestled them around Mikha's body. "For good measure."

Hadn't she worried someone would see him back there . . . ?

"That should do it," I said, keeping my real thoughts to myself.

We had rolled him in a sheet and a flowered comforter to carry him out the house. And under the cover of a black starless sky—one of the blackest nights I could remember— we now unfurled him and put him behind the steering wheel. She doused him and his car with gasoline and set it all afire.

"How is this supposed to look like an accident?" I asked. I had to hold my hand up to cover my eyes from the bright orange flames.

"His car was in a recall." She collected the gas cans and threw them into the flames.

"Yeah. And?"

"A recall because the engines on his kind of car explode. Spontaneously." She pointed to the burning car. "They'll think that was what happened to him."

An accident. I shook my head. If that wasn't the dumbest thing I'd ever heard. Almost as dumb as me agreeing to help her out.

"I gotta go," I said, standing up straight. I brushed glistening snow over where I'd gotten sick with the toe of my shoe.

"Thanks," she said as I ambled over to my car.

I had to get back to the station, sign out of my computer, retrieve my cell phone, and let Sergeant Rutherford see me leave.

She had a genuinely grateful grin on her face. "I didn't want to have to go to jail," she said.

It took our forensic team three hours to identify the victim of the car fire after it was discovered the next day (dental records). Twenty-four hours to identify the murder weapon (bullets don't burn in a fire). The same amount of time to determine the owner of the registered gun (Mikha Ahmed). And twenty minutes for his wife to spill on who he'd given it to ("that little tramp").

Just three days after the fire, the East Cleveland prosecutor drew up an arrest warrant charging one Tianna Moore with aggravated murder, tampering with evidence, and abuse of a corpse.

The day they found the body, I'd made sure to stop by the crime scene. I'd left my DNA there and didn't want it found.

"Hey Nicks, what you doing over there?" Jared Francisco yelled over at me. He ran forensics. Collected all the evidence.

I was back in the same spot. My stomach still wasn't in the best of shape, but today I had to make myself throw up. Right where I had the night before.

"Are you contaminating my crime scene?" He was shouting.

"Sorry," I said, standing up and moving the snow to cover my deed again.

"Leave him alone," someone called out. "He ain't been feeling good."

"I'm fine," I said. "It's just that this is a lot to take in." I nodded to the scorched remains of the car and body.

"Get out of here, man," Jared said to me, shaking his head, then turned to another officer. "Tag that spot so we don't go picking up any of Caro's DNA."

As I pulled out, chomping on Tums, I passed by the county's arson specialist pulling in. I knew then they'd find everything that Tianna thought she'd lose in that fire.

It had started snowing as I came out of the park. Heavy. Big fluffy snowflakes. Sticking to the bare branches of trees. I headed up Hayden to Superior and turned right. I was going to see Miss Pruitt. Let her know she had another granddaughter going to prison. This one for a much longer period of time.

Grandma Pruitt met me at the door. "Officer Nicks," she said as I stomped my feet on the outside mat. She waved me in and I detected a strong odor of bleach.

"Don't mind the smell," she said. "Tianna done spilled some bleach all over her bed. Ruined the comforter and everything." She was fussing as she headed back to the kitchen. "Had to throw everything out."

I pulled out a chair and sat at the table. "That's why I'm here."

"Something about Tianna?"

"Yes ma'am."

"She ain't dead, is she?" She pulled out a chair and sat across from me.

"No."

"She do something illegal?"

It was like déjà vu.

I had been sitting at that same table when I'd come to tell her about Diamond. How she'd been caught with drugs. How she was going to prison.

Nothing much scared me out on the streets, but telling Pearl Pruitt about Diamond had made me more jittery than a crackhead in need of his next hit.

Diamond had taken my breath away the first time I'd seen her. Big legs. Wide eyes. Her skin was light and creamy and her cheeks dimpled every time she smiled. Some nine or ten years younger than me, so I waited until she got to be legal age before I went after her. She was a good girl. Smart. Hard worker. Had a sweet personality just like her grandmother. And nothing like Tianna had turned out to be.

And I gave her everything she wanted. That was easy because she didn't deny me a thing. She didn't care I was white. She didn't care I was a cop. And she didn't care I was dishonest and unprincipled.

She probably should have.

I could have maybe gotten Diamond a better deal. If I'd gotten to her first. But by the time I found out she'd been caught, she'd tried to rip the eyes out of the arresting officer. After that—assault on a cop—there was nothing I could do. She got the maximum.

And even with that, she never said a word about me.

"Can you get Tianna out of it?" Miss Pruitt asked.

"No ma'am. There's no getting her out of this. But I will do everything I can to help her. You have my word on that."

I was glad she didn't know that my word wasn't worth much.

Then I told her what Tianna had done. Even threw in a lie or two, hoping Tianna wouldn't have time to verify. I told Miss Pruitt how I tried to stop her from going through with the plan to dispose of the body and how I'd followed her there to make sure she was okay.

"She just wouldn't listen to me," I said.

"That girl don't listen to nobody," her grandmother said, tears starting to well in her eyes.

"I'm sorry. I just wanted to let you know before, you know, they come to pick her up."

"I appreciate that."

"It probably would be best if she don't try to run. Maybe not tell her?"

"I always make sure my girls do right, even after they've

done wrong." Miss Pruitt nodded her head and stood up. "I'll make sure she stands up for what she's done. And keep your name out of it." She hung her head, swiping away tears. "God knows I tried to raise them two girls good."

"I know you did. But raising them here. In East Cleveland. I don't know, Miss Pruitt." I stood up too, ready to take my leave. "This ain't the best environment."

"I'm learning that," she said. "It's bad around here. I just wanted to make it better."

"You did the best you could."

"I did. And we got you." She chuckled. "Cracking the whip."

"I try."

"Now we just have to make sure justice gets served. It's the only way to turn these streets around."

"You're right about that, ma'am." A brief silence passed between the two of us. "Well." I looked at her. "I'm going to go."

"Hold on," she said. "I have something for you." She went to a cabinet.

That made me feel bad. Here she was trying to take care of me when I hadn't taken good enough care of either one of her girls.

"I made this batch yesterday."

I held my hands out to stop her. "No, you must've made them for someone else."

"But I'm giving them to you," she said, and pushed a plastic container with a blue top into my hands. "Eat 'em. I know you like 'em. They your favorite."

"Sugar cookies?" She nodded. "I do love them. Thank you."

I reached in my pocket to give her more money, but she wouldn't accept it.

"Being able to share that with you is payment enough,"

she said. "Now go. Take care of what you need to in them streets. I'm going to be fine."

Three days later, they brought Tianna into the station, wrists cuffed behind her, her grandmother following her in, saying the lawyer would be there soon.

They may have been on their way in, but I was on my way out. I didn't feel good and it made me feel worse to see the two of them. I'd taken a half day and I was going to spend it peering out the window that overlooked Lake Erie in my Bratenahl condo and nurse myself back to health.

My stomach was cramping and the Tums had stopped working. The tingling in my fingers hadn't been relieved from wearing gloves and I'd been stressing more than usual, which gave me a headache.

I made it home just in time to puke up my morning coffee. I laid on the couch with remote in hand and dozed off.

I jolted up when the buzzer rang.

It was Miss Pruitt.

I buzzed her in and waited at the door for her. She had a big pot of chicken soup and a bag of cookies. A comforting smile on her face.

"I heard you weren't feeling well."

"Yeah. Everyone is trying to get me to go to the doctor, but I'll be all right."

"I know you will after you eat my soup. It'll cure you of all your ailments." She went into the kitchen and called back to me, "You sit down. Take a load off. I'll get a bowl of it piping hot for you."

"How did you know where I lived?"

"Diamond," she said. "She always let me know where she was when she wasn't coming home at night."

I smiled. That was my good girl.

"Here," she said, handing me a bowl and a spoon. She sat on the ottoman across from me. "Eat up."

So I did. It felt good in my stomach. Warm. Easing up the cramps. Even the heat from the bowl helped the tingling in my fingers.

Handing her the empty bowl after my second helping, I asked, "What was in the bag you brought?"

"You know." She smiled at me.

I pushed myself up and she fluffed a throw pillow behind my back. "Cookies?"

"Your favorite," she said. "*Sugar* cookies."

She retrieved them from the kitchen and handed them to me. I dove right in, but after eating five or six of them, nausea started to rise in my belly again.

"You gone back to feeling bad?" she asked.

"Yeah. Probably from stuffing my face." I smiled up at her. She smiled back, but then it faded.

"Or maybe from the arsenic I've been putting in the sweets I've been making for you."

"The what?"

"I've been poisoning you since sometime after you got my Diamond in trouble. Little by little. That's why you've been feeling bad. But this batch got enough to kill you right now."

"Oh my God."

"He can't help you none." She shook her head slowly. "I've been asking around about you. Diamond wouldn't tell me, but people on the street were happy to give me the lowdown on you and your dirty dealings. And now that I ain't got none of my girls, which I think had a lot to do with you, I see no reason not to finish the job."

I looked at my phone sitting on the table between us. But before I could reach for it, she placed her hand over it.

"You won't be calling for help. It's time we take back East Cleveland and get all the bad out." She smiled. "Including you."

JOCK TALK

by Sam Conrad
Parma

"What'd you and your shrink talk about, Biscuit?" asked my dad, police officer Franco Rossi, after picking me up from my psychiatric appointment. His mood scared me. As mom used to say, "When trouble in camp, wise old Indian keep eyes open, mouth shut." I hated being called Biscuit. My mom, a Massasauga Chippewa, named me Bis-ka-ne, meaning "the fire is burning." The Ohioan Parmense called me Biscuit, as if I were edible.

I pretended deafness over the din of his car radio as we cruised through the West Creek Reservation. He tuned into the play-by-play of his beloved Cleveland Indians. The Indians were already on their usual losing streak.

Dad dressed in a wife-beater undershirt and a Chief Wahoo cap. Mom used to complain about how my cop father reeked of grimy sweat even when he was off duty. I cracked my passenger window for fresh air, sticking out my head like our German shepherd, Max.

Riding in his squad car, I prayed he would be proud of me just this once for seeing Parma Community General Hospital's premier psychiatrist, Dr. Vernon Everhart. I was more excited to cruise shotgun through the scenic late-April tree-studded landscape in Parma on the southern border of Cleveland. My seventeen-year-old body was jonesing for summer vacation.

Three months free from the deafening war-whoops of Parma High School's Red Men. Those snot-nosed white kids drove me *witkotkoke* with their fake headdresses and war paint. Bullying me, calling me Arrowhead. Half Breed. Feather Head Nigger. Before big games, a posse of Neanderthal jocks would ambush me after band practice. They'd strip me to the waist, paint my face red, stick a feather in my hair, and parade me into the gym chanting, "Chief Wahoo Junior!" Almost killed my spirit, eating me alive.

Mom went with me to complain to the assistant principal. He brushed her off saying it was all in fun, no harm no foul, boys being boys, skin-shaming us into being good sports. But soon leisure pursuits would fill my days with everything teenage boys crave, even a mixed breed like me. Dad was an Italian Catholic. Franco Rossi never let me forget his Ellis Island immigration heritage.

"That kid ain't no Chippewa off the old block," he would joke to his buddy cops in front of Mom and me, getting a side-eye from Mom.

I looked out of Dad's car window and dreamed of last summer with my Ralphie. He said I was his *tawicasa*, Lakota for boyfriend. I said he was *witkotkoke*, crazy. We were like an indigenous Huck Finn and Tom Sawyer, going shirtless and hunting for arrowheads together on the banks of the Rocky River where ancient Indians once buried their dead. Sometimes we brought my dog Max along to romp in the woods. We explored bordering suburbs for ancient mounds built by real Cleveland Indians. Backlot baseball. Outdoor basketball courts to shoot a game of horse.

Ralphie's real name was Ohitekah, Lakota for "brave standing bear," but the white townies nicknamed him Ralphie. A white drunk driver with a dozen previous DUIs orphaned Ohitekah when he smashed my friend's folks in a crosswalk on Pearl Road, a primeval Indian trail. Road kill. Ohitekah became a ward of the state at the Berea Children's Home, an orphan asylum run by the Episcopal Methodists, famous for the slogan, *Kill the Indian, save the man.*

I first met Ralphie at the big annual Berea High School vs. Parma High School football game. Braves vs. Red Men. I spotted him slouching on the top row of the bleachers, sitting alone. I risked getting my ass kicked by the Berea jocks by entering rival territory to climb up and sit next to him. Neither of us spoke. Without uttering a word, he brushed his hand along my thigh and across the side of my dick. Nobody would have noticed his deft maneuver. I nearly came; my face flushed from embarrassment. I could barely breathe when he motioned for me to sneak off with him to chew some fat. He had eyes like a grizzly bear with that lean and hungry look. My man, my man.

When I got home, Mom could tell I'd met someone special. We spoke with our eyes the way our people do as she tossed my shorts into the washing machine. The last thing she ever said to me was, "Whatever you do, never tell your father his name. He would kill you."

The Episcopal Methodists enrolled him at Berea's Loomis Elementary School, named for Elisha Scott Loomis, kin to the Loomis clan of historic Indian fighters. Ralphie felt the insult and the injury. He read to me from the memoir of Loomis, who bragged about his ancestors who torched the nearly seven hundred elderly Pequot men, women, and children in the dawn while they slept in a longhouse. The settlers sold those who escaped the conflagration into slavery on ships bound for the Caribbean.

"So what are you going to do, Pilgrim?" he mocked in

his best John Wayne voice, snapping the book closed and leaning over in my face. I pushed him back, jumped on top of him, and rolled around in the dirt.

Ohitekah later attended Berea High School, erected on the ashes of an Indian village. It too boasted a degrading Indian mascot. The Berea Brave was a cartoonish, bare-chested, big-nosed dude brandishing a tomahawk with three feathers in his hair. At BHS, Ohitekah escaped the racial cruelty by excelling in sports and his studies, cultivating a thirst for Native history. The real deal. Not fake whitewashed pablum.

This summer, there would be no Ralphie. No Ohitekah. He was dead. Killed last month by a care worker at the Berea asylum who called him a flaming faggot after putting him in a chokehold for insubordination, crushing him to death. I heard some snitch called in a tip to the headmaster, who searched his stuff and confiscated his diary with sexually explicit love letters addressed to me. Letters I never received. Despite Berea's finest on scene with their thumbs up their asses while the terrified kid gasped for air pinned to the ground, no charges were filed.

I was alone in a world of *wašícus*, Lakota for white people, literally translated as "he who takes the best meat." Ohitekah taught it to me a couple of weeks before they killed him.

I was alone with my father. My mom had died of cancer the previous year. Her Indian name in Chippewa was Ta-ma-sha-ka-we-zee, meaning "woman of strength"—but Dad called her Wheezy, as did everyone else. She shielded me from the wrath of the *witkotkoke* white man she married.

Mom swore that she'd contracted cancer from breathing bad medicine at the General Motors plant. Her doctors discovered a lump when a broken arm landed her in the hospital after she "fell" down the stairs. By then, it was too late. The only person who tried to warn me to run away while I still could.

A few days before she died, Mom told me in a whispered deathbed confession how she'd met Dad, how Dad was the first on scene after a nosy neighbor called 911 over a domestic dispute gone south. How Dad had pulled her drunken boyfriend off her and got him cuffed and stuffed. Later, in processing the scene, Dad had ushered her to the grimy plastic backseat of his panda—his black-and-white police cruiser—to take her statement. One thing led to another. First time with a man, so as a fifteen-year-old, she was surprised to deliver me nine months later. Her statement wasn't the only thing he took. I remember how she would sneak downstairs in her nightgown after he was dead asleep, open the front door, and sit on our stoop, looking up at the moon, crying. I'd sneak down to sit with her, my head in her lap, crying with her. We'd sing a Chippewa lullaby, swaying in rhythm:

Hey, hey, watenay
Hey, hey, watenay
Hey, hey, watenay
Kay-o-kay-nah
Kay-o-kay-nah

"Boy, what'd you and your shrink talk about?" Dad demanded.

"I beg your pardon, sir?"

"For Christ's sake, show some freakin' respect. Pay attention when I ask you a goddamn question. *Capisce?*"

It was none of his business. Why should I reveal humiliating details about Dr. Everhart making me strip naked each psychiatric session? The doctor wired my dick to a plethysmo-thing-a-ma-jig while showing me pornography of men screwing each other in the ass. He asked me how often I jack off, and then ordered me to stop.

Everhart looked my body up and down. He studied my lanky arms and legs. He wondered at my uncircumcised penis. I felt uncomfortable with my scant chest hair and peach fuzz above my lip. I was an odd half-Injun, half-white manboy, hoping my weightlifting packed on some muscle. The guys in the showers mocked me. Being closeted devalued my man card because the guys suspected me of being gay. They pegged me for queerbaiting and made me the subject of bathroom-stall graffiti.

"Sir, yes sir," I said, unable to remember his question.

"I've been paying out my ass to Everhart since your mom and your little friend died. Shouldn't the fucker have come up with a treatment by now?"

"Doc calls it talk therapy, Dad."

"So talk," he said.

Resistance was futile without Mom. "Dr. Everhart mentioned a treatment today," I said, squirming in the front seat, wondering what it was like for Mom to be raped in the backseat of a cruiser. Powerless and exposed.

"'Bout friggin' time. What'd Everhart say?"

"Everhart wants me to get an operation," I said. I had a waking dream. Unbidden, I remembered a story my mother told me about Pochockow, aka John Omic, a Massasauga Chippewa, who was the first person hanged in Cleveland in 1812. The townsfolk had framed him for murdering a white fur trapper trespassing on Indian land. Another dead Indian.

"What operation?" Dad asked.

"I dunno. A *bilateral* or *key* something," I said, unable to recall the medical term Everhart used. He'd explained it so fast that I didn't catch it.

"Oh yeah, a bilateral orchiectomy," said Dad. "It was routine in the service. Common procedure, minor surgery."

Service? Dad was never in the military. Unless you count his silly weekend warriors of Ohio's national guard as part of the real armed forces. He'd bivouac with his buds on weekends playing GI Joe and Soldier Boy and come back all gung ho spouting crap like killing commies and gooks. God bless America. And bragging about his trigger-happy commanding general, Sylvester Del Corso, a proud Berea Brave and, like Dad, Italian Catholic. Credited with his heavy-handed quashing of the Glenville shootout and Hough riots two years earlier.

"Whatever," I said, rolling my eyes, still not wanting to talk about it as my mind wandered out the window where the polluted industrial air didn't smell like ass.

"It's how they treat guys who play for the other team," Dad said, spitting a wad of man cud out the driver's-side window.

"Huh?"

"Ya know, pansies. Homo. Sexuals, Queers. Like you," said Dad, lowering his voice. "Everhart called me with yer diagnosis: latent homosexual. Look it up. I always pegged ya for a little fruity in the man department from all the funny woo-woo Indian shit yer mother stuffed in yer feathered faggot head."

Busted. By my own father? Over what shrinks termed my deviant tendencies? Mom said I was Two-Spirited—a gift from our Creator. Now I felt dirty and defective. Good as dead. Must have been a big heap of embarrassment before Dad's über-macho cohorts. And God.

I sweated bullets by the time we turned off the Metroparks and drove past Parma's little white-frame houses, each one looking identical to the next with green lawns and

American flags. Idyllic. If you were a robot or a clone—with not a colored person in sight.

"So, how d'ya feel?" Dad asked after a long silence.

"About what, sir?"

For a second, Dad sounded like my shrink, inquiring about how I feel. About having Two Spirits. About losing my *tawicasa*. About having a dead mother who was Native American. About being half white—that meant, since 1931, in the eyes of the law, society, their community standards, and family values, they considered me colored. About the torment I endured in school. About Vietnam and having to register for the draft the following week when I turn eighteen. About my dream of attending Kent State after high school. About his hero, the antichrist, Richard Nixon . . . About my recurring dreams of murdering him in his sleep. Dad, not Nixon. Okay, Nixon too.

"How do ya' feel about gittin' surgery?"

"Dunno," I said.

"What did ya tell Everhart when he brought it up?"

I cleared my throat. "Said I'd think about it."

"What'd he say?"

I shrunk down in my seat like a withered piece of fruit. "Everhart said I must decide soon since it's impeding my progress."

"Everhart described yer procedure?"

"Said it's simple and easy. Painless. Overnight in the hospital a day or two."

"With upcoming finals," Dad said after a pause, "say ya went in after school on a Friday, git home Sunday, never missin' a lick of school."

"Everhart told me it's how all his guy patients get it done."

"Can't beat that," Dad said, looking at me funny. "So, what d'ya think?"

His radio blared, babbling about his Indians. The Tribe this. The Tribe that. Wahoo whatever.

I watched towering old-growth trees disappear from the landscape to be replaced by a barren suburban carpet of white folk. Parma was a great place to raise kids, my Dad always said. *If they're white*, I wanted to say, but bit my tongue for fear of getting my head smashed in.

"What would you do, Dad, if you were in my shoes? Would you get it done?"

"Hell, if I was sick, and someone like Everhart offered a cure, I'd cut off my right arm for a chance to git well."

"Everhart said it ain't no cure, Dad."

"Biscuit, I'd cut off both arms for an incurable disease."

I twiddled the radio dial, turning down Dad's jock talk, unsure that I was the sick one. "You want me to do it?"

"It's yer decision, kid. I'm telling ya what I'd do if it was me with an incurable mental illness. I'd man up. Git it over with. ASAP. Take one for the team, Biscuit. Couldn't hurt." He snorted and again spat out his window.

"I guess," I said, feeling they were rushing me into this, although I failed to fathom the urgency.

We stopped at a long red light. I grew hot and clammy in the motionless car. Afraid I'd pass out, I resisted an urge to jump from the vehicle and run for my life, never looking back.

"So, you'll git yer surgery? Right, kid?"

"If you think it best, sir," I said, picturing him assaulting Mom in his backseat, suppressing a queasiness in the pit of my stomach. My head spun.

"Okay, when we git home, I'll phone Everhart so yous can tell him ya decided to have yer operation. Deal?"

I squinted at Dad as though time stood still, grappling over what was going down.

"Deal?" he repeated, reaching over and extending his hand.

"Deal," I whispered, shaking his hand with reluctance and regret, followed by disgust over how these filthy paws groped Mother.

"It'll fix ya up in no time flat," Dad said, patting me on my shoulder. I quelled an urge to brush off my T-shirt. "You'll be a new man by this time next week."

"Next week?"

"Freudian slip," he said, half stammering, like he and Everhart had planned this ahead of time since he knew squat about Freud.

As soon as we got home, Dad beelined for our kitchen telephone and called Everhart while I peeled off my sweaty T-shirt and tossed it over a kitchen chair.

"Yo, Dr. Everhart, Franco Rossi," Dad said. "Yup. He did. I see. Okay. He's right here. Hold on." He nodded and handed me the phone.

"Hello," I said. "Yes. Dad and I talked it over. Uh-huh. If you both think I should get it done . . . Uh-huh. Okay. I get out of school at noon on Friday. Parma Community General Hospital? One o'clock? This Friday? For real? Like, day after tomorrow?"

My face flushed crimson and my ears burned hot as I handed the phone back to Dad, trembling like Max going to our vet.

"Right. Can't eat or drink after midnight the day before?" Dad turned to me. "Everhart says wear yer jockstrap."

"Do I need my cup?" I reached down, adjusting my balls.

Dad laughed his deep dago laugh, shaking his head, not bothering to ask.

"They'll shave 'em? *Che bello!* Better them than me doing it, Everhart."

Dad hung up the phone and breathed a sigh of relief. Like he'd feared I'd chicken out and disappoint him further. "Good to go, kid. Nuthin' to eat or drink tomorrow after midnight. Everhart says to shower real good Friday morning. I'll pick ya up after school for yer trip to the hospital to git'cha fixed."

"Whatever," I said, stroking my mustachette, puzzled over why it needed a shave.

"Never guessed you'd be down for it," Dad said, half talking to himself, fixing dinner as I set the table. Fried onions and garlic with pierogies, a favorite nosh in Parma, those doughy dumplings slathered in putrid greasy slime. I'd prefer a cup of Mom's corn soup and her cornbread. "Not in a million years. *Fantastico!*"

"How come?"

"For real? Vinnie down at our precinct laid 1,000-to-1 odds against my queer kid agreeing to git his balls cut off." He shook his head. "Biscuit, your old man just hit the jackpot. Winner, winner, chicken dinner."

"What?" I couldn't believe my ears. The kitchen twirled like the carousel at Cedar Point in Sandusky.

Dad sneered at me. "Hello? What'd ya think an orchiectomy was, dumbass? Everhart didn't explain ya?"

"Not so much." My mouth gaped wide in shock and awe.

"Neutering? Nutting? De-sexing? Caponize, sterilize, *castrato*—snip, snip. *Finito! Capisce?*" He flailed like orchestral tyrant Toscanini guest-conducting the Cleveland Orchestra at Severance Hall. He always got his way—with Mom, his "Glenville niggers," me. Notches in his gun belt.

"You mean . . . So, you knew all along? You—and Everhart—were in cahoots this whole time to castrate me? How could you, Dad? I ain't no animal, Daddy. I'll be good. Sir, I promise—please!"

My hands slid down, cradling my crotch, now aware of what he and Doc had been scheming all along. I glared at the carving knife Dad held, slicing onions. It wasn't my mustache they were going to shave. I froze in fear of strangers wedged between my legs wielding razors, scalpels, and scissors, peeling and dicing my man bits like an onion.

"So that's how ya feel, ya little homo." The vein in Dad's forehead bulged out like a pink balloon weenie dog. "It's what'cha git for being mentally ill—not yer fault yer a sick piece of rotten fruit," Dad snarled, then waved his frying pan like the American flag.

"Listen up, fruitcake. I am yer father and yer legal guardian, for Christ's sake, and I am trying to help ya, ya fucking ungrateful little degenerate. I work my ass off for ya. To put a roof over yer head. And clothes on yer back and food in yer mouth. Yet here I am. For the first time, proud of ya. For having the balls to git yerself fixed. Some man you are. Yous shook on it. Go ahead and be a baby and weasel out, numbnuts. Ya always disappointed me, so why should this be any different? I can still have ya committed to a Catholic insane asylum like Parmadale for feeblemindedness, ya revolting little cocksucker. And yer going to hell. Just like yer whore mother.

"Ya think ya got it bad? The Sisters of Mercy would strip ya naked and tie ya down and shave yer head and jam an ice pick up yer nose before they administer shock treatments leavin' ya a drooling zombie after which they would slice off yer berries without anesthetic so ya could watch 'em fall to the floor one by one. How'd ya like those apples, ya filthy-fudge packer? It's yer choice, Mary."

Our windows were open. His voice thundered so neighbors could hear. I remembered Ralphie once asking if I knew why teen suicide is four times higher than the national aver-age for Native American youth, higher than any other ethnic group.

Mom hated his habit of sleeping naked with his loaded ser-vice revolver tucked under his pillow. That night, I lay awake until I heard him rise to use the john. I snuck into his room and reached under his pillow. Before I could grab it and suck its barrel down my throat, the lights snapped on.

"Lookin' for this?" he asked, standing stark naked with a big angry boner, pointing his Glock at me. "What'cha gonna do, ya little fairy, shoot me? Turn around, Biscuit. Bend over. Take it like a man."

He collared me and spun me around, ripped down my shorts, bent me over, and held my arms tight behind my back, all with such swiftness that he must have done this a thou-sand times before. He thrust so hard and fast I feared I'd split in two as a searing burn charred my insides, rising to my head.

"Open up! If this is what'cha want, ya got it, bitch. Daddy's home."

My eyeballs bulged out, rolling up behind their lids. Be-tween each teeth-rattling thrust, he hissed in my ear with breathless rhythmic pulses.

"Hell of a tight little fucker . . . Unlike your dead mother . . . Shouldn't've married that skanky old squaw . . . Sick of her bitchy whining . . . *I don't feel good* . . . *I don't love you* . . . Jesus fuckin' Christ . . . You fuckin' tight-assed faggot . . ."

I uttered not a peep, then crumpled to the floor, oozing effluvium, drenched in the musky metallic smell of his sweat, as he dismounted to take a shower.

I must have passed out. It was pitch black outside when I

woke on the floor to the sound of the shower running and Father belting out strains from Verdi's *Il Trovatore*. Ralphie couldn't fight back. My mother wouldn't. I was going to fight back and win.

I grabbed the service revolver from his dresser, then snuck into the bathroom and bludgeoned him with it during his rendition of "Coro di Zingari," the "Anvil Chorus." I remember his snide little smirk with blood bubbling from his lips as he gurgled Mom's name, "Wheezy, Wheezy, Whee . . ." so I hit him again. For her.

I kept striking him in the head after he was dead.

I cleaned the gun. Standing over his dead body, I washed his blood off me. Everhart said to shower good in the morning. Besides, after what the old man did to my backside, I needed a shower.

I reached under Father's bed to pull out his smelly old duffel bag. The one stuffed with untraceable C-notes from his shakedowns, corrupt Parma City officials, councilmen, judges, the usual. They fit neatly in my gym bag . . .

It looked like a home invasion gone south. I unlocked the back door and left all the windows open with the lights off. Any vagrant could have walked on in. I put a note on the refrigerator:

You were asleep, so didn't want to wake you. Changed my mind after our talk. Left to spend the summer with Mom's peeps out west. Got a ride with some friends. I love you, Daddy.

Knocking over some kitchen chairs and ransacking our bedrooms in the dark added a professional touch. Pulling out dresser drawers and flinging the contents to the floor without worrying about who was going to clean up the mess was as epic as it was cathartic. Freedom really is another word for nothing left to lose.

Ralphie often spoke about the St. Regis Mohawk Reservation, back east in upstate New York, on the Canadian border. An hour south of Montreal. An eight-hour drive from Cleveland. Since the currency of the open road was gas, ass, or grass, I figured my oral skills would get me anywhere without batting an eye.

By then, I'd be safe in the bosom of a sovereign Indian nation—whose muscular tribal council would forbid extradition of any of its Indians to federal or state authorities. I could easily pass between the US and Canada, as our people had been doing since the Ice Age. Nobody could raise a finger to stop me.

BITTER

BY ANGELA CROOK

Hough

Sadie stood in front of the old house, the dark empty windows staring back at her like the empty eye sockets of the dead. A hundred years ago the house had been a symbol of wealth, proof of some white man's achievement. Its wide porch, a place for ladies to sit and fan themselves while sipping iced tea, while their husbands smoked cigars and talked politics nearby. Now it stood alone, its only neighbor a vacant lot, surrounded by hills made from the dirt of long-abandoned projects to reclaim the neighborhood.

The porch, once the pride of the house, sagged under the weight of time and disrepair. From where she stood on the snow-packed sidewalk, where so long ago she and her brother had drawn hopscotch squares onto the cracked concrete, she could see the red sign marking it for destruction—finally— and it made her glad. In her pocket she carried the check for $25,000, paid to her by the city, for the rights to wipe clean the last remaining evidence of her mother's failed life.

Wind blowing across the vacant lot cut into her skin like diamonds on glass. Tears welled in her eyes from the bitter cold and the pain that refused to dim, despite what people said about the power of time. She barely felt it. Behind her, cars crept by, careful not to slide down the street, which anyone who knew anything about Cleveland could tell you hid enough ice to cover an entire ice hockey rink.

A few cars took enough interest in the solitary woman staring into the near darkness to blow their horns, but not one stopped. This was East 79th and Lexington after all, a place where people had been groomed to mind their own business.

She closed her eyes, sending a trail of tears sliding down her frozen cheeks as she inhaled the bitter cold. When she opened her eyes, the house in front of her shimmered as if she were looking at it through the warped glass of a fun house, and she started to walk, each step taking her back in time. She stepped onto the porch, her feet automatically knowing to avoid the soft spaces, and laid her hand against the door, pushing it open with the smallest effort, as if it had been waiting for her. The sound of her brother's laughter surprised her, but just for a moment. She had always known he would be here for this final act.

Turning away from the open door, she looked back into the night. The dark, snow-covered streets had gone, replaced by the brilliance of a bright spring day, the sun shining with its first true warmth as it hovered on the brink of summer. A small boy and a girl who was not much bigger than the boy sat on three-speed bikes that looked like they would be too big for either of them to ride, grinning at each other, plastic bags hanging from their handlebars. How young they had been, she nearly twelve and he two years younger, that summer of 1984. She closed her eyes again, falling into the memory.

That had been the summer she and Brian had become best friends, not simply brother and sister. Just the two of them, most of the time. They had made an adventure out of surviving, collecting old bottles in the neighborhood, turning them in for a nickel apiece. Sometimes, if they were very lucky, they would find a big bottle worth a quarter.

When they had collected enough, they would ride around the corner to Phil's and buy four chicken wings for a dollar. Sometimes Mr. Phil would throw in the fries for free. Or if they were really lucky, they would have enough to share a soda. They would take their prize and ride to Thurgood Marshall Community Center and find a spot away from the bigger kids and eat, dreaming out loud with each bite about how different their lives would be one day.

Now she shook her head, fingering the check in her pocket as she thought of him, her little brother, her responsibility, and the smallness of their dreams.

"When I grow up, I'm going to have a whole chicken every year on my birthday. And I'm not sharing it with nobody," he once said, the grease and sauce from the chicken covering his face.

"You not gonna share with me? Well, forget you then."

"Naw, Sis, I'm not gonna share with you, 'cause you gonna be so rich, you gonna have *two* chickens. Where you think I'm gonna get mine from?"

They had laughed so hard then, neither of them really believing the words they were saying. How much had the woman gotten for his life? In the end, how much had he been worth? She shook the thought away, the pain of it tearing through her body. Turning away from the street, she stepped inside, shutting the door on the outside world, along with the past.

Inside, the air was as frigid as outdoors and even with the gauzy light from the moon reflecting off the snow and through the windows, it was still almost too dark to see, but she didn't need her eyes. If God were to strike her blind, she could still find her way around this house, where she had spent so many years of her childhood.

She had been six years old when her parents brought them here. She thought it was a castle, it seemed so big then. If she closed her eyes, she could still see how the sun shining through the windows onto the white walls made the whole house seem to glow so brightly that during the summer they rarely needed to turn on the lights.

Now, the walls were covered with gaping holes where scavengers had come in and stripped away the copper pipes to sell, allowing the wind to rush through the house unimpeded and piles of snow to gather in the corners of the empty rooms. Kids had tagged the walls with gang signs and lewd messages. Even the old stove that had served as the house's main source of heat so many winters, and seemed too heavy to ever be moved, had been taken.

Out of habit, she turned the lock on the door before walking into the living room, pausing in the center of the room to listen. When she was sure that she was alone, she continued through the house until she stood in front of the narrow door that led from the kitchen into the basement, her hand hovering above the doorknob.

She could turn back now. Walk away and let God or karma have its say. She could rejoin her life and maybe work through the grief until she was a whole person again. The person who loved a laugh, a glass of wine, and a nice chicken dinner on Sunday. Maybe it wasn't too late for her and Emil to work things out. She imagined that, if she let him, he would welcome the old her back with open arms. They could give up their trendy apartment on Shaker Square and finally get married, buy a house on Larchmere with a wide front porch and a big backyard, and fill it with babies, maybe even a dog or cat.

Or maybe she could accept that job in Seattle that she had worked so hard for. That would be something, a girl from Cleveland's Hough neighborhood becoming the dean of communications at a fancy university in Seattle. Surely, that would be worthy of her picture on the wall of fame at her old elementary school, Mary B. Martin. They'd probably even invite her to be the guest speaker at the career day assembly, where some other little Black girl would hear her story and learn to dream bigger, just like she had done after hearing Councilwoman Fannie Lewis speak in that auditorium so long ago.

A noise, like a wooden chair scraping against a concrete floor, broke the tomb-like silence. She grabbed the knob and pulled the basement door open. She could only see the first few wooden stairs before they disappeared into the blackness.

She lifted one of the battery-operated lanterns she'd brought with her, sliding it open so that a beam of white light illuminated the path in front of her. With each step the old wooden stairs threatened to give way under her feet, sending her crashing into the concrete wall at the bottom. Still, she kept going, reaching out with her free hand to grab hold of the banister. As she stepped off the final stair, she paused, releasing the breath she hadn't even realized she'd been holding. She stood there, the lantern in one hand, her other hand clenched into a fist at her side, her feet refusing to move. At any other time, she would have prayed for strength, but God would not be with her tonight.

Music, distant at first, seemed to float in the air around her before filling her head, pushing away her fear, as her eyes again filled with tears. She knew the song. How could she not? When it had always seemed to be on his lips that summer. It had been their secret favorite. Two Black kids from the hood had no business knowing who Cyndi Lauper was, much less loving her music.

But they had, him even more than her. "Time After Time." Even before she fully understood the lyrics, the song had burrowed its way into her heart. These days, she couldn't hear it without feeling on the verge of a breakdown. But tonight, its gentle lyrics of love, loss, and hope gave her the strength she needed to do what had to be done. So, as she turned the corner and stepped through the doorway into the room, she hummed along with the words, feeling her doubts die.

It was quiet. The air so bitterly cold, it seemed impossible that anyone could survive for any period of time. Everything that could be used or sold had been removed, taken by scavengers, leaving the floor of the room strewn with garbage and useless debris. In the center of the room, a wooden fold-up chair and the milk crate across from it were all that remained, along with an iron grate between the chair and crate that held the long-cold ashes of a makeshift fire.

She barely glanced at the chair as she bent down to grab dry old branches from the floor beside the crate, tossing them into the iron grate. She didn't look at the chair as she busied herself making the fire. When the fire began to consume the branches, she picked up a thicker piece of wood and placed it in the middle of the fire before settling on the crate and finally looking at the chair.

"Hello, Melanie," she said, not expecting and not receiving a reply. Ignoring the silence, she continued talking, her eyes resting on what looked like a mound of rags piled high on the chair: "You don't look so hot. I suppose I wouldn't either. It's cold as shit out there, more so down here. Cleveland winter. I swear, I don't know why we choose to live through this. Maybe it's the beauty of fall that keeps us here, huh? You think that's it? You know, Brian loved fall more than anything. Most people think of spring as a time for renewal, but not Brian. He loved fall. He called it the gateway to all the great things: Halloween, Thanksgiving, Christmas, and of course his birthday."

The mound of rags moved, just a little but enough for her to know that the woman was still alive. Sadie remembered when Brian had first introduced her to Melanie. In his eyes, she had been the most beautiful woman in the world. All Sadie had seen was a plain, slightly overweight white woman with dull stringy brown hair that didn't take kindly to curling, and splotchy skin that she used too much makeup to try to hide. The only thing she had agreed with him on were her eyes. They had been a strange grayish-blue color that reminded Sadie of the sky right before rain.

Now, all the color was gone from her skin, leaving her looking as if someone had drained every ounce of blood from her body. Her once-plump cheeks sagged like old, deflated tires. And those eyes, once so strange and beautiful, were flat and colorless as dead fish. What would Brian think of her now? Sadie wondered.

"I brought you something. You'll like this. I got it from your own apartment," she said, reaching into her pocket and pulling out the half-full pill bottle and shaking it like a baby's rattle. "Nope, you don't look good at all. And just between you and me, you stink. I could smell you as soon as my feet hit the floor. I imagine it won't be too much longer now. It's the last time we'll see each other at any rate."

"Let me go. Swear I won't tell anyone. Just leave. Won't see me again. Please," Melanie said, her voice disappearing into hoarse sobs.

Sadie watched the tears roll down the woman's cheeks where they seemed to gather on her dry, cracked lips until they spilled over like drool, and felt nothing. Neither pity nor satisfaction stirred her heart, but that was good too.

"Gladly, honey. All you have to do is tell the truth. Here, you need this. How many would you like? One? Two? All of them?" Sadie shook the bottle again. "How many did he ask for in the end?"

"Please," Melanie said.

Sadie got up and moved the short distance to where Melanie sat. Lowering herself to her knees, she reached into the pocket of her coat and pulled out a switchblade made in the shape of a bat. With a flick of her wrist the blade sprung open. Melanie jerked upright in the chair as if she had been slapped, her eyes growing wide.

Sadie reached down and slid the blade under the rope, releasing Melanie's arm in one flick of her wrist. Melanie didn't move, just let her arm dangle at her side as if she had forgotten how to use it. Sadie grabbed Melanie's wrist, holding it up while she shook two OxyContin pills out of the bottle and into Melanie's trembling palm. Sadie sat back down on the crate and watched as Melanie jammed the pills into her mouth and swallowed.

They sat in silence, both waiting for the drug to work its way into Melanie's system, numbing her pain, at least for a moment or two, even giving her an unreasonable glimmer of hope that Sadie could choose mercy. When Sadie saw Melanie's body relax, her head dropping forward, Sadie exhaled, letting the calm spread through her like a healing balm on an open sore. It would all end tonight. She was glad.

"You know, Brian and I were only two years apart. But in many ways, he was a lot older than me. Or maybe he was just more street smart. I tried, I really did, to keep him out of trouble. It was my mission, even though I was just a kid myself.

I failed though. Did he tell you about that? Did he tell you what it was like growing up in Hough?"

At first it seemed like Melanie wouldn't, or maybe couldn't, answer, but then she nodded her head, just once, enough for Sadie to see that she was still listening.

"My mother came to Cleveland from Selma, Alabama, part of the Great Migration, right after Bloody Sunday. She was still a teenager, but she was determined to leave the cruelty of the South behind and make a new future for herself.

"I think she had dreams of being the next Billie Holiday. Instead, she ended up working as a maid during the day, a waitress at night, and scrubbing toilets at the hospital on the weekends, just to afford to live in a tiny roach-infested apartment on East 83rd. She said she watched out of her apartment window as the neighborhood burned during the riot. She met our father shortly after that, got married, and somehow they managed to buy this house.

"Sadly, their marriage burned out long before some of the fires did. You know all these years later there are still so many empty spaces where there used to be thriving Black businesses? Phil's made it though. And a good thing, for us at least. Did Brian tell you about Phil's? The best damned chicken in Cleveland, although no one will ever know it, unless you grew up around here. I wonder if it would still taste as good today."

"Let me go," Melanie whispered, and Sadie could see that the tears had grown to two small streams running down her cheeks now.

"We'll get to that soon enough," Sadie said, shaking the bottle back and forth, smiling at how Melanie's watery eyes followed the bottle in her hand with as much attention as a cat stalking its prey.

"I'm sorry," Melanie said, seeming to use all of her strength to force her eyes to meet Sadie's.

"I went to Mary B. Martin for elementary, same as him. After school we used to ride our bikes up to the Quik-Pik on 79th and Chester and get a quarter's worth of Colby cheese. That and a pack of twenty-five-cent crackers was a whole meal for us sometimes. I know, to someone like you, it must sound terrible, but for us, it was the good old days. Can you understand that?" Sadie paused long enough to allow Melanie to respond, but all she seemed to be able to manage was another weak nod.

"Here, this will help," Sadie said, leaning forward to grab hold of Melanie's hand, dumping two more pills into her filthy palm.

Sadie was quiet while Melanie choked down the pills.

"When I was fifteen, my grandmother came up to Cleveland from Selma. She took one look at how we were living and insisted on bringing me home with her. I didn't want to go, but she didn't give my mom much of a choice. It was either let me go to Alabama with her or have Children and Family Services swoop in and take us away."

"He told me you abandoned him," Melanie said, her words slurring.

"Yeah. I'm sure that's how it felt. You know how many times I wondered how things would have been different if I hadn't left? For both of us?"

Quiet descended on the basement as they sat there staring into the fire, Melanie slumped over in the chair, her chin resting against her chest, a line of drool hanging from the side of her mouth.

Again, Sadie thought about getting up and walking away. She saw herself heading up the stairs and out the front door.

The Quik-Pik was still there, so she could use the pay phone and call 911. If Melanie told, she could claim emotional distress, maybe even temporary insanity.

"He cried for you in the end." Melanie's words floated across the tiny space between them and ripped through Sadie with the ferocity of a knife slicing through her gut, as she tried to make sense of what she had heard. "He wanted you to save him like you did before, remember?" Melanie choked on her own laughter as she stared at Sadie, her eyes suddenly bright and alert.

Sadie held back the tears that filled her own eyes.

"He told me that story so many times I feel like I was there myself. How you came back from Selma and walked through the whole neighborhood pounding on doors, begging for help. How you found him and pulled him out of a crack house and convinced him to go to rehab. How he promised never to do drugs again. He kept his word, you know. Even in the end, he kept his word." Melanie broke into a coughing fit as she lost control of her own laughter.

Sadie picked up a brown paper bag from the floor beside her. Without looking up at Melanie, she reached inside and pulled out a pair of latex gloves. Moisture from the sweat on her palms forced her to tug at the gloves to get them on. For a moment she was sure they would rip before she could get them completely over her hands, not that it really mattered anyway. She knew that if anyone cared to look that hard, the trail would lead back to her fairly quickly.

She reached back into the bag and pulled out the full syringe and the small dingy-looking rubber hose she had brought from Melanie's apartment. The fear mixed with longing in Melanie's eyes brought a smile to her face.

"I brought you a present," Sadie said, waving the syringe

around. "It's all yours. All you have to do is tell the truth."

A loud crash from upstairs, followed by the sound of scurrying feet seeming to come from inside the walls, shocked Sadie onto her feet. Melanie tried to yell, her voice coming out in hoarse breathless bursts as she flung her body from side to side in the chair. Sadie stood rooted to the spot, waiting for the sound of feet pounding down the stairs coming to rescue Melanie, and take her to jail. But after a few moments the silence returned, except for Sadie's heart crashing against her rib cage, the sound of it filling her ears.

As Sadie's heart slowed, she sucked in a deep breath, letting the cold moist air of the basement fill her lungs, cooling the hot blood rushing through her body. She collapsed back onto the crate, her legs too weak to hold her any longer. Melanie's mouth opened and closed like a fish dragged from the water, but whatever last bit of strength she'd found at the thought of a reprieve had died, leaving nothing but pitiful mewling whimpers of despair.

Sadie watched her as she sat rocking back and forth, as much as the ropes would allow, her chest heaving with noiseless sobs. Any hint of pity she could have felt was wiped clean by the thought of her brother alone, helpless, probably terrified, dying slowly at the hands of the woman he had loved. The woman he thought had loved him.

Sadie had never been fooled though, not really. She could still remember that day almost a year ago. It had been his birthday. He had walked through the door holding Melanie's hand, a nervous smile on his face as he greeted the family. Sadie had tried to convince herself that the unease she felt when he introduced her was simply surprise, since he had never brought anyone to his birthday celebrations before. She had even considered that she might be a little jealous.

Melanie had said all the right things, but her smile didn't reach her eyes and there seemed to be something off in how she clung to Brian, never leaving his side. Even her laugh had seemed cold and forced. When Sadie finally managed to pry Brian away from Melanie's side to try to find out more about the woman he was so sure he loved, his answers had been short and vague, until he finally told her to mind her own business.

They hadn't talked much after that. It seemed that every time Sadie tried to reach out, he either didn't pick up the phone or he would put her on speaker where Melanie could listen in or join the conversation. Then had come the call, Melanie informing her that her brother was gone, her tears as fake as her laugh.

"When they told me that Brian died of a drug overdose, I talked to the doctor, told him it was impossible. I could tell he felt sorry for me, the poor delusional sister. He said it probably took about three weeks for the drugs to kill him. Twenty-one days. That's a long time. The thing is, at any time, even on that day before, if you would have called someone—a doctor, me, anyone—they could have saved him. What kind of person can watch someone die for three weeks and do nothing? I thought about that a lot before we ended up here. I suppose I hoped I was wrong, because a person capable of that isn't really human at all, are they?"

Melanie didn't answer this time, the hatred blazing from her eyes brighter than the dying fire.

"So I did some digging. Turns out Brian wasn't your first. You've had such a tragic life. Five marriages to five different Black men in five different states. All under the age of forty. All with troubled pasts. All dying for no real reason under the care of their loving wife."

Melanie's eyes widened and she shook her head as Sadie continued to talk.

"Oh yes. The names changed, but you're still the same monster, whether you call yourself Jade from Oklahoma, Tammie from Minnesota, Patricia from Denver, Renee from Albuquerque, or our own little Melanie from Cleveland. Still the same monster."

"What about you? How is what you're doing any better?" Melanie asked, the words soft and mushy, trailing off as her head rolled forward.

"You want to know something weird and honestly a bit sad? No one is looking for you. Not really. Your family seems to think you just moved on. I guess they're used to that. Made my life a hell of a lot easier, I tell you. Honestly, my plan was to give you your drugs and leave you down here to die. I'm sure our friends in the walls would enjoy the feast. But you're right, I'm not you. So I have a proposition."

Melanie forced her head up, fighting to hold it steady.

"Yes, that's right," Sadie said, smiling as she watched a tiny new spark of hope grow in Melanie's eyes. "You can live, if you choose to."

"What do you want?" Melanie rasped.

Sadie didn't answer at first, just stared back at Melanie, enjoying the war between fear and hope that raged across Melanie's face, until the woman's head started to droop forward again.

"Restitution. That's what your life will cost. Restitution and the truth. You're going to tell me how my brother died and you're going to give every nickel of the blood money you stole back to the families of your victims."

An odd clicking sound seemed to come from deep inside Melanie's chest as she shook her head from side to side.

"I don't know what you're talking about. Brian was sick, I helped him. I don't have nothing to give anyone."

"I thought that might be your answer," Sadie said, turning and reaching into her pocket to pull out the switchblade again. "I found this in Brian's things. I gave it to him for his birthday one year. He loved Batman. He carried it everywhere. It's still sharp after all this time. If I cut you, just the tiniest bit, just enough for the blood to flow, I wonder how long it would take for them to come feed off of you. Will they wait until you're dead? Passed out? Asleep? Or maybe the smell of it would be too much for them to hold back and they'd ignore your screams in favor of a fresh meal."

"No," Melanie whispered.

Sadie stood up, clenching the knife in her hand so tightly she could feel her fingers start to cramp.

"Okay," Melanie said as Sadie took a step toward her, "I'll tell you everything."

"Start talking, you're running out of time." Sadie lowered herself back onto her seat, taking a deep breath to fight back the wave of nausea that seemed to come out of nowhere.

As the night ticked away, Sadie sat, barely breathing, as Melanie talked, her words colder than the wind blowing off Lake Erie during a February blizzard. How she had slipped the heroin into his food, a little each day at first, increasing it over time, until he didn't know who he was any longer. How she had watched his body, which he had once been so proud of, waste away, as he lay stinking in his own filth, no longer caring about eating, unable to even make it to the bathroom on his own. How he became sick when she took it away. How he begged in the end for Sadie, for their mother, for God, and finally, for death.

Each word sliced through Sadie, opening up a new wound

until she could barely hear anymore over the screaming in her head.

Silence reclaimed the room when Melanie finished speaking. Sadie touched her face, surprised when her fingers came away dry. She had spent months since Brian's death searching for the truth. A part of her had never really believed that she would ever find it, but now that it was here, there was no rage, no pain. Nothing but an emptiness that left her feeling exhausted.

Turning away from Melanie, she reached back down into the bag and brought out a single sheet of paper and a pen.

"A deal is a deal." Sadie said. "Sign this and you'll never see me again."

"What is it?" Melanie asked, her voice as empty as Sadie felt.

"An agreement turning over all of the proceeds from the insurance policies you took out on your husbands to their families, including the $250,000 you received from Brian's death to the Hough-Norwood Family Health Care Center and the Thurgood Marshall Recreation Center."

Sadie watched as Melanie struggled to sign the document with her shaky free hand. When she was finished, Melanie passed the paper back to Sadie.

"A deal is a deal," Sadie said. "But first, I think you deserve a reward, don't you?"

Sadie stood, grasped the switchblade, walked around the fire, and knelt beside Melanie.

"I wish you an eternity in the pits of hell where you forever have to face the same torture you inflicted on so many." Sadie squeezed Melanie's hand in hers until she could feel the bones grinding against each other as she cut the ropes from around her other wrist.

Melanie slumped forward, sliding onto the floor without the ropes to keep her upright.

"You want it?" Sadie asked, holding out the syringe and the dingy piece of rubber.

For a moment, it seemed as if Melanie might find the strength to refuse. If she had, Sadie had prepared herself to accept God's will and walk away. But it only took seconds for Melanie to ignore her gut and grab the syringe from Sadie's hand.

Melanie struggled to tie the piece of rubber around her arm and jab the needle into her vein. When the convulsions started, tossing Melanie around the floor like a rag doll, her eyes rolling back into her head, foam frothing from her mouth, Sadie did not move.

When it was over, and Melanie lay on her back, sightless eyes staring up at the ceiling, Sadie picked up the folding chair and slammed it onto the basement floor again and again until it splintered into pieces. Taking her time, she spread the wood over Melanie's body, before moving around the basement, gathering up old newspapers, garbage, and pieces of broken furniture, adding them to the pile.

Reaching into the paper bag for the final time, she pulled out a bottle of Everclear 151, opened the cap, and poured it on, tossing in the bag and rope before setting it all on fire.

For a moment, she stood at the bottom of the stairs watching the flames inch across the floor, devouring everything in their path, before turning her back and walking away. Outside, the wind had strengthened with the promise of the first real blizzard of the season. Already the swirling fat snowflakes were so thick that Sadie found it hard to see more than an arm's length in front of her face. The streets were deserted now, and that was good. Without looking back at the house, she crossed 79th and headed the short distance to Martin Luther King Jr. High School, where her car was the only one left in the parking lot.

As she sat in the vehicle waiting for the engine to warm up, she thought about all the days they had spent there as children, playing hide-and-seek, or hide go get it. Watching the older kids play basketball. She looked across the street and wondered if old Mrs. Tyler still lived in the big green and white house. Her first boyfriend had lived there, Mrs. Tyler's grandson. Elliot? Arnold? She couldn't remember his name, but she remembered he had been her first kiss.

When the windshield was clear enough for her to see, she pulled out of the driveway. She could still smell the smoke, and soon anyone who happened by would be able to see the flames shooting through the vacant windows. But on a night like this, by the time the fire department was notified, there would probably be little left.

As she drove slowly down the ice-encrusted road, she thought she heard the distant sound of sirens. She reached over to turn on the radio. Klymaxx was singing, "*I miss you, there's no other way to say it . . .*"

This time, when the tears came, she let them fall.

PART III

THE TRENDY

TREMONSTER

BY D.M. PULLEY

Tremont

I hear his laugh before I see him.

A giggle from somewhere over my shoulder. I open my tear-crusted eyes to an old episode of *The Fresh Prince of Bel-Air* playing on the television. The laugh track titters in the background, but that wasn't it.

I unkink my neck and scan the room. Saltines and dead cigarettes litter the coffee table. Toppled bottles. Open wine. I must've passed out on the velvet couch we found at that garage sale. Our bedroom door stands open, but the queen-size air mattress is empty.

Dan left.

The door slams again in my head, and everything I drank in the two nights since he stormed out rolls to the top of my throat, lurching me up to my feet.

That's when I see him.

His dark face peeks in through my living room window, catching me midcrouch like a bathroom stall intruder. I yelp and cover myself, eyes darting to the front door, the open window, the empty bedroom.

But . . .

This little Black boy can't be more than nine years old. I follow his gaze to the television where Will Smith is dancing like Carlton. He props his elbows on my windowsill and presses his nose to the bug screen, ignoring the hungover white woman gawking at him.

I must've left the window open the night before. I can't remember. I can't remember how I got home. I remember the martinis at the Lava Lounge down the street. I remember the song that was playing. Tracy Chapman telling me to run.

The boy laughs again, but not at me.

"Hey," I say.

He looks at me, looks at Will Smith, and then vanishes without a word.

Flabbergasted, I gape down at myself. I'm wearing Dan's old T-shirt and nothing else. Bare legs. Loose tits. Crumbs on the floor. Crumbs on me. Mortified, I run to the bathroom and throw up last night's vodka.

It takes most of the day to pull myself back together again. My head stops pounding around five. I'm able to hold down food by six. I clean up the evidence of my bender—the bottles, the ashtray, the spilled wine—thinking of that kid and what he saw.

And what he must think of me.

Because that wasn't me. Not the "me" I show people. I graduated from CWRU at the top of my class and landed a job at a well-respected software company downtown just this spring. Yes, I drink from time to time, but so what? It's practically a prerequisite in college.

And after you're left for dead by the love of your life.

Dan and I were supposed to get married. One day. After three years of dating, we signed a lease on this apartment. Just the two of us. Just four months ago. Our landlord, Mr. Lewandowski, called the newly renovated duplex a "love nest" while eyeballing my chest with a wet-lipped smile on his bloated Bible-salesman face.

Our first apartment.

Tremont was supposed to be the perfect place to start our grown-up life together. This little neighborhood across the river from downtown had everything we wanted—monthly art walks through galleries like Asterisk and Doubting Thomas, vodka infusions at the Treehouse, culinary wonders at Michael Symon's Lola. We wanted nightlife and free street parking. We wanted the "real Cleveland" despite my mother's qualms about the crime rate.

But now Dan's gone.

I scan the street outside for the little boy again. A loose dog runs down the sidewalk. In the late summer haze of 1999, Tremont's a fancy dress with broken heels and smeared mascara. Ragged houses stagger listlessly between painted flipper-uppers and flashy new townhomes. Rusted chain links stumble into plastic picket fences. The Realtors call it a neighborhood "in transition." The residents call the yuppies driving up rents "Tremonsters."

And maybe they're right.

Frank Sinatra starts crooning through the ceiling. Our upstairs neighbors like to blast their vintage record player while cooking gourmet food. Katie and Roger moved in the same week we did, and the four of us would've been fast friends if life was an all-white sitcom. Katie's an MBA from the East Coast, and Roger's in law school or something (I forget). Our first attempt at hanging out, they drank herbal tea instead of cheap wine and found none of Dan's jokes funny. Now, we mostly mock them and their pretentious music.

Dan and me.

I don't see the little boy again until the next Saturday.

All week long, I check the front windows, paranoid,

while I watch reruns on Dan's dorm-room television. He said I could have it. He took nothing with him but a suitcase. He didn't say where he was going, and he's not anywhere I've looked. There's no number to call. His old answering machine sits on my kitchen counter, waiting for the phone to ring.

He's probably stoned in some coffee shop, studying the patrons. Dan fancies himself a freelance anthropologist. What my dead father would call a "bum." He plans to get a real job when his grandmother's inheritance runs out. In the meantime, Dan majored in philosophy and studies the "art of life."

He'd keep me sane, he said. He'd keep me honest.

I stare out the windows and picture him dead in a car crash. I replay our last fight over and over in my head. The moving in together all happened too fast, he said. He can't deal with my anxieties and perfectionism. He can't fill the hole left by my father's heart attack and my mother's depression. Not anymore. I'm too broken. I drink too much. I remind him of his abusive father. Because he had to say something that hurt enough to make me throw him out.

Fucking coward.

God, I miss him. I love him. He was like air. The lack of it drags me down to the couch again, and I can't breathe. This is how dying must feel, I think. If it wasn't for work, I might just lie here and rot.

Judge Judy rolls her eyes at me from the TV screen. I down my whiskey and check the windows again. The sun has faded behind the big Catholic church on the corner. A warm breeze blows in through the screen, and I see him. A small head at the edge of the windowsill. He's just a kid, but it's like the eyes of God are on me.

"Hi," I say.

He frowns at me like I'm the one peeking in windows.

"What's your name?"

"Landon," he almost doesn't tell me.

"Nice to meet you, Landon. I'm Reenie."

That's the most I've said to another person outside of work in a week. I consider inviting him inside, but that would be inappropriate. Right? I debate offering him a pop, but I'm not so sure I want to commit. He might come back and expect food or something, I think, and then hate myself for comparing a boy to a stray cat. I don't want to be that kind of person.

What would the person I *want* to be do?

The two of us watch Judge Judy yell at people for the next twenty minutes in silence. By the time I make up my mind to offer the kid a drink, he's gone.

That night, I lie on the floor where Dan and I had planned to buy a bed and stare up at the ceiling. A steady stream of voices passes by my window. New couples and old friends chatter and laugh and stumble to and from the bars. I should be with them, I think. I should be out there living my life.

But Dan was my life. All my Cleveland friends are Dan's friends. I didn't bother making any of my own after freshman year. Some feminist I turned out to be.

A stray ant crawls over my arm, and I flick it away.

The damn bugs survived the renovation. Despite the fresh paint and new carpet, they lingered along with that musty smell wafting up from the basement on humid nights. It smells like something died.

Dan was supposed to call Mr. Lewandowski about the ant problem.

Every half hour or so, a shout or scream somewhere outside makes me jolt up. I stop breathing and listen, straining to hear sirens or a call for help, but then it's quiet again.

* * *

The next time I see the boy, I open the door and step outside with two glasses of water.

"Hey, Landon. You thirsty?"

He takes stock of me. He takes stock of the glass. He looks over his shoulder at the empty sidewalk and the cars parked along the curb. Only then does he take it.

"Thanks," he says.

I plop down on the front steps because Dan and I never got around to finding porch furniture. I haven't had a sip of alcohol in two days, and I feel it. Not withdrawal exactly. It's something else. Boredom? Despair? I should be inside making up ads to find a roommate. I should be hanging pictures and organizing shelves. I should be finishing that project for work.

"Is your mom or dad around?" I ask.

"No."

The August heat wraps around me like an itchy sweater as I wait for more. He just looks away. What a shameful, presumptuous question, I think. Not everybody has parents. My own father's dead.

After an awkward silence, I try again: "Are you staying with family around here?"

"Auntie Felice." Landon points to the dilapidated pink house next door. The one Dan and I called "the crack house."

Our gallows humor makes me wince inside as I look over there again. Bags of trash are piled on the front porch. Scattered garbage and weeds litter the muddy yard. Most of the windows are covered in newspaper. The day we moved into the duplex, a scraggly old white guy limped over to our U-Haul and said, "Watch out for that house there. It's full of drugs!" He pointed to his makeshift eye patch. "One of 'em got me with a bat."

Dan and I nodded and slowly backed away, later agreeing that Eye Patch was the neighbor to avoid, but the warning stuck along with the shitty nickname. Our third day in Tremont, two cop cars and an ambulance pulled up to the pink house and camped out there for two hours.

We installed a security system that afternoon.

Maybe it's my suburban upbringing, but I hurt for this poor, sweet kid. He doesn't have his mom or dad around. Or a TV. God only knows what that pink house is like inside.

"You hungry?" I ask him.

"Nah. I should go."

He hands back a half-empty glass, and I see a drawing, a portrait in blue ink, on the back of his hand. It looks like . . . me. There's a perfect hummingbird on his forearm and more doodles on his sneakers. Flowers, dragons, tears.

"Did you draw all those? They're really good, Landon." And disturbing, I think, seeing my face on his skin.

He shrugs and lifts a worn backpack onto his shoulder before crossing the narrow driveway and disappearing into the pink house. Felice's House, I say to myself. Auntie Felice. A part of me is relieved he left, and the other part thinks about him for the next four days.

The following Tuesday night there's a knock on my front door.

It's after nine, and I'm in pajamas because I don't have the energy to go out and "have fun." I barely had the energy to open another bottle of wine. Dan still hasn't called, and I'm beginning to think I'll never see him again.

"Hello?" I say through the locked door, and turn on the outside light, hoping against hope it's him. That he's come back.

Through the keyhole, I see the outline of a small boy, pacing in the shadows. I unbolt the security door.

"Landon, what's wrong?"

He pushes his way into my apartment without asking, clutching that worn backpack to his chest and looking scared for his life.

"I'm sorry to bother you, Miss Reenie."

"What happened, honey?" I shut the door and crouch down, scanning for cuts and bruises. "Is it your Auntie Felice? Should I call someone?"

"No! Don't. Just take this and keep it safe for me." He thrusts his ratty backpack my way.

"I don't know, Landon." I lean back. "What's in there?"

"Nothing bad. It's just . . . private. Keep it for a day. Please? I can't let him find it."

"Him? Him who?"

"Nobody. I have to go."

"Landon." The bag is heavy. Heavier than a kid's backpack should be. "You can't just leave th—"

The boy shushes me like someone's listening, and we both stand still. He snaps off the porch light and checks the front windows, scanning the dark street. A pack of Tremonsters stumbles down the block to the bars on West 14th.

Without another word, Landon opens the door and slips out into the night.

My mouth opens to yell after him, but the whole episode has left me speechless. I close the door still holding the backpack, which smells like cigarettes and old cheese. Feeling duped, I carry it to the bathroom and set it down in the tub, not wanting it to touch my carpet or my furniture or my life. It might be infested with roaches or bedbugs. Or worse.

It sits there like a bad omen, watching me, daring me to

open it. But I don't want to get involved in whatever this is. He said it was private. I silently curse the moment I offered Landon a glass of water instead of shooing him off my porch.

The next day, I get home from work, turn on the TV, and wait.

Every few minutes, I check the windows for a pair of brown eyes. I check my messages. Nothing from Dan. Nothing from my mother. She still doesn't know we broke up, and I can hear her voice nagging me all the way from Muncie, Indiana: *He's the best thing that ever happened to you, Reenie. I hate to think of you living in that city by yourself.*

I check the windows again.

After an hour of this, I go into the bathroom and open the cheap cabinet under the sink to make sure Landon's book bag is where I threw it so I could shower.

It's still there, crouching like a cornered spider.

I close the cabinet again and start pacing. If I unzip the bag, I'll have to do something about it. I can't claim plausible deniability if it turns out to be bags of heroin. Or a severed head. I can't say it's none of my business.

Opening the bag makes it my business.

If he's not back tomorrow, I'm throwing it in the trash. I didn't sign up to be an accomplice to some sort of heist or whatever this is. I didn't sign up to be this kid's friend. I'm not the one squatting on other people's porches. I'm sorry, Landon, but this isn't my problem.

When I don't see the boy the next day, I start to worry.

He's not there in the morning as I walk to the 82 bus station. He's not in Felice's muddy yard when I walk home, but the dark windows of the pink house watch me pass by. I hear a baby crying somewhere inside.

He was scared of someone that night, I think, scanning my empty porch. I grab my mail and unlock the door. Bills. Fliers. More junk mail for the last tenant that didn't get forwarded correctly.

Landon talked about a "him." The police? A drug dealer? A bully? I pull the backpack out from under my sink and look at it again. Whatever this is can't stay here. Maybe I won't throw it in the trash, but I need to get it the hell out of my apartment.

I wait until the sun goes down to carry it (in a nondescript trash bag) outside. I check the sidewalk and the papered windows of the pink house again before scuttling up the narrow driveway to the laundry door in the back.

During his flip, Mr. Lewandowski did almost nothing to the basement but throw a cheap washer and dryer in the corner and call it a day. The crumbling brick walls sweat mildew, and deep cracks run through the badly patched and undulating concrete floor. The ceiling hangs low enough that Dan has to duck.

Dan.

There's a six-foot hole inside me as I scan the room. The basement never frightened me until now. The shadows. The spiders. That terrible smell. I tell myself it's just a dead mouse or two hidden behind a wall.

I squeeze the trash bag in my hand and make up stories about the backpack inside. *I've never seen that bag before in my life, Officer. Someone must've broken into the basement. Maybe my neighbors forgot to lock the door.*

I'm a terrible liar.

Dan said it was the thing he loved most about me. He'd laugh when I pretended to like his cooking or said work was "fine" or swore up and down I only had one glass of wine.

Remind me to never rob a bank with you, Reenie.

God, I can't breathe right. I can't sleep. My boss wants a "meeting" tomorrow, and I can feel my grip on things slipping away. I used to be able to function on my own. I had actual bones in my body. That's the problem with loving someone.

And what the hell am I going to do with this bag?

Katie and Roger won't do laundry until Sunday. Sunday is *their* day. They told us so the week we met so we wouldn't try to sneak a load into *their* routine. Fine. Whatever. I stuff the bag behind the dryer and scurry out of the basement like I'm being chased.

The next morning, my boss sends me home with a handful of pamphlets for counseling services after HR walks me through the procedures. I have two weeks to show improvement. If I'm suffering from alcoholism, I need to enroll in a support program right away.

The first thing I do when I get home is drink two shots of vodka because fuck them. The second thing is check on the damn backpack still hiding behind the dryer. The third is to find Landon.

I stand on the sidewalk in front of that damn pink house, working up the courage to knock. It's been three days since the boy dragged me into this mess. Three days without a word. I step onto the creaking porch and tap on the door.

No one answers. A baby's car seat lies on its side in the corner.

I knock again, and a small head appears in the doorway. It belongs to a stringy-haired blond girl, maybe six years old.

"Hi," I say. "Is Landon home?"

A voice bellows from inside, "Who is it?"

"Hello, Felice?" I call back. "I'm your next-door neighbor?" I'm already regretting this. I have no good excuse for knocking or to be looking for a nine-year-old boy. She's going to think I'm a pervert.

"Toni, let her in."

The girl sizes me up with her doll eyes before opening the door wider. A cloud of cigarette smoke, garbage, air freshener, and cat piss hits me square in the face. The house smells just like Landon's backpack. Fast-food wrappers litter the floor along with an assortment of broken lawn furniture and cardboard moving boxes.

Through the kaleidoscopic mess, a gaunt white face glares at me from the back corner of the living room. No lips. Hard eyes. Hair pulled back so tight it hurts my scalp.

"Who the hell are you?"

"I'm Reenie. I live next door."

I look around for the little blond girl, but she's vanished into one of the corners or maybe down the hall to my right. Landon's nowhere in sight. There's a baseball bat leaning against the woman's couch.

"What can I do for you, Reenie?" She picks up a glass pipe and takes a hit. A skunky cloud drifts over the room.

"I was looking for Landon? He stopped by the other day. I told him I'd . . . lend him a book." The lie makes me grimace. "Are you his aunt Felice?"

She stares at me, deadpan.

I shift my feet.

"He's not here," she finally says.

"Oh. Do you expect him back anytime soon?"

"Can't say. He just stays here sometimes since his mama . . ." Her voice trails off with a telling shake of her head. "You can leave the book for him."

I look down at my empty hands. "Right. Shoot. I'll go

. . . Or just . . . let him know I stopped by? So sorry to have disturbed you."

I back my way out of that house, half expecting the woman to bolt up and take the bat to my head.

I walk into the Lava Lounge that night feeling too foolish and frightened to be alone.

"How's it going, Reenie?" Nuke asks from behind the bar. "The usual?"

I nod and plop down on a stool while he mixes a vodka martini with two blue cheese olives. Nuke's cute in a washed-up-surfer kind of way. He likes telling people he dropped out of business school and never looked back.

"You make it home okay last Friday?" He winks and sets down the drink.

"Yep. No worries," I say, but the wink makes me cringe.

I wonder what histrionics he witnessed the night Dan dumped me. I wonder if I threw up on the floor or tried to kiss the poor man. I wonder if I cried.

Sipping vodka as slowly as I can, I light a cigarette and look around. In true lounge fashion, everything there is upholstered red. A local artist painted swirling neon murals of faces staring from the walls and bodies dancing on the tin ceiling.

Scanning the booths for friends I don't have, I debate calling the police to report a missing child, but I don't even know for sure if Landon's missing. Maybe I should report Felice to child services, but she'd know it was me. Right? I might get an eye patch to match my neighbor's. Besides, the police have already been inside the pink house many times over the last three months. They must know what goes on. And I don't know who else lives there. I never bothered paying attention to the comings and goings. Just the police cars.

And Landon.

He needs help, I think. He needs a grown-up who gives a damn to be there for him, and for an indulgent moment I daydream that grown-up is me. We'd be friends. Landon and me. I'd help him with his schoolwork. I'd keep him out of trouble. I'd help him find a real home. Maybe even mine.

"You want another one?" Nuke asks.

I nod. Who am I kidding? I can barely take care of myself, and Landon didn't ask to be rescued. He just shoved that filthy backpack into my hands and took off.

Halfway through my second martini, a scraggly white man with an eye patch lumbers into the bar. He takes the empty stool next to mine and waits for Nuke to hand him a light beer before turning to me.

"Ain't you my neighbor?"

"Yep," I say and wish to hell I knew someone else there.

"What happened to your fella?"

I glare at him and don't answer.

"Too bad. You shouldn't be in that house by yourself."

The last thing I need is a well-meaning misogynist's advice. I roll my eyes and turn away, hoping he'll take the hint.

"Last woman to live there alone met a bad end. That's all I'm sayin'."

"I'm sorry?" I glare at him like he's nuts. Because he is.

"Last girl went missing." Eye Patch leans in. "I heard a hell of a racket one night, screaming like bloody murder, and then she was gone. I wouldn't be surprised if those druggies next door got her."

"Did you call the police?"

"What good would that do?" he asks like I'm the crazy one. "They take about a year to show up. Besides, you think I want one of them coming to *my* house?"

"Who, the cops?"

"No. One of *them*."

Disgusted, I push my drink aside and pay up.

On my way out the door, he calls after me, "You be careful now, girlie!"

The whole walk home, I think of things to say back. If Dan were here, he'd tell me not to overreact. He'd remind me that Eye Patch is batshit and fighting with old men is pointless. I keep my head down passing Felice's house, feeling murderous eyes peering out those dark windows. What was I thinking going in there?

I grab my mail and hustle inside, locking the door behind me. Coupons. Political flier. A *Final Notice* for a *Letitia Murray* stops me cold. It's not the first time we've gotten unforwarded mail for Letitia, but it's the first time I've given her a second thought.

Is this who Eye Patch was talking about? I look at the notice again. It's from a collection agency.

I turn on the television, mind buzzing with vodka and unanswered questions about this missing woman. And Landon. Every slam of a car door, every footstep, every voice makes me flinch. The street doesn't go quiet until well after two in the morning, and the quiet's almost worse. I stare at my closed curtains and imagine Landon peering in through the seams. I shut my eyes and hear Letitia screaming.

Eye Patch didn't even call the police. Maybe no one did.

The next morning, I startle myself awake on the couch. My eyes and head feel swollen as though I've been crying.

In the bathroom, I try to work up the courage to call the police about Landon. The thought of Felice and her baseball bat next door makes me hesitate. I stagger to the side windows and peek through the curtains at the pink house.

Oh no.

Three police cars block the street. No sirens. No lights. Two uniformed officers patrol the sidewalk. There are two more on Felice's front porch.

He's dead, I think. Landon.

The cops lead a skinny white woman out of there in handcuffs. She turns her head toward my window, and I duck behind the curtains.

Fuck. She'll think I called them.

When I dare to look again, little blond Toni emerges holding a lady officer's hand and a blue teddy bear. She's escorted to a police car along with a black trash bag (her clothes, maybe), and I think of the one hidden behind the dryer in the basement.

Two of the police cars pull away.

Panicked, I gather a laundry basket together and rush up the driveway, stealing glances at Felice's house, looking for shadows in the windows, wondering who's still inside. A scary drug dealer with the baseball bat? Landon?

The black trash bag is in the basement right where I left it. Landon's big secret. He trusted me to not look inside, but I need to say something. Do something.

Bag in hand, I approach the remaining police car at the curb. The officer behind the wheel stops writing on his pad and looks up. He's a handsome Black man with kind eyes. Eyes like Landon's.

"Can I help you?"

"Yeah, hi. I live next door. What happened?"

"That's a private matter for the family, ma'am."

"Right. Sorry. I just was worried about a little boy that stays here sometimes. Landon? Is he okay?"

The officer studies my face and then his notes. "We don't have a record of a Landon here."

"Nothing? He's about nine years old? I saw him Tuesday." I look down at the bag in my hand. Proof of Landon and God knows what else. "He said he'd come back to visit me, but I haven't seen him since. I'm worried he might be in trouble."

The officer flips to another page and takes down a description and the timeline. "We'll keep an eye out, ma'am. But I have to be honest. If he's not in the system, there's not a lot we can do. We don't even know his last name."

This is when I should hand over Landon's backpack and tell the officer the whole bizarre story. But I don't. Landon said the bag was private. It might incriminate him. More importantly, it might incriminate *me*. There could be unregistered guns or bags of crack in there, and I smell like vodka and look insane. I should've opened it and checked.

"Okay, thanks," I say but hesitate to leave. "I'm sorry. This is totally unrelated, but do you know anything about a Letitia Murray? She used to live in my house."

"Can't say that I do. Lots of people come and go around here."

"My neighbor told me she disappeared awhile back. After he heard screaming?"

"Doesn't ring a bell. I can make a note of it." The officer writes Letitia's name down and tells me to have a nice day.

I watch him drive off still holding Landon's backpack hidden in a trash bag. Because I'm a fucking coward. And not the person I want to be.

Alone in my apartment, I drop it on the kitchen counter disgusted with myself.

There's a message waiting for me on Dan's machine. The first message in weeks. The little red light pulses with hope, and I'm almost afraid to press the button. Worried my heart can't take it.

"*Reenie? It's Dan. I'm sorry. About everything. I just couldn't do it anymore. I'm out in California now . . .*"

My eyes lose focus as Dan rattles off a forwarding address and a half-hearted goodbye.

I wait for the tears to come, but they don't. It's heavier than sadness. It's like falling into a deep, dark pit. I can barely see daylight as I pick up the phone and dial a number from the fridge.

A recorded voice answers followed by a beep.

"Hello, Mr. Lewandowski? It's Reenie Williams on Auburn. I need to talk to you about the lease. Dan's gone and I don't feel safe here anymore. I need to leave. Today. Please give me a call."

I hang up and stare at the black trash bag. Landon. All alone. Alone like me. He was the closest thing I had to a friend in this city. How pathetic, I think, and a fat tear escapes down my cheek. I didn't even know him.

"Why did you pick me, Landon? What were you running from?" I whisper. After a moment's hesitation, I grab the backpack out of the plastic and pull down the zipper.

A pretty Black woman smiles at me from behind a square of glass. The same woman sits with a little boy on her lap. Landon? There are photos with extended family. Grandparents? Cousins? Picture after picture of a life. Landon's life.

At the bottom of the bag, I find envelopes, maybe thirty of them, and a worn notebook. I dump it all out onto the counter like pieces of a puzzle. Junk mail. Bills. It's all addressed to Letitia Murray. I look from the envelopes to the photographs of Landon and his mom. Letitia and Landon Murray. Oh my God.

This is his house.

The phone is in my hand before my head catches up.

"Cleveland Police Department. How can I help?"

"I'd like to report a missing person. Two persons."

"Please hold."

I put the cordless phone on speaker and open Landon's notebook. It's full of drawings. Beautiful pencil sketches and color portraits of his mother, an old man, a cat, a car. He truly is an amazing artist. I wonder if his teachers know.

God, don't be dead, Landon.

As I flip through, the drawings grow darker and more frightening. A balding man's white face glowering in a window—puffy lips, comb-over, hauntingly familiar like I met him once somewhere. Then there's a shadow of a man in a doorway. A broken chair. A body lying crooked on the floor. A knife in the sink. Dark stains dripping down the walls and onto the floor of an empty room.

Did Landon see these things?

The implications race through my mind. The scream Eye Patch heard. The unforwarded mail. That telling shake of Felice's head next door. *He just stays here sometimes since his mama . . .*

Warnings about meeting a bad end scream through my head as I stumble into my room to pack up my things. I'm going straight to the police station with Landon's bag and then I'm going to a hotel. It isn't safe here.

Ants scatter out from my pillow like little harbingers of death. They're all over the carpet, racing under the air mattress. A trail of them follows an unpainted brown streak under the loose baseboard and disappears under the brand-new carpet. Landon's drawing flashes in my mind as I claw the rug back.

The wood subfloor is swarming with ants. Thousands of them gathering over a reddish-brown stain. Blood.

A faraway voice says through the phone in the kitchen, "This is Sergeant Albers. How can I help?"

I can't move. Three months. I've slept inches away from all this dried blood for three months. The ants. The smell. Letitia Murray. My stomach rushes into my throat. She died here.

"Ma'am, are you there?" the tinny voice asks. Then I hear a click and a dial tone that drones on for what feels like hours.

A knock at the front door snaps me out of my stupor. Terrified, I don't answer it. It could be anyone. It could be Letitia's killer. Shaking, I throw clothes into a bag, hoping whoever it is goes away, but the sound of the dead bolt sliding back stops my heart.

"Hello?" a voice calls out. "It's Hal Lewandowski. I got your message. Anybody home?"

"Uh, yeah," I call back with a breath of relief.

I poke my head out to see my landlord's stocky frame wander over to the kitchen counter where the contents of Landon's backpack lie strewn. I only met Mr. Lewandowski once and couldn't pick his average white face out of a crowd, but I recognize it now as he turns my way. The fat wet lips. The greasy comb-over. The bloated cheeks.

It's the face from Landon's sketchbook.

Mr. Lewandowski renovated this place. He covered up the bloodstained walls and floor with paint and carpet. He knew Letitia Murray.

"Where did you get this?" he asks, holding up his ominous portrait.

"I, uh, found it. Under the porch," I lie.

"Huh. Do we have a problem, Reenie?" There's a tool

belt around his waist—claw hammer, screwdriver, drywall saw, duct tape.

My blood drops. "No. It's fine. I was just leaving."

I know then with mortal certainty that I should've said more to that police officer. Given him the bag. Opened it sooner. Tried to help Landon instead of myself.

"We don't need to play games." He curls his wet lips into a semblance of a smile. "Letitia Murray was a pretty girl. Wasn't she? Not as pretty as you, though."

I swallow hard and look at the front door and the security keypad next to it, but his large frame is blocking the way.

"A pretty girl like that shouldn't have been in this house all alone. No husband. No friends or family nearby. Real shame. So many women go missing in this city, but what can you do?"

"Did you, um, call the police?" I ask, searching the floor for a weapon and finding none.

"They said she ran off."

I nod, backing up.

"You know I got this house at the sheriff's auction for a song? That's the beauty of Tremont: foreclosures. You just need to be patient. I've had my eye on the house next door for a few years now."

He called the police on Felice, I think through the adrenaline roaring in my ears. He's probably done it more than once. To get her in financial trouble. To steal her house.

"How long have you been buying real estate?" I ask, buying time, inching closer to the window.

"Oh, ten years or so. I just love house hunting." His wolfish grin spreads to bare his teeth. "Among other things." He steps into my bedroom with a plan forming in the dark light of his eyes.

"Where's Landon?" I whisper the name like a prayer.

"I don't know who you mean," he says, but I can see that he does and my heart goes cold.

Not even the dogs are barking outside. Katie and Roger are at work. The bars down the street are closed. Over his shoulder, the photos of Letitia and Landon gaze up at the kitchen ceiling like bodies in their graves.

When I scream, maybe someone pauses and listens. Maybe someone wonders. But the screaming stops, so they keep driving or watching old reruns on TV. Because it's really none of their business.

I would've done the same.

THE BOOK OF NUMBERS

BY MIESHA WILSON HEADEN

Fairfax

Add *$1,155.*

Kaye Hatcher would be $1,155 the richer at the end of the day.

Standing next to the senior pastor's designated parking space, Kaye looked up at Pastor George who stared down at her from her office window. The senior pastor of Mt. Moriah Baptist Church waved. He always seemed to turn up in her office whenever she went on a smoke break. He disapproved of her smoking. She'd been smoking fifty-five of the sixty-nine years of her life. No sense in quitting now.

The church bookkeeper, Kaye pushed up her vintage horn-rimmed glasses and smoothed the high bun on her yellowing gray hair. She snuffed out her cigarette on the sidewalk and moved to the other side of Pastor George's Cadillac Escalade, obscuring her from the church's back-lot security camera.

Walter Goode Jr. took her lead, angling his body and mouth away from the camera. Walter was one of those guys who was good with figures and mechanics but barely graduated from high school. After a short and unfruitful career as a thug, he had returned to his natural proclivity. He was a jack-of-all-trades handyman, including roofing, which is why Kaye had put him on her rotation of fraudulent church contractors.

Kaye grew up on Kempton Avenue, the same street as Junior in Glenville. Kaye was there when his mother died of lupus, when his daughter was killed by her boyfriend, when the remaining siblings lost the house to foreclosure. She knew Walter. She knew he needed the money.

"Did you fix the roof leak, Junior?" she asked.

"I did as best I could," he responded. "That roof has to be over twenty years old. Mt. Moriah is old as hell. The rot is inside. I can only do so much. I mean, I put some thick tar and boards over the holes. It'll hold for a minute, not through a heavy storm."

"It's not going to look right if plaster falls on the choir members' quick weaves, and then I call you back in three months for the same job. The trustees will complain, ask me a bunch of questions."

"Kaye, that's the best I can do with the little bit of money you're sliding me."

"Write an invoice to the church for three thousand dollars."

"How much of that do I get?"

"Two-thirds of the invoice in cash, the usual. Don't be greedy. Be glad you're getting paid for half-assed work. I need the roofing invoice by three p.m. Tell your nephew Brandon I need the cleaning service invoice too. Today, before the pastoral anniversary."

"About that: Brandon wants a better cut, maybe like 75 percent. His crew wants more money to clean the church each week. People aren't showing up. Leaving him hanging. He's trying to keep up his end of the bargain. You know what I'm saying?"

"Brandon wants a better cut." Kaye cocked her eyes at the camera and lowered her voice. "If Brandon wants a better cut, then he can get a barber's license or chop food in some-body's kitchen with the other convicts."

"Somebody said something about how people in glass houses shouldn't throw stones," said Walter.

"Make Brandon separately invoice the church for five hundred dollars in COVID cleaning. I'll charge it to the Cleveland Foundation COVID-19 grant. Get me the in-voice. I gotta go."

She'd have $1,155 by the end of the day. She needed a bit more. A good thief, if only a petty thief, she took what she needed. A little here, a little there. She calculated the small numbers in her head, like an old-school bookie.

She walked back within view of the security cameras and glanced up to her office. Pastor George still sat there at her desk, typing away on her computer, replying to emails in the church's general account. Pastor George buttered her up. He told her that the church could not continue without her. She was the church's longest-serving employee at twenty years. She knew the ins and outs of the church better than anyone.

Kaye adored Pastor George. For the past five years, he'd offered relief from fifteen years of serving under old Pastor Booker, who had treated her with biblical disregard. There were only two audible words she, as a woman, could speak to Pastor Booker—*yes* and *amen*.

When Pastor Booker announced his retirement, Pastor George had appeared out of nowhere. He understood the assignment when he showed up with his expensive-looking wife, Monica, and his three Jack-and-Jill-type children. Kaye remembered Pastor George's rousing sample sermons during the parking lot tent revival. He performed. George pulled out all the stops in those sermons: the elegance of Reverend Otis

Moss, the prancing of a Pentecostal, and the voice of Andraé Crouch. He inspired confidence.

As a pro forma measure, the trustees had asked Kaye to run the requisite criminal background check. Pastor George had never been charged with a felony; he was not a pedophile. His credit score was low and his debt seemed high with a house note, car notes, credit card debt, department store debt, and school loans. Forgive us our debts. A lot of people were in the same boat in those days. Kaye contacted the church in Illinois where Pastor George had previously served as senior pastor. The Illinois church took so long to reply that the trustees of Mt. Moriah moved forward without the recommendation, unanimously approving his appointment. Pastor George had been a blessing to the church ever since.

Subtract $60,000.

Pastor George, Gina Douglas, the recently elected treasurer of the Mt. Moriah Board of Trustees, and a fussy man stood outside Kaye's office. The unidentified man sported a tweed jacket, round spectacles, and a grayed, receding hairline. He smelled of mothballs and cedar. An accountant. Solo practice. She recognized her own kind.

Her bookkeeping gig at the church should have been temporary. TRW Automotive in Lyndhurst had employed her as a staff accountant for sixteen years, making $60,000 per year with benefits. She wore smart suits from Macy's to work. Each workday morning, the TRW guard waved her through the parking lot gateway. Her employee badge, always clipped to the lapel, granted her entry to the most secure parts of the building. Her colleagues, global engineers and capitalists of the automotive industry, respected her presence. Rolling into the ten-acre wooded campus was utopia. She soon escaped

Glenville. She bought a three-bedroom house in South Euclid off Belvoir Road. Her son Andre graduated from Brush
High School in South Euclid–Lyndhurst. She made good.

Utopias never last. She swallowed bitter root thinking of
how TRW's modern design, respectability, and salary dulled
her hustle, her sense of self-preservation honed as a Glenville Tarblooder. She had suspected something was wrong in
2000 when the CFO, Steve Byrne, requested more metrics,
more historical data, more microanalysis. Gently questioned
about the purpose of the new assignments, he chuckled about
the capricious demands of the CEO. His ice-cold blue, lying
eyes. When TRW sold for $1.5 billion to BFGoodrich, Byrne
received a million-dollar golden parachute, and Kaye, then
fifty years old, received a six-month severance package.

For a pittance, she accepted a bookkeeping gig at Mt.
Moriah to help old Pastor Booker in her spare time while she
looked for another accounting job. No one wanted to salary
a fifty-year-old Black woman. Puzzling through the church's
haphazard finances, sitting in the pews of the sanctuary staring at the cross during lunch, she asked God why and how.
She never heard an answer. She did discover that the church
made a lot of money. The widows' copper coins amounted to
a fortune.

Kaye breathed a sigh of impatience. She hadn't expected
the board to appoint an outside accountant so soon into Pastor George's tenure. Pastor George put a big hand on Kaye's
shoulder, nearly pinning her to the wall.

"Kaye," he said as they entered her office, "I'm sorry to
barge in on you. I'd like to introduce you to Grady Smith.
Gina and the other board members hired Grady to help you
catch up on the past-due tax filings. I told the board that it
was unnecessary. You do everything. You are in charge. I told

Mr. Smith that you are the most important person in this church, and we don't do anything without your approval."

"Hello, Miss Hatch," said Grady, extending his hand. "Like Pastor said, I'm just here to help. We can finish the three years of tax returns in no time. If you give me access to the church's QuickBooks account, I can finish most of my job offsite."

"She doesn't use QuickBooks," said Gina. "She barely uses a computer."

Gina Douglas was part of the thirtysomething crowd who had recently joined the church. They were young, professional, well-educated, and rude. Gina ran for a board seat on a platform of financial stability and transparency. Beatrice Heath, an eighty-year-old mother of the church who had served on the board for twenty-five years, withdrew her candidacy, allowing Gina to lord into the position.

"It's not a big deal," said Grady. "Really, as a church and nonprofit organization, you can only run into criminal liability for theft of employer withholdings."

"The church contracts with Paychex," said Kaye, "a payroll company, for weekly employee deposits and employer withholdings. They send me a weekly email to tell me how much money to transfer from the operating account. The withholdings have been in a separate account for years. It's so automatic that I rarely review it."

"The church has only one email address: administration@mtmoriahfairfax.com. Kaye monitors it," explained Pastor George.

"Miss Douglas knows that I do my accounting the old way: in my head, on paper, and in Excel," said Kaye. "That's the way I learned it. I've been doing this job for twenty years."

"Okay, that's fine, you can share those documents with me," said Grady.

"I don't put all church's accounting on the Google drive because I don't trust the digital security. I can print the detailed financial statements for you, but it's going to take time because I'm very busy around here."

"Maybe I can start with spot-auditing some of the receipts," said Grady.

"You are welcome to it," Kaye replied, motioning toward a mountain of bankers boxes.

Grady will find nothing, thought Kaye. The receipts recorded legitimate purchases of supplies and equipment from legitimate vendors. Kaye then fenced the church's supplies and equipment to local businesses for a nice discount. She thought of herself as a financier in the underground economy. She gave Black businesses access to capital. This side hustle pulled down about a hundred dollars per week.

Add $745.

"Hey, little sweet pea," said Kaye, kissing Amaya, her granddaughter, on top of her two braids still slicked down after a whole day of third grade. They walked up the eroded steps of the church. Such a pretty girl with a round face and honey-colored skin. She was already fine with a protruding behind and thick legs. *She looks like her heifer tramp mother*, thought Kaye.

"Grandma's got things to take care of," said Kaye. "Be a good girl and go on down to aftercare with the other children." More backpack than girl, Amaya skipped to the 1950s wing of the church were the classrooms were built.

Be a good girl, Kaye thinks. *Not like your mother, who landed my son, your daddy, in prison. Christie. Who names their kid after a strip club?*

James got fooled by a big butt and a smile. Kaye paid for it. She imagined James parked in front of Christie's house at night, waiting. Christie came home after midnight with another man. The guy pulled a gun on James, and James rammed his car into the guy's car while Christie was still inside. One moment, one fit of rage, crumpled his life, Amaya's, and Kaye's. What was he thinking?

Attempted murder, felonious assault, criminal damaging, aggravated menacing, the Cleveland Police charged. Judge David Alighieri of the Cuyahoga County Common Pleas set the bond at $50,000. Kaye bonded him out with five thousand from her savings. Still, James lost his job for taking an unexcused week off work. The court appointed a public defender, but when he showed up with a luggage full of other cases, Kaye found an attorney in private practice. Criminal defense attorney Charles Willis required a five-thousand-dollar retainer to be paid before the preliminary hearing.

She owed Willis two thousand by the end of the week. Still $745 short. Attorney Willis, who once got a heartless felon off after actually holding a smoking gun, made plain that he would start working on the case after he received his money.

Kaye deducted $745 from the Cleveland Foundation COVID grant. She wrote the check to Northeast Ohio Whole Health, an epidemiology consulting firm, for training the staff on ending health-care disparities in underrepresented communities. Northeast Ohio Whole Health was a DBA account for Geraldine Knew, her dead aunt whose checking account Kaye still controlled. She stamped the check with Pastor's signature.

Old Pastor Booker had treated her with the special dismissiveness Baptist preachers reserve for sidelined women of the word. But young Pastor George was a wellspring of charm. He immediately offered to let Amaya attend the church's aftercare program free of charge after James's arrest, after her son and granddaughter moved into her house. Not that Kaye would have paid, but she appreciated the grace.

Add $60.

Pastor George appeared at her office door. "For my fifth pastoral anniversary on Sunday, I had a suit made for me at Christophier in Lakewood. Is my suit an allowable church expense?" He handed Kaye the invoice for nearly $3,500.

Kaye's fingers flinched at the cost. Apparently, he had ordered a custom-tailored suit and two custom shirts. Pastor loved fine clothes. To his credit, he looked fine in them. A few months ago, he had given Kaye a bill for a $1,350 pair of shoes from a store called Church's on Chagrin Boulevard. She buried the expense in travel reimbursement.

"I could expense the clothes to the pastor's fifth anniversary fund," said Kaye.

"I hoped to use that fund to take my first lady on vacation." He winked.

"I guess I could charge it to the general fund if you wear it underneath your clerical robes."

Pastor George gave a conspiratorial laugh, then said, "Kaye, I have a favor to ask of you. All the ministers are gone today. The church's van is on empty. We need it tonight to deliver meals for the sick and shut-in. Could you spare a moment to fill the tank? I'd be grateful. Plus, you almost never leave this building. You deserve some air."

"Yes, Pastor, some air would do me good. I'll fill the tank." Kaye stood from her desk and slid the church's credit card into her pocket. She could fill the van and then fill up her own car to tide her over until the next paycheck. "Do you want me to grab you a Popeye's sandwich on the way back?"

"I could eat," said Pastor George. "I'll be doggone if I didn't leave my computer at home today. Hey, do you mind if I use your computer to post some pictures of the food drive on Facebook and read the church email?"

"No worries, Pastor, of course." Kaye never left anything incriminating on her computer. She was an analog girl in a digital world. She left no electronic footprint. "You must have deleted a lot of emails recently. I noticed the nearly empty in-box. Why don't you let me set up your own account?"

"I make folders and filters for the contacts I need," said Pastor George. "One email account is fine. It gives me an excuse to hang out in your office."

His dazzling smile confounded Kaye. He probably kept her on as the church bookkeeper because no one would suspect sexual shenanigans between them. She was old, but she wasn't dead. She committed a bit of adultery in her heart.

Add $83.

Pastor George was still typing on Kaye's computer when she returned. She handed him the Popeye's chicken sandwich, no spice, green beans, and a Diet Coke. Like Kaye, he stayed in the church long hours, skipping dinner and neglecting the time he should spend with his manicured wife and three teenaged children. Pastors' wives put up with too much.

"For my fifth pastoral anniversary, I want you and your family to sit on the front pew with me." He spoke like he preached, as if his words were a fresh revelation. He electrified his audience with his earnestness.

"I'd be honored, but I don't want to get you into trouble.

There's people who have been sitting on those pews for as long as the tree grew that made them."

"They'll be all right. It's time to recognize the workers who get things done around here." Pastor George squeezed Kaye's shoulder in confidence. She felt his warmth run through her body.

"Thank you, Pastor."

"I'm going to make a guest appearance at tonight's AA meeting. May I have the password to the God box so that I can put in the cash offerings before I go home? . . . Oh, I forgot, the Cleveland Foundation called while you were gone. Something about the first COVID grant distribution. I told them you would call them back."

"No problem, I'll call them back," said Kaye, as she wrote the passcode to the God box on a slip of paper and handed to him. "You should go home more often."

"My son plays winter and spring sports at University School. My two daughters participate in every imaginable club—robotics, mock trial, entrepreneurs—at Hathaway Brown. I pay so much in private school tuition for the three of them, I could start my own charter school. They barely notice I'm missing." Pastor George chuckled and walked away.

Cleveland Foundation could wait until tomorrow. Pulling out the church's checkbook, Kaye paid the Illuminating Company from the general fund by adding the amount of the church's utilities to her personal bill, placing both invoices in the envelope. One check, two accounts. With James and Amaya living with her now, she had to keep the lights on. She had to be careful because that damn Christie would look for any excuse to snitch to the caseworker, take custody of the little girl, and stop paying noncustodial-parent child support.

* * *

Not one more penny.

The spirit of the Lord led Kaye to check up on Brandon, Walter's lazy-ass nephew. He was not cleaning the bathrooms. He napped on the couch beside the second-floor bathrooms. He looked like a giant baby—cute, fat, and stupid—if babies smoked Black & Milds, one of which dangled from the corner of his mouth.

Kaye opened the door of the lady's bathroom. Still dirty. She saw muddy tracks on the white tiles, hairs near the sink, and a doo-doo snug on the side of the toilet bowl.

For weeks, Monica, first lady of the church, had been murmuring complaints to Kaye about the indifferent cleaning of the bathrooms. Monica wanted the bathrooms perfect, like her hair, her Yale doctor of divinity husband, her prep school children, her Audi A6, and her house on North Park Boulevard. The bathrooms needed to be spotless for Pastor's anniversary on Sunday or there would be hell to pay.

Kaye was worldly wise. She knew pussy wins over proficiency. If Brandon messed up the bathrooms, Pastor might be obligated to dismiss Kaye to please his wife. Kaye's stomach turned thinking about the difficulty of covering her tracks if the church ever fired her.

Brandon needed to get out. She would find someone else to appreciate a two-thirds cash deal on the cleaning job before the pastor's anniversary. Cash, the gift of unreported income. Money discreetly hidden from child support, creditors, or the Cuyahoga Metropolitan Housing Authority.

She regretted picking Brandon for the cleaning job. Walter's sad story about his nephew who had just gotten out of prison for a petty crime swayed her. Brandon was a corner boy—too dumb to be a kingpin. Too stupid to run.

Kaye pulled out her phone and opened the church's security app. Pastor was also logged in. *He is so absent-minded,* thought Kaye. *He forgets to log out.* She disabled the camera.

"Brandon, put the spliff away while you are in the church," said Kaye.

"Okay, miss lady. I was looking for you." Brandon rubbed his droopy eyes and palmed the cigarette.

"No, I'm not giving you one more cent."

"Wow. I'm here to talk business. I deserve more. You got your hustle, I got my own. We can come to some kind of arrangement so that, you know, other people don't have to get involved." Brandon nodded to the security camera.

"Are you threatening to tell Pastor?" Kaye asked, laughing. "No one will believe you. You are a felon with multiple convictions—larceny, weapons, assault. Is that all of them or were there others that were dismissed with your plea deal?"

"You do too much," said the young man.

"Go on and get up out of here, Brandon."

"Trust and believe: if I go to prison, you will be with me." Brandon hefted himself off the couch. The church's worn marble floors echoed as he stomped to the stairwell.

Subtract $25,000.

Kaye opened the church's security app and swiped through the camera views. She saw the cars of Gina the trustee and Grady the accountant in the parking lot. Pastor George must have let them in through the side door. She swiped again. Someone had disabled the boardroom security camera.

She followed Brandon's trail down the back staircase to the first floor. She walked down the hallway, knocking on the boardroom's heavy wooden door. Pastor George opened the door wide and greeted her. Gina and Grady sat at the table with laptops and stacked papers.

"Kaye, I'm glad you're here. You were tied up with Brandon a moment ago. I meant to tell you that Gina and Grady scheduled a meeting. They have a few minor questions for the finance committee. God did not gift me with the discernment of numbers, except the Book of Numbers. That's why you control all the accounts. Could you please answer their questions while I prepare for the anniversary on Sunday?"

Kaye's suspicion about a secret meeting evaporated. Pastor George consoled everyone with his humble demeanor and convivial nature.

"Kaye, you are coming to the anniversary, aren't you?" the pastor added. "I want you right up front."

"I wouldn't miss it for the world," said Kaye. Pastor air-kissed her on the cheek and waved goodbye to Gina and Grady. Light and warmth exited the room with him.

Kaye took the chair at the head of the table.

"Thanks for taking the time," said Grady. "I need to make sure I understand your procedures. Who authorizes transactions and transfers between funds?"

"I'm happy to help," said Kaye. "The pastor endorses checks, authorizes transfers of funds, and approves the accounts payable. He's our spiritual and lay leader—"

"Really, it's you. Effectively, it's always you," interrupted Gina. She locked eyes with Grady. "You have digital, administrative access to all the church's bank accounts and funds from your computer. You control what comes in and what goes out. For physical checks to contractors and vendors, you have a stamp with the pastor's signature. You transfer the payroll payments to all the church's employees."

Gina just showed her hand in her tirade, thought Kaye. *The poor woman misunderstands basic accounting controls. She's got nothing.* Feeling confident, Kaye relaxed and cracked her neck.

In all her time working at this church, she had never filched more than $25,000, and from time to time she repaid some.

"Bless your heart, you are confused," said Kaye. "But it's my fault. With so many new board members, I should have insisted on an orientation training to teach the newly elected basic accounting procedures. Gina, you're a social worker at Children and Family Services, right?"

Kaye gathered the power in the room to herself. She blinded them with numbers; she belittled Gina with complicated accounting terms. She lectured at length, leaving no room to ask a question. They knew nothing about the contractor kickbacks, the phony vendors, the double utility payments, or the gas cans. They could conjecture but not prove anything.

"Kaye, what about employer payroll withholdings?" Grady asked.

"We use a payroll service, Paychex. I told you that in our first meeting."

"Do you have administrative access to the employer withholdings account?"

"Yes, but it's automatic. The money runs through a separate bank from the general fund. The payroll service pays employees by direct deposit and sends the employer withholdings to the State of Ohio. I rarely even look at that account."

Add $2,833.

Back at her desk, she searched for emails from the payroll provider in the church's general inbox. Grady's questions made Kaye nervous. She wondered what he'd noticed that she'd overlooked. The general email held over fifty undeleted emails from Paychex but nothing unusual.

"Kaye, it's Cleveland Foundation on the phone. Would

you mind if I transferred the call to you?" Pastor's voice startled her as he appeared out of nowhere. He closed her door behind himself.

"Hi, Kaye, thanks for taking the call," said Alan from the Cleveland Foundation. "I told the pastor that we need to demonstrate impact in our grant funding. Impact boils down to the number of people of grantees reach with their programming. Could you explain how many residents of Fairfax you served with back-to-school supplies, PPE, and Chromebooks during the COVID lockdown? Your outreach far exceeded those of the surrounding churches, which is great. I'd like to verify this for the annual report."

"Our congregation and its outreach have grown exponentially since Pastor George started," said Kaye. "He is a blessing to the church and the community. I can verify the numbers for you."

Verify Kaye did. She pulled out her handwritten notebook, her own off-book accounting system. She told Alan all the good things he wanted to hear. She'd spent two thousand dollars on Chinese N95 masks from Amazon with grant funds. She then procured free disposable masks from another agency, returned most of the N95 masks to Amazon, and pocketed the change. She bought two Chromebooks for $1,000 and sold one. She paid $1,000 to Heavenly Transportation to deliver food from the Cleveland Food Bank to the homebound elderly and sick. She charged Heavenly Transportation her usual one-third fee.

In total, the church served 250 residents of Fairfax, the historically Black neighborhood sacrificed to Cleveland Clinic's expansion. Kaye rooked $2,833. The American Rescue Plan proceeded with dazzling efficiency. Kaye genuinely took pride in her work: People received aid. She provided for her family. The church's reputation grew. No one got hurt.

Kaye decided to go home that night at five p.m. although she rarely left before eight. There was practically a contest between Pastor George and Kaye to find out who would stay later. The day had been good. She'd dealt with Brandon. She'd shut up Gina. She'd told the Cleveland Foundation the kind of fairy tales they liked to hear. She felt content.

She'd pick up barbecue and fries from Beckham's B&M Bar-B-Que for her son and granddaughter. She'd pull weeds out of her long-neglected front yard. She'd enjoy the improvements to her home made for the showy benefit of Children and Family Services. She might even purchase a new church-lady outfit for the pastor's anniversary.

Pastor George's black BMW X5 stood alone in the parking lot as Kaye drove away. She glanced up at his office window where he stood waving at her. He was always there, like the Holy Ghost.

Add scores.

Pastor George's anniversary was a huge success. People squeezed into every square inch of the wooden pews in the six-hundred-person sanctuary. Guest Pastor Stanley from Bethany Baptist Church lauded Pastor George and kept the crowd lively.

A chunk of plaster crumbled from the ceiling to the right of the choir stand. Kaye could see the rot remaining beneath where the plaster had been. A few women in the choir preemptively dusted their wigs, sew-ins, and silk presses. Kaye twisted her head to give the evil eye to Walter, who'd done a crap job repairing the roof. He sat directly across from her in the next aisle. Brandon sat beside him. They didn't usually attend church, but, she supposed, they came to honor Pastor George's anniversary.

In response to the falling plaster, Reverend Stanley hollered from the pulpit, "This is the Lord's house! You didn't hear me! I'll say it again: This is the Lord's house! Satan can't steal my joy!" He was met with boisterous agreement from the congregation.

"We gather to praise Pastor George on his fifth anniversary at Mt. Moriah Baptist Church. The message I deliver today is taken from Numbers 5:5–7. God told Moses that if any man or woman sins, he must confess and make restitution. Now, you all are church folks, so you might not know about sin. Maybe a few of you do. Some people, somewhere, have been known, brothers and sisters, to lie, cheat, and steal. The devil is busy." Reverend Stanley got the crowd going.

Strange topic for a pastoral anniversary, thought Kaye. *Not very gleeful.* Pastor George was sitting next to her on the front pew, just as he had promised. He patted her hip near her side pocket. First lady Monica, in a Chanel tweed suit, sat on his other side with his three kids farther down the row. Kaye's granddaughter sat to her left and leaned on her lap with her dad next to her. The little girl was hot and fidgety. Truth be told, Kaye felt claustrophobic.

"Sin, said Moses, demands confession," preached Reverend Stanley. "Tell the truth, shame the devil. You can't blame Ray Ray and them. Stand before the face of God. Admit your wrongdoing. Jesus declared the wages of sin is death, but the gift of God is eternal life. Can somebody praise God today?"

Whenever Kaye came downstairs to Sunday worship, she sat in the back row. Quietly in, quietly out. Now, the attention drawn to the front row burned the back of her neck, like piercing eyes. Gina and some other trustees sat in the second and third rows. Kaye caught a glimpse of Grady in the third-row aisle seat.

Pastor George placed his arm around her and looked backward. Unabashed, Kaye swiveled her torso around. There were a number of white faces in the crowd. One white face belonged to Alan from the Cleveland Foundation. Two white faces were Cleveland police supplementing the church's rent-a-cops. Could there possibly be two white men in black at the back of the church? *No, no, no,* thought Kaye. Her heart raced; her ears rang.

"Here's the hard part, the hard road. Once confessed, the man or woman must make restitution. That's a big word. It means you've got to pay it back with interest. In this world, God ain't going to let you get away with it. But in the next life, Jesus promises that you will sit at his right hand, and in his Father's house there are many mansions."

Kaye knew she was surrounded. They were going to bring her in. She pulled out her cell phone to access the church's Google drive to tidy up anything potentially incriminating.

Then she saw it, she saw the score. Someone had repopulated the church's general email inbox with scores of warning notifications from Paychex about withdrawals from the employer withholding account.

$150,000. Gone. Zero balance. The account was empty.

Everything fell into place. Pastor George had used her computer IP address, her email account, her account passwords, her office. She stared at him in horror. He had gutted the account. He had conned her. He had framed her. Kaye was petty, but Pastor George was grand.

A man in black touched her shoulder and took her cell phone. "Ma'am, can you come with us? You are under arrest for theft of employer withholdings as the manager responsible for the employer's fiscal responsibilities."

Gina, Grady, Alan, Brandon, and Walter quickly gathered around to witness the kill.

"I'm not guilty," said Kaye, though she knew that no one would believe her.

"If we claim to be without sin, we deceive ourselves and the truth is not in us," said Pastor George.

"We have to leave this in the hands of God," said Gina. "I'll pray for you."

THE HOUSE ON FIR AVENUE

BY ALEX DIFRANCESCO

Gordon Square

"Why the fuck did we have to move into this shithole?" Winston asked as we unpacked in the tiny two-bedroom apartment on Detroit Avenue. He had recently begun to curse without punishment and did it as often as he could.

He was thirteen, thin and wiry, nearly as tall as me. I suspected he was doing drugs—in fact, I knew he was smoking pot and hoped that that was as far as it went. I'd found a plastic baggie of marijuana in his sock drawer when I was putting away his clothes.

"Because your mother died," I said flatly.

He looked at me like I'd punched him. Somehow, in both of our suffering, we'd forgotten to care much about each other. It was more my failing, really, as his father. I didn't know what to do, suddenly, without my wife Colleen, with a newly teenaged son. And so, I was as blunt as he was. I was as casually awful as he was. I was a bad father, suddenly, when fathering had been my whole life.

"No shit," he said under his breath. "You think I wasn't there for that?"

I flashed back, and maybe he did too, for a second, to the final days in our old house, the disarray we'd left it in, the hurry to pack up and move to our new, tiny apartment.

There hadn't been a chance to say goodbye, to get closure. Now, here we stood.

"Winston," I said, relenting, deciding to be the adult, "what would you have liked me to do? Even if we'd wanted to stay, we couldn't. I fell too far behind with the bank when your mother got sick. It wasn't my choice."

"Well, you didn't have to pick such a shithole."

"We're lucky we're not completely out on the streets," I said. "It'd be pretty hard to get to your soccer games if we were sleeping in a tent."

He didn't hear me. He was ripping open boxes, tearing things out of them to put in his room. "I'll never be able to bring my friends over," he said grumpily.

I decided that, for my part, the conversation was over. I opened my own boxes, maybe with a little more force than necessary, ripping the cardboard along with the tape.

We'd lost the house on Fir Avenue, the house we'd lived in since just before Winston was born, just after Colleen lost her fight with lung cancer. She'd been a smoker, and over the years I had tried again and again to get her to quit. When the diagnosis came through, she cried, I cried, we looked at each other and all that would be lost. We threw all the packs of cigarettes and lighters away, or I thought we did. Winston, who was drawing away from us in near-teenage angst anyway, had been acting out since her diagnosis. I focused on her, to my son's detriment, to the detriment of everything, really. Even with my health insurance, medical bills mounted. The mortgage became a secondary concern, even when we started getting letters from the bank marked *FINAL NOTICE*. I hid the letters from Colleen and told her everything was fine, that she just had to focus on getting better. She kept getting worse. She died in 2000, just after the turn of the century and millennium. Shortly thereafter, I got the letter from the bank that said we had officially missed so many payments they would be kicking us out of the house and selling it at auction.

It's just a house, I kept telling myself as I fought the bank's decision and squirreled away money toward the inevitable move we'd have to make. But it wasn't, it never had been. The house we bought in 1986 had represented all our hopes, all the bright futures we thought we were owed by the universe. Colleen and I were young, just married, and in love when we found it. Back then, Gordon Square was just Gordon Square, not the Gordon Square Arts District with its theaters and hip coffee shops and art galleries and juiceries where you paid five dollars for a shot of something green and viscous that tasted like a million pea shoots all condensed into liquid. Back then, everything was derelict and abandoned. People thought we were crazy for moving there, into an old house that was structurally sound but needed repair, especially with a baby on the way. I remember the days before moving in, when my wife was pregnant and we were living in a cheap one-room apartment while repairs were finished on the house, as some of the best days of my life, as some of the days most full of promise and light and future. If we lived in a world where your best memories could be bought from you for millions of dollars, I wouldn't sell those days, ever.

The first few years in the house were the best. Winston arrived, and Colleen and I were the happiest we'd ever been. We babyproofed the place, cordoned off the rickety wooden stairs up to the second floor, put plugs in all the old outlets, stripped the original paint we feared contained lead, and put new coats on everything. Our house was warm, scattered with toys and diapers and little tiny hooded sweatshirts and footie pajamas. Winston was the light of our lives. We were in love. We didn't care about the people hanging out on the corners, we didn't care that half the houses on the block were abandoned, we didn't care that we couldn't walk in the Fir Street Cemetery after dusk. The inside of our house, that living room and kitchen and dining room, those upstairs bedrooms, the two bathrooms—they were our entire world, and we were happy in it. We had a security system on the locked doors, and when our cars got broken into, our stereos stolen, our CD cases disappeared, we thought, *C'est la vie, if this is the worst life has to throw at us, we can withstand anything.*

Those walks to the Cleveland Public Theater, the trips to Detroit Avenue to get Winston ice cream, the days spent in the reading room of the public library, the sunny days we had picnics in the cemetery—they came to an end far too soon. Not just because our son grew older—he did, playing sports, finding us insufferable, spending more and more time away from home, but that wasn't the death knell to our happiness. Colleen and I still had each other. We, older now, padded around the house in our stocking feet, tended a little garden in the backyard as Winston practiced throwing a ball against the heavy brick foundation of the house; we were still so happy. Around us, the neighborhood was "cleaning up." Our house, nearly paid off from the bank, increased in value. We were pleased, even though we mourned our old neighborhood as the theater brought more businesses into the neighborhood, as speculators bought up more real estate. We knew that if we ever wanted to move after Winston was grown and off to college, we would have much more money from the sale of our house than we'd put into it.

Then Colleen was diagnosed with cancer, and just like that everything went to hell.

A few weeks after her funeral, I told Winston the news

that we'd be moving soon. He looked at me, as he had for months, with barely concealed hatred. He had lost his mother when he needed her the most, and I, his father, had all but disappeared from his life too, to take care of my dying wife. We stood there, in the living room, strangers to each other, when I told him the bank was taking the house away and we were moving somewhere smaller, more manageable, until we got back on our feet.

"Bullshit," he muttered then, and walked away. A minute later, I heard the heavy thunk of his baseball on the foundation of the house. The noise had once comforted me. Now it drove me crazy.

We left the old house in a hurry. We packed up boxes, and I found one of Colleen's old lighters and a half pack of cigarettes in the attic. I put the lighter in an old velvet jewelry bag and forgot about it. Winston and I fell into a routine of mutual yet separate misery in the new apartment. Winston started staying out later. He quit sports. Even with the tininess of the apartment, he managed to stay away from me most days. I kept working at my job. I worked, I finished, I came home. I watched television in the living room. From Winston's room, I heard first-person shooter video games and smelled incense that cloaked whatever was really going on in there. He was falling further and further into whatever hole he'd stumbled into upon his mother's death.

Unpacking the boxes, I found the small velvet jewelry bag. I dumped its contents into my hand. I clenched it in my palm, the plastic slick with my sweat.

I'm not sure what made me go to the house on Fir Avenue one night after work. I remember it was wintertime, and the tree branches were like skeleton fingers in the sky. It was cold, but not so cold that I didn't take a detour while walking down Detroit Avenue, telling myself I'd just head a bit south. Before I knew it, I was standing at the edge of the cemetery on Fir, out in the darkness, looking into the warm yellow light of the home I'd lived in. I could see a man there, walking around. I'd followed as much as I could of the bank auction, found out that it was sold to a middle-aged man who planned to live in it until he flipped it for more money than even we would've been able to, had things turned out right. The changing neighborhood was ripe for such things.

I stood in the cemetery that night among the crooked gravestones and watched that man walk through my house. He extended a measuring tape across doorways, walls. He was making plans, thinking of changes. Anger bubbled up inside me, fierce and volatile. I thought about what it might feel like to hammer his head with a rock. The image was fleeting, but the emotion stayed. This was my home. The place I had raised my son, the place where my wife had died slowly. What was happening wasn't right. I could blame the bank, sure— maybe I should have. But this man was standing in my home, in the flesh, and made such a convenient target.

That first night, I stood there shaking. I told myself it was the cold, my opened peacoat, the long workday. But when I stood there shaking night after night, I knew that it was so much more.

"You're a shitty father," Winston mumbled under his breath.

We were sitting at the dinner table. It was one of the few nights I'd persuaded him to eat at the table with me instead of his bedroom. He'd asked for a favor—twenty dollars to "go to the movies," though I suspected the money would go directly to drugs. That's when he put down his fork, looked me in the eye, looked down at his plate, and said what he said.

I reached out across the table and slapped him across the face. I couldn't control myself. The anger—with the man who'd bought the house, with my wife for dying and leaving me, with my son—was too strong to resist.

It was not something I'd ever done. It was not me. I had been raised by gentle, thoughtful parents who talked everything through calmly. I was not violent. The violence had been building up in me every night as I walked through the Fir Street Cemetery, looking through the windows of my old house. I brought binoculars to see better. I still shook every time. I thought of fighting, punching. I thought of ambushing the man. I thought of a lot of things I knew—hoped—I would never do in real life.

Winston didn't look sad or shocked. He looked furious. Then he smirked. "Like I said, a shitty fucking father." Then he went to his room, slamming the door, lighting his incense.

My right hand stung from where it had made contact with my son's face. It shook a little under the table, where I held it on my lap. The hand slid into my pocket, where I felt my wife's lighter.

The first act of sabotage was flattened tires. I slunk out from between the gravestones and took a pocketknife out of my coat. My shaking hands unscrewed the caps of his tires and depressed the valve core. The air hissed into the night like a snake. When the tires were flat, I walked away casually, as if I hadn't been in the shadows of his driveway doing wrong.

I headed to the cemetery early the next morning, before work, to watch him curse in my front yard. He didn't suspect anything. The neighborhood, while improving, was taking its time. Petty crimes were still committed. And he hadn't been quiet about telling his neighbors about his intention to flip the house. He was nonplussed because it was such a minor sabotage, so small and easily fixable.

As my crimes mounted, so did his anger. Next, I smashed a breaker box outside the house. I took a rock and knocked off the padlock, then I crushed the levers and switches inside. My hands were bloody when I finished, cut at the knuckles and red around the nail beds. The man in the house on Fir was out of town that weekend, it seemed, as he had been gone when I went there on Friday and still on Saturday. That night, as I stood waiting and watching, the seed of an idea full of malice blossomed in my mind. I knew it had to be committed.

I cut phone lines, I got into the basement and sabotaged pipes. Hate burned in my heart. Every few weeks, I came back to see what I'd done. I watched the man in my old house grow more and more angry as the damages piled up. He was watching his investment dissipate, and he must have been wondering who could hate him so much. Because by a certain point, it would probably have become clear that these things were no accident.

At the apartment, Winston became more and more detached. I caught him sneaking in one night with his pupils dilated and confronted him about drugs. I wanted to grab him, to shake him, to hurt him in ways that I knew he would remember, think about the next time he defied me. He laughed in my face and slammed his bedroom door shut, locking it. Loud music echoed through the house for the rest of the night. He did not sleep. I did not sleep.

I couldn't bring myself to care. I was so caught up in my sabotage of the house on Fir that I thought about little else, even that I could be caught. The neighborhood still had bigger problems, though, and while the police were called a few times, they made notes and did nothing, walking off to take care of the murders, the rapes, the grand thefts. No one cared about an inconvenienced house-flipper, not with what he represented in the death of the old neighborhood, not with the way things were going. Stores opened along Detroit Avenue, businesses filled in, rent went up. This man was just a part of that gentrification.

That night when the idea of burning the house down first came to me, I was lying awake in bed in the wee hours of the morning, disturbed by Winston's loud music pumping through the walls. My thoughts were hard to control, and many of them were of violence, of escalating crime. The man had to pay. I thought of all the ways he might. I imagined him tied to a chair, me torturing him. This thought had occurred to me one day, and it hadn't abated. It grew in my mind like a little sapling watered with my hate, my despair, my sadness and anger over the death of my wife. It had been a year and a half, by then. Winston was fourteen, taller, angrier, skinnier, pulling further and further away from me. My life was a dark shipwreck of what it once had been. Going down in the midnight waters, I was consumed by the desire to pull everything down with me. In my sleepless bed, I turned the lighter over and over in my hand.

As I stood outside the house in the cemetery one night, I began to make plans. I began to think of ways I could do it and not be caught. I began to think of the ways that it could all be over. The night was cold and dark. The yellow light from the house seemed miles away, a campfire seen through distant trees. The streetlights down the block were like torches flickering in the gloom.

The next day, I began to prepare.

* * *

I wanted to make sure the man who'd bought my house wasn't in there when I did it. I didn't want to commit murder, I'd finally decided, despite my torture fantasies. I just wanted the house to be gone, for both of us, for all of us. I couldn't bear looking at it anymore. I couldn't watch the man make the slow upgrades and changes. I couldn't watch the place where my wife and I had once lived happily disappear. I would make sure it was gone once and for all.

I sat in my office on my lunch break or at the library, reading newspaper articles about arson. I was too smart to look them up on my computer—I knew how easily trackable that would be if I came under scrutiny. I assumed I would. I had to do this right.

I showed up in the graveyard night after night with a backpack full of items I would need. The man was always, frustratingly, home. I went there for weeks. Finally, a night came when he was gone.

I knew every inch of that house. In the dark cover of night, I slid my backpack off my shoulders in the backyard by the door. I went to a casement window in the foundation, high up in the basement, and pried it open. My heart was beating faster than usual, but my movements were calm. I shimmied down into the basement, felt around in the darkness until I made my way to the stairs. At the top, I found the door unlocked. Not that I couldn't have opened that too, but I was thankful for small blessings. Less for the fire investigators to find amiss.

I quietly opened the back door and grabbed my bag. I knew from all my reading that most accidental fires start in the kitchen. I rolled newspapers into logs, drenched them with grease from the messy kitchen. Shaking, I made my way in the darkness through the kitchen and placed the logs of newspaper on the stove. I took Colleen's lighter out of my pocket and lit the edges of the paper.

Within thirty seconds, the fire was licking the walls behind the stove. When the wallpaper caught, I made my way out the back door, the closest exit, locking it behind me. I watched for a moment from the graveyard, just for a moment, as the Halloween-orange flames danced up the walls inside the kitchen. I wished I could have stayed to see the whole thing burn. But I ran. I ran back home.

When I got there, Winston was in the living room watching television. I was smudged in soot and I smelled of grease. I was disheveled. As I stood there looking at my son looking at me, I paused in my insanity for the first time in a long while. Who was I? What had I done? What had become of me? What was becoming of my child? I felt my wife's lighter in my pocket.

"Dad?" he said. He knew something was wrong, but he didn't, couldn't, know what.

As I stood there, I began to cry. "Winston," I said through my tears.

"Dad?" he said again. He sounded lost. He sounded like he had when he was a little boy, running through the house on Fir Avenue, and had fallen down, or lost a favorite toy.

"I miss her so much, Winston."

I don't know who moved toward whom. Maybe it was both of us. But we were in each others' arms crying.

"I do too, Dad."

"We're going to fix this, Son," I said. And I meant it. "We're going to get the help we need."

The police stopped by, once, after I'd started taking Winston and myself to family therapy. The kind officers let me know immediately it was a formality. And I was just a grieving widower, trying my best to raise his son. Of course I knew nothing about the blaze, the ongoing sabotage. Of course I was just trying to do the best with the mess I'd been left with. In my pocket, I flicked the lighter, though no flame was left in it.

I read the newspapers. Eventually, foul play was ruled out in the fire that burned the house on Fir Avenue to the ground. The fire had started in the kitchen, on the stove. I breathed a sigh of relief that the insanity that had overcome me would not ruin my or my son's lives.

In therapy, Winston and I did a lot of crying. Summer was there, he was out of school, and he spent those months in an outpatient rehab for his drug use. Watching my son come back from the angry teenage boy that had swallowed him was like a small miracle. Watching myself come back from the darkness was no less miraculous. I thought a lot about the man whose life I'd ruined, about the house on Fir Avenue and the dreams it represented for him. I tried not to dwell on it, but it lurked in the back of my mind even as my son and I moved more and more out of the darkness. I walked down Fir Avenue when I didn't have to, looked at the leaning remains of the house, its charred beams. The man wasn't there and never would be again. I felt so many feelings on these walks—fear at who I'd let myself become, guilt at what I'd done, and accomplishment that it was all over now. I still held Colleen's spent lighter in my pocket. It was useless now, having done its job. Sometimes I dreamed about the fire. Sometimes I simply wondered who the victim was in the situation: the man or me. I never had any answers.

Two years later, when Winston was sixteen, things seemed

almost normal again. He'd gained weight, gone back to playing soccer and baseball. His teams welcomed him back like
a prodigal son. I kept going to my job, saving money. A few
months after Winston's sixteenth birthday, I bought him an
old car, a '93 Mustang convertible. I don't know if I've ever
seen the joy on his face that I saw the day I handed him the
keys.

I taught Winston how to drive in parking lots of Wal-
greens and Metroparks. He was a fast learner, eager to get on
the road with his friends and the lovely young woman he'd
begun tentatively seeing.

He passed his driving test on the first try, and with a car
already in the driveway, he began looking around on the In-
ternet for good deals on insurance. He was set up in the living
room on our home desktop when I heard him call out to me.

"Dad?"

"Yeah, Son?"

"Why are these quotes so high?"

"You're a sixteen-year-old boy," I said with a laugh.

"No, Dad, they're, like, *really* high."

I looked at the different tabs open on the computer.
Something was wrong.

In the next few days, I found out about the credit lines,
the open warrants, and the tax fraud committed under my
son's name. I had no way to prove it. But I recalled quite viv-
idly the rush we'd left the house on Fir Avenue in after Colleen's death. If something of my son's had been left behind—
something with his Social Security number—wouldn't it be
the perfect crime? Wouldn't it be the perfect revenge for a
man who surely suspected me? Wouldn't it be something that
would take years to find out?

I called the local police to report what was happening.

They sounded bored and unconcerned as they took notes—I suspected I'd never hear back from them. Winston sat at the table, maybe thinking, as I was thinking, about the life that had been taken from him before it even started, what it would cost in time and money and fight to get that life back.

I wondered again who the victim had been in the battle over the house on Fir Avenue. And as it turned out, it hadn't been me or even the man who bought it—it had been someone I'd never suspected it would be.

THE LADERMAN AFFAIR

BY J.D. BELCHER

Lakewood

Melissa Hinton hurried, cautiously tracking a couple the private investigator handed down to her as a first solo assignment. The profile information that Louis Bustelo, her boss at the private detective agency, gave her included biographies and headshots of Nora Auletta, the female subject, a beautiful part-time model who also worked as a financial advisor with Key Bank downtown. According to a news article she found on Google, Nora had been married five years to her husband, Jean Laderman, a very handsome, middle-aged, self-made millionaire who owned a mansion in the Gold Coast, Lakewood's exclusive Lake Erie shorefront district on the west side. Melissa remembered how she had caught herself studying Laderman's face, noticing his gentle green eyes, wanting to stroke his thin beard, running her finger along the slanted scar just above his brow. Louis said the tycoon suspected his wife of screwing some other guy and wanted proof.

She had been tailing the couple for three weeks. They kept a similar routine, eating at diners on Madison or a little farther up Detroit, followed by a stroll in Kauffman Park. The evenings always concluded with them doing the deed at his place, a beautiful brick home on French Avenue.

This evening, Melissa passed through the glass doors of Lakewood Hospital, where she had been hiding, and out into the brisk cold of Detroit Avenue in pursuit. Forecasters called for an overnight accumulation of snow, so she had disguised herself in orange knit gloves, a brown wool sweater, and a scarf thrown around the exposed parts of her neck. She felt awkward as she always did at work because she was packing a gun, but Louis insisted.

Her subjects suddenly departed Forage, an American gastropub, as she surveilled them from across the street. Although she had been on the case for nearly a month now, she was still a bit nervous, afraid of making a mistake or doing something out of protocol which might land her in hot water with Bustelo.

As she followed the doting couple, she sent her lover, a man named Jansen Monroe, a quick text—*Can I come over after work?*—then slid the phone in her back jeans pocket and kept walking.

An hour before, she had hid in her Honda Accord, parked at a side street meter next to Forage's main entrance, then walked around the block, taking random pictures with her camera—a Canon T7 with a telephoto zoom lens—of the surrounding architecture, art murals, and bicycle racks. At just the right time, she nailed the damning snapshots of her unaware assignments, snuggling up for an embrace. Afterward, she had ducked back inside the hospital lobby.

With her phone, Melissa now took a final discrete picture just as it pinged with Jansen's stinging reply: *I'm tired and going to go to bed early. How about tomorrow night?*

She sent Jansen another text: *Fine, I'll call you tomorrow.*

The couple turned into Root Cafe, a trendy cubbyhole coffee shop in the middle of Lakewood's quaint downtown district, one crammed with vogue eateries, dive bars, and boutiques. Melissa followed them inside, standing two people behind in line, adjusting her coat to make the handgun less noticeable. Jansen was on her mind. She thought of the evening, a year ago, when their lips touched for the first time in the park across from the Cleveland Museum of Art, underneath a white sculpture that looked like giant walls of melted pickup sticks, with the wind chasing dead leaves around their feet. Instantly, she had fallen in love.

Her mother always told her that men showed up in twos and to be careful to choose the right one—the one sent by God—because that's exactly how she had met Melissa's father. Perhaps the next might be the real deal, her mother suggested, to no avail. It was too late; Melissa was already smitten.

Her phone beeped again, another text from Jansen: *I love you*.

The couple took a seat at a table in the rear of Root Cafe behind a bookshelf. Melissa made herself inconspicuous by ordering jasmine tea and an almond biscotti. Her memories of Jansen fluttered like the wings of a butterfly, stopping at flower thoughts, fertilizing each memory with longevity, tasting the sweet nectar. Once, Jansen had smiled and taken a swig of Dos Equis from a tall glass while they sat in the Sauced Taproom, not far from where she was now. She could still see the satisfaction on his face; he *knew* he had her trapped securely in his grasp. Then back to *that* kiss again, recalling how soon after they both danced around their special but awkwardly shared experience. To her, it was the kind of thing that pulled a man and woman together lickety-split, in one fast, miraculous moment; something like in the twinkle of an eye.

Sometimes, she considered why Jansen even bothered with a woman like her. Melissa wasn't gorgeous, and it wasn't like he lacked opportunity. She thought of herself as a plain Jane with fair skin, naturally light-brown hair, a nice round bottom, but breasts that were too small. Often, she mused about why God had given them to her at all. Jansen, however, was striking. He wore a perpetual five o'clock shadow that gloriously contrasted with his enchanting eau de nil eyes. The product of an interracial couple—his father, a white pastor, and his mother, a Black college sweetheart at Oberlin—Jansen had been raised with the meticulous teaching in the church under them both. He could probably have any woman he wanted. But he was now hers, she knew, and ever since that first kiss, she couldn't stop imagining tying the knot, buying a home, and moving in together, confirming her hopes that her mother's intuition had indeed been incorrect.

She could never be a treacherous whore like this woman she had been following, Melissa thought to herself. She texted Jansen back: *I love you too*.

Melissa had found this gig while perusing the Indeed app around the same time she and Jansen started getting serious. The simple title, *Private Investigator Assistant*, seemed unappealing until she scrolled down and found keywords like *agent*, *espionage*, and even *covert* laced throughout the job description. What sold her was a little detail she noticed at the bottom: *Photography experience highly preferred*. She used to belong to the photography club in high school and had even worked for the *Cauldron* while studying for her undergraduate degree at Cleveland State. After sending in her résumé, she'd received a call back three days later from an elderly man named Louis who said he'd be willing to pay thirty dollars an hour *and* offer training.

His office was hidden in a yellow-brick building directly

across the street from St. Edward High School. It housed an Arab barbershop, a bridal store—which she planned on visiting after Jansen proposed—and an antique furniture boutique on the storefront level, each donning a black awning advertising their business in white letters. A door with checkered square windows at the end of a petite front entrance foyer, one with golden brass mailboxes on either side and along the trim paneling, had buzzed open after she pressed a button under the number 310. She climbed the unlit staircase, running her hand along a smooth mahogany railing up to the third floor, passing watercolor portraits of flowers in vases of different shapes and sizes at the crest of each flight, until she found the correct door.

"You must be Melissa!" Louis had greeted her with a gravelly baritone voice. "Please, come in. Have a seat."

She sat on a burgundy leather sofa with her feet pressed together upon a cerulean Persian rug covering the hardwood floor. A coffee table nearby had various magazines fanned out across the glass. Louis plopped down at a cluttered desk near the window and lit a cigarette. There was a separate workstation with an empty chair and computer positioned adjacent to him, which she assumed was ready and waiting for the new hire. He was a fair-skinned older gentleman with long wavy hair that stopped short of his shoulders. Wire-rimmed glasses perched atop a nose that looked as if it had been repeatedly punched in former boxing days, or severed and sewn back into place at some point. She couldn't pinpoint the man's ethnicity, and flashes of ideas appeared and disappeared on his face, like revealing spirits. Melissa only smiled, watching him fumble through papers. For some reason, the entire scene humored her, yet she took comfort knowing people probably thought the same when they considered where she might be from or what kind of mix produced her specific racial makeup. She and Louis could pass for close relatives.

After brief introductions, Louis settled into the interview, gave his philosophical spiel about the seriousness of being a private eye—from its origin via a French soldier named Eugène Vidocq and the ensuing popularity of Pinkerton Agency, to his connections with the city's law enforcement. At first, she thought Louis had the intention of trying to scare her away, using his anecdotes to weed people out who might not have true interest in the work.

Despite his bizarre tangents, she accepted the job. The first few months involved nothing but completing a lot of paperwork: getting references, signing up for insurance, obtaining FBI background checks, a US passport, and, surprisingly, applying for licenses, including a gun permit, and registering for firearm training. That was the most fun of all. She was delighted to have a choice in which weapon she wanted to carry, eventually settling on a Glock 43, mainly because of its small size. It took some time getting used to all the equipment—her camera, binoculars, the gun, a cell phone, and a laptop. She ended up toting them around easily, snugly stored in separate compartments of her backpack, just like Louis suggested.

Though he constantly voiced his opposition to her going out into the field alone too soon, which perturbed Melissa because she took it as downright chauvinism, they still got along well, working mostly evening and late-night shifts from the office, drinking tons of coffee, and eating everything off the numbered menu from China Express. He even gave her a key and a private parking space in the back of the building so she could work as much as she liked.

Louis's advice burned impressions into her long-term

memory. "The most important part of the job," he'd say, offering proverbs like a wise professor, "is keeping it a secret from everyone." He'd give pointers about safety, harping upon the life-or-death necessity of staying unseen. "An investigator blowing his cover could not only turn into a disastrous situation, but also might cost a life."

During other instances, his wisdom seemed aloof and strange. "People are unbelievable!" he once blurted out from his desk after hanging up from a call with a client, while she inputted information into a database. "I'm warning you right now, this job may not be what you think."

"What do you mean?" she asked, flinging her ponytail to one side.

"It's like you enter through a door into this magical place—to the other side of the mirror, so to speak."

"A magical place, huh?" she responded, trying not to giggle.

"Yes, a land filled with jerks and douchebags." Louis raised an index finger. "It just gets right up in your face. Trust me. You'll see what I mean."

By the time Melissa finished the tasty tea and biscotti, Nora Auletta and her man stood up, put their dirty dishes into the plastic return tub, and started for the door. Melissa paused and stationed herself a dozen steps behind. She watched them pass the register toward the exit. When the door opened, a bell at the top of the doorframe jingled.

It was then that the mirror and the magic of which Louis foretold happened. Humungous snowflakes began falling out of the sky like weightless cotton balls. Outside the café's storefront window, Melissa saw Jansen, her soon-to-be-fiancé, kiss another woman while walking down Detroit Avenue.

Seeing this was like taking a bullet to the chest, sucking all the breath out of her lungs. She gasped and felt as though her heart had stopped, thinking it couldn't be true. Maybe it wasn't Jansen. How could that man be him? Melissa forgot her clandestine subjects and began a pursuit in the other direction.

Outside, she confirmed that it *was* Jansen—the argyle scarf she bought him last Christmas, his black peacoat, his confident, sexy gait. A furious, sizzling anger overcame her equilibrium so strongly that it made her sick. Melissa's stomach turned and she nearly vomited before swallowing down the bile. Jansen cradled the woman's hand as an ambulance siren approached in the distance. He intertwined his fingers with hers in a seductive maneuver Melissa recognized all too well.

Other people along the way, phantasms beneath the glow of the streetlights—a teenager blowing out mist from a vape pen, a red-mustached cyclist in full winter gear waiting for the traffic signal to change, a mother in a beige minivan—all turned to peek at Melissa striding down the block as if they knew something had gone awry.

Across the street, a grungy man with a full beard smiled and waved to her. She thought he looked like an older, Black version of Jesus Christ. It seemed as if he wanted to cross the street and walk toward her, but the ambulance passed, the light changed, and cars steadily filled both lanes.

Melissa stopped and reached for her cell phone. She decided to intervene another way, and sent him a text: *What time should I come over tomorrow?*

Paces later, Jansen looked at the screen and returned it to his coat pocket without responding. The other woman turned to him and spoke, as if she also sensed what the pedestrians and the driver and the cyclist and the Black Christ had, and Melissa wondered if Jansen noticed it too.

She followed them from behind, riding an emotional wave of rising hatred, mesmerized by the never-ending signage as she passed each storefront—a Dave's Hot Chicken joint, Great Clips, Rozi's Wine Store, Deagan's Kitchen and Bar, First Federal Bank, Geiger's Clothing. They crossed at the light and turned left down Warren Avenue. By the time Melissa reached the other side, Jansen, still holding his lover's hand, strolled into a parking lot directly behind Forage. When he reached his silver Lexus and unlocked the car with the automatic key fob, Melissa jogged up from behind and pushed him in the back as he opened the driver's-side door.

"What are you doing?" she screamed. "What the fuck are you doing?"

Jansen fell into the seat, clumsily banging his head on the interior frame. For the first time, she glimpsed the face of her boyfriend's paramour from the opposite side of the car. Their eyes connected; she had a beautiful face, the cover-girl type, but one that exuded both fear and wonderment. Jansen jumped up and lashed out, striking Melissa with a hard smack to the cheek.

"What is your problem?" he yelled before realizing who had shoved him.

When his mistress drew near, Melissa had already removed the concealed gun from inside her coat and fired two rounds into Jansen's chest. She then turned to the woman and pulled the trigger twice more. Without hesitation, Melissa returned the weapon to its holster and left the scene, tucking both hands in the pockets of her coat like nothing had happened.

She tried to remain calm as a torrent of thoughts flooded

her mind. *Someone saw me and called the police about shots being fired. They are on the way. I'm going to prison. Where did I park the car? What should I do now?* She was afraid to look back and pressed forward, encountering an ebony-painted parking meter at every other stride. Then, to her horror, almost like a trick of the mind, she saw a man dressed in all black, leaning against the last meter at the far end of the lot, grinning at her as she went by.

At the corner, she turned right onto St. Charles and smiled meekly through the falling snowflakes at a passing woman, who reciprocated with a concerned glance, and again she felt a horrid sickness growing in her stomach. She couldn't shake the smiling man's uncanny familiarity, like she had seen him before, but couldn't quite put a finger on who he was.

Just ahead, across the street, was Lakewood Hospital, and around the block, her car. She kept a steady pace, resisting the urge to turn her steps into a full-out sprint. Even though time seemed to stand still, she quickly reached the door to her vehicle. As she turned on her car, her cell phone startled her by chiming, and Louis's name showed on the screen. Melissa answered on impulse, hit the speaker button, and instinctively made a right, driving down Detroit Avenue toward the office.

"Hello?"

"Melissa, where are you?"

"About ten blocks away."

"Stop by the office, I need to talk to you about something."

"Okay, I'm on my way now."

The feeling of the inevitable trouble she now faced because of her rash move became unbearable. Torn, she considered the escape of heading to the nearest highway ramp and making a dash to who knew where, juxtaposed with gambling on the safety of hiding out in the office. Being hunted by a police mob was the last thing she wanted, a deadly situation she had seen gone awry far too many times on television and online news clips. Acting as if nothing unusual had occurred, she figured, might be the best option for now. Perhaps a better idea would come later.

Instead of parking in the back lot, she put the car into a metered space directly in front of the building housing Louis's office. After exiting the car, she was suddenly taken aback by the three mannequins in the bridal shop's storefront window: one wore a white wedding gown, the other two sapphire sequined bridesmaid dresses, all of them mocking her. Once inside, she bounded up the staircase two steps at a time, and as she advanced toward 310, she hesitated, took a moment to compose herself, then slowly opened the door. Forcing a grin and still contemplating whether she should do an about-face and run back to the car, Melissa hung up her coat and scarf on the brass coatrack next to the door. When she sat at her desk, police sirens could be heard racing down Detroit Avenue, as always, but now the tocsins dug a dagger of fear directly into her heart.

"Melissa," said Louis, taking out a cigarette, striking a match, and letting out a puff of smoke, "I think it's time to wrap up the Laderman case. We have more than enough for this guy."

"Okay," she replied, shrugging her shoulders and frowning. "Do you want me to send you the files?"

"What happened to your face?"

"I don't know, what's wrong with it?"

"You have a bruise under your eye."

She touched her cheekbone and winced; Jansen's slap must have left a mark. "Oh, I tripped and fell coming up the steps," she said, guffawing. "Is it swollen?"

"You might want to put ice on it. I have some of those instant cold packs in the closet. Don't worry, it happens to the best of us. Are you hungry? I was about to order some Chinese."

Melissa began to relax.

The next day, she received a call from Jansen's sister Heather, who broke the news about her brother being shot. Heather apologized profusely, giving information she had gleaned from the police about a possible robbery gone bad. They both cried over the phone.

To Melissa's surprise, nothing else really transpired over the next several days except that she carried around an incessant paranoia, prompting her to be overly alert during every waking second. To no avail, she tried to exorcise herself of this by continuing to attend her usual Zumba and spinning classes at the YMCA, but ultimately concluded that only one remedy would cure her ills. She planned to retrace her steps, return to the scene of the crime, and go back through the magic door.

A week later, just before she left work on the day of her revisitation, it snowed, another foreboding sign. Louis had dropped the interesting news, which she couldn't help but connect to her unfortunate dilemma, that Nora Auletta and her boyfriend had been found shot to death in Kauffman Park. Louis suspected that Jean Laderman was somehow behind it. He asked, "Have you read the *Plain Dealer* article about a similar double murder not too far away from the same location?" She said that she hadn't. To divert Louis's attention from the subject, she abruptly asked about an upcoming assignment, then reminded him that she had a doctor's appointment and needed to leave a little early.

When Melissa approached her car in the back parking lot, she was shocked to see writing in the frost on the driver's-side window: *I KNOW WHAT YOU DID.*

She grabbed the ice scraper from the backseat and cleaned off the windows and windshields, hoping no one had seen. It was occurring again: the magic thing Louis had spoken of. Feeling a greater sense of purpose and destiny which told her she desperately needed to erase this terrible memory, she put the car in gear, turned out of the alleyway, and drove up Detroit Avenue. But it wouldn't go away. Everything seemed to be manifesting itself in *twos*, a reminder of the two people she had killed: two empty plastic soda bottles drifting in the middle of the road; a man walking two dogs in each hand down the sidewalk; the same color automobiles arriving in pairs at each stoplight. Even when she pulled into the lot behind Forage, wanting to park in the same space where Jansen and his significant other had put the silver Lexus, she was forced to park between two vehicles of the same year, make, and model.

Without drawing too much attention to herself, she searched for signs of blood on the pavement, or anything else left behind from the crime. A few faint blemishes on the blacktop were all that she spotted. The idea came to push further and return to Root Cafe. More than anything, she desired a place of solace. She threw her scarf over her face, keeping her head down as she passed each storefront, hoping no one driving along the avenue would take notice.

The shop tables were crowded and bustling. She ordered a cup of Brazilian and a scone, then spotted an empty seat in the back, behind the bookcase. As soon as she sat down, took a swig of coffee, and dropped her head in her hands in exhaustion, a man with a paper cup filled with steamy java swept in, placing himself in the opposing chair. He smiled, and the first thing that came to Melissa's mind was that this stranger was an undercover police officer and her time had come. But like a Russian doll opening the shrouds of his exterior, she recognized a distinctive feature which might have otherwise gone unnoticed—the scar over his right eyebrow. In all of the photographs she had seen of him, he had worn a beard; now, he had a clean-shaven face and a surprisingly younger visage.

"You're Jean Laderman," she said.

"And you're Melissa Hinton," he responded with a smirk, showing his teeth. "Just as you have been watching me, I have been watching you."

"What do you want?"

"Do you know the phrase *carpe momentum*, my love?" he said with a hint of a British accent, briefly glancing over his shoulder. "Perhaps you're not paying attention. I'm a little better at this than you, I think. But you see, we must act now."

"What are you talking about?"

"If you haven't noticed," he whispered, leaning closer, "before long, we're both going to be on Cleveland's most wanted list."

Jean began unraveling a plan: they would both board a fueled-up Cessna at Burke Lakefront Airport and head to an apartment in Caracas. It all made sense: he *was* behind the killing of Nora and her lover. Melissa knew that she too sat on the edge of a very steep precipice. The police were probably right then compiling footage from security cameras and doing forensics on the shell casings from her Glock. And if higher-ups got involved, satellite imagery might blow her cover in no time.

"Come with me," he said.

"This is so crazy. I don't have anything ready. I mean, damn, I have to pack a bag or something. There are things I need."

"Don't worry, I have lots of money." He pulled out his phone. "And an Uber waiting outside. I can just as easily add a stop and we can both leave this place forever."

"I don't know . . . Why me? Something's not right."

"Melissa, I can't answer that," said Jean, reaching out a hand in an act of submission, almost begging. "All I know is that it *is* you. I'll ask one last time. Please come. Believe me, this is your best and only option. We don't have much time."

Melissa stood, took a deep breath, and grabbed his hand. Then together they walked through the door, tinkling the bell atop the frame, and out into the brisk, snowy block of Detroit Avenue.

PART IV

THE HEIGHTS

MOCK HEART

BY JILL BIALOSKY
Shaker Heights

If I lean down into memory, it's riding in your jeep,
plastic windows, like the sound of Hitchcock's birds,
flapping, wheels grinding on troubled gravel,
past prim gardens & whitewashed houses.

If I look closely, I see our river burst from oily waste
into blaze. You had my youth, my virgin not-knowing,
isn't that enough? To escape tributaries, restraints,
mothers in wallpapered prisons, fathers trimming

The divide, haves & have-nots, in the inner ring
where the Shakers once settled, you were my ride out.
If I lean down farther, I was your devotee, like a choir
to a church, my accomplice, my suburban failure.

In noir, there's always a cynical hero. And a love story
as twisted as a girl who gives herself to a demon lover.
A noir can be a dream. In mine, we're at a motel,
darkness, board games, cards on the filthy

Dismantled bed, your door open across from mine,
showing up always, just when I've forsaken you,
desire, an act of cruelty. Always some girl with you—
at the track where you groomed the horses—

Blackness is where we lodged. A cement-block tack
room those nights I didn't want to go home.
I'd sneak out to the girl's room, find her in the mirror
in jeans & boots, combing her hair, my dark doppelgänger.

Even in my dream she's there. You don't have money
to pay the motel bill, riotous, rapturous,
you've figured out a way for me to see, even in dream,
that you're still wild, that the rules do not apply—

That you still possess me. Nothing made you want
me more than when I agreed to slip underneath
the burgundy velvet rope of the Vogue Theatre,
your hand guiding mine in the pitch black.

Criminal, triumphant, nowhere were we more in sync—
your smell the scent of a forbidden,
never-to-fully-taste fruit—than when I betrayed myself
for your attention. Buried in the undergrowth,

Deep in my mind, rooted in my consciousness,
I can't retrieve it, grows the existential meaning
of what bound us. My lonely mock heart,
your cruel logic. In my dream you're drunk, possessed,

I'm washed in a sweat, ashamed that I still believe in you—
phantom of my youth, my desperation, down in the cellar
where we dwelled, my crimes, my tawdry oblivion.
Why do you keep coming back? To make me see

That you've chosen a life of squalor over me?

THE FALLEN

BY THRITY UMRIGAR

Cleveland Heights

At the front door, I hesitate.

Ali is still in bed and for a moment I waver, wonder if I should go back into the house and ask her to join me on my run, as she does most mornings. But then I think, if she'd wanted to, she would've set her alarm, right?

I'd slept in the guest bedroom last night, too angry to lie next to Ali after the shit she'd pulled at the party earlier in the evening. Even now, remembering the way she'd flirted with Jan, I feel my throat tighten. We'd left early, after I'd feigned a headache and said I needed to get home. She'd known that I was faking it, but maybe she understood she'd gone too far this time, had seen the glint in my eye and knew better than to argue in front of our friends. Still, as soon as we were in the car, we'd turned on one another. We fought the whole way home from Lakewood to Cleveland Heights, my rage growing by the moment as she accused me of being jealous, of having a suspicious mind, swearing that she didn't have the slightest interest in Jan, trying to convince me that I'd imagined the glances and giggles that passed between them all evening long.

I listened dully as she tried to turn the tables on me, saying that I'd embarrassed *her*. After eight years, our fights had a certain rhythm and cadence, as if we were both reading from the same dog-eared script. But Ali never knew when to stop.

We were a mere two blocks from home when she twisted in her seat to face me. Even in the dark of the car, with my eyes on the road, I could feel the heat in her eyes. "I'm sick and tired of your jealousy, Samantha," she said. "For fuck's sake. I'm not your father. I'm not abandoning you, okay? I'm allowed to go to a party and talk to a friend without you—"

"Enough." My hand hit the steering wheel so hard, my nerves buzzed for a few seconds. "Enough with the gaslighting. This isn't about me or my dad. It's about you being a shameless little slut."

I regretted my words almost immediately, but I was tired and my head was hurting for real by now. Also, one thing about us O'Mallys—you can punch us in the face and we'll forgive you by the next morning. But words . . . I have aunts who haven't spoken to their sister over an inopportune remark made forty years earlier.

I turned onto Lee Road, and we rode in silence past our beloved Cedar-Lee movie theater, past the art galleries and restaurants, until I made a right onto Corydon. Home. Ali opened the car door before I'd even pulled all the way into the garage, as if she couldn't wait to get away from me. She was almost out of the car when she said, "I'm telling you, Sam, I've just about had it with your jealousy. I wasn't doing a damn thing except being friendly and polite to Jan, mostly to make up for the last time you acted out in front of her. This is your issue, not mine. So deal with it. Just fucking deal with it."

"Fuck you," I said.

She flinched. I stayed in the car until she let herself into the house.

I sat there, staring straight ahead. Already, a feeling of incredulity at how out of hand this fight had gotten was sweeping over me. I felt numb and hollow, regret needling through my body. When had we begun to fight this ugly? How could I treat the person I loved most in the world in this fashion? Slowly, I got out of the car and let myself into the house.

I stayed in the study for an hour to keep out of Ali's way, but the lines of the novel I was reading kept blurring and I had to read them over and over again. Mostly, I kept tabs of the sounds coming from upstairs, where Ali was getting ready for bed. I waited until the sound of the running water ceased and I heard the creak of the floorboard just outside our bedroom. I waited another fifteen minutes and when I was sure she'd gone to bed, I went upstairs. I was turning on the light in the guest room when I heard her call my name. "Sam?" she said. "You coming to bed?"

God help me, relief and gratitude sparked in my heart. But then I remembered the shitty things she'd said about Dad and I stood still, unsure of what to do.

"Sam? Will you come in here? Please?"

I made my way down the hall. "What?" I said, standing in the doorway of our darkened bedroom.

I heard her fumble for the bedside table lamp. The sudden light made her dark hair glow. Her beautiful face looked small and I knew she'd been crying. As I watched, she sat up and leaned against the headboard. "Will you come lie with me?" she whispered. She removed her left hand from under the covers and held it out toward me.

I felt myself soften almost immediately. I always did. From the time we'd met in grad school almost eight years ago, I've never had any defenses against Ali, especially when she turns those luminous eyes on me. But this time I thought, *Not so fast.* This time, I remembered what my therapist had said to me a few weeks ago—if you give in to her every time, you're simply rewarding her bad behavior. Ali was an incorrigible flirt and she knew it hurt me terribly. Still, she did this, time and time again. I had to lay down some limits.

"I'm sleeping in the other room," I mumbled, forcing myself to meet her eyes. "I told you, I have a headache."

Her lips thinned at the obvious lie. But she rolled onto her side and turned off the light. I stood in the sudden dark for a second and then made my way to the guest bedroom. "Good night," she called after me, but her tone said, *Fuck you.*

A strange sort of satisfaction gripped me as I got into bed. I had drawn blood and it felt good.

I'm not what you'd call a lucky man.

In school the other kids beat me up every goddamn day of my life.

My old man died when I was seven years old.

I developed a speech impediment the next year and it followed me all the way through college. You may as well kiss the prospect of any serious girlfriend goodbye when you stutter like a fucking loon and have to wear braces at twelve.

Joining the army saved my life. Not only did the men I served with in Iraq and Afghanistan help pull me out of my shell, the army provided the therapy I needed to get over my speech defect. No way my widowed mother could've paid for that. The army felt like a homecoming because for all the talk about rules and discipline and codes of conduct, the fact was the military ran on the two things that I understood best—anger and violence. And the kind of brotherhood I never had with my own kin. I would've gladly stayed for the rest of my life, but life had another plan for me. They threw me out with a dishonorable discharge after I'd done one tour in Iraq and two in Afghanistan, for trying to teach some fucking Afghani warlord a lesson. I figured that's what we were there for in the first place, to fuck them up so that they wouldn't dare come fuck with us stateside. But Obama had won reelection a month earlier and everybody knew his heart wasn't in the fight.

Now, I stand in the driveway, debating whether to go back in and wake Ali up for our morning run. Or, better yet, get into bed with her to snuggle for a few minutes and leave behind the madness from last night. We depart at three to pick up Sally and Maureen from Cleveland Hopkins International Airport and we need to find our way back to one another before company arrives. This is our annual ritual—every July 4 holiday, Sally and Mo fly in to spend time with us. The fact that we're expecting visitors makes this a shitty time to not be on speaking terms.

I bend to retie my shoe laces. I don't want to wake up Ali if she's still asleep. And I need to clear my head, rid it of the tangle of last night's angry thoughts. A good, vigorous run, my body trembling with exhaustion and dripping with sweat, will do the trick. I love running with Ali, it's one of our favorite things to do together, but at five foot four, her stride is shorter than mine and her pace slows me down. I take after my big Irish father; I'm five eight.

It's a beautiful Sunday morning in July. As I run, the morning sun filters through the canopy of trees. The sight is so glorious that my immediate thought is, *I wish Ali could see this.* As if last night's fight hadn't happened. As if the sun is boring holes into the last of my resentment. This is what years of living with someone does to you. It messes with your head.

The birds are wide awake, sounding as brash and self-important as kids on their way to school. The sunshine and the feeling of my feet flying across the pavement are beginning to fill my body with a liquid joy. I know I have to do a shorter run today—Sal and Mo will be here for ten days, and we still have to clean the house and go grocery shopping. As I run, I notice an old-fashioned lemonade stand on someone's front porch. The lights in the house are off and it will be hours before they set it up on the sidewalk. In any case, all I have on me is a credit card to pick up bread from Stone Oven after the run. But the truth is, even if I were carrying cash, I wouldn't stop to buy lemonade from the kids. Whereas if Ali accidentally drives past a lemonade stand, she makes a U-turn and hands the kids a dollar or two. Selling lemonade in the summer in her old neighborhood in Columbus is one of the few pleasant memories that she has of her childhood, back when her mother was still alive and her life had not turned to shit.

Truth be told, Ali is kind not just to children but to all living creatures. I can't count the number of times she's had me dig small graves in our backyard to bury the robins and squirrels and chipmunks that she's been unable to nurse back to health. I kid her about how every injured or sick creature finds its way into our yard, as if news of her carries its way through some underground network shared by all the feathered and furry creatures in our Cleveland Heights neighborhood.

Khandhar Province, December 2012. Eight days before Christmas. My unit was caught in an ambush that took the lives of three of our men. Back at the base, we were pissed off, seething, cold, and homesick. Well, most of the men were homesick. All except me. As far as I was concerned, if I never saw that miserable little ranch in Wyoming ever again, it would be too soon. I'd seen a bit of the world during my R&Rs and I'd begun to fancy myself as something more than a hick from Hicksville, USA. Way I figured, there were a million places worth visiting before I'd return to the crappy town where I was born.

Maybe it was my idea. That's what the others said after they turned on me, but honestly, I don't know. My mind fritzes out. All I remember is the five of us walking into that Afghani home just around dinnertime and lining up the warlord and his family. The women had their heads uncovered, I remember that. There was an elderly man there and he kept begging us to allow the women to cover up. But that only made us laugh and leer at the cringing women. None of us knew what exactly we were planning on doing, but then the teenaged boy threw himself onto my buddy Terry and next thing I knew, I'd spun around to pistol-whip him. I watched in fascination as his face bloodied. I heard a scream and his older sister came up to me and clawed the heck out of the left side of my face. And here's the weird thing—even as my face stung, I was aroused. It had been six months since my last R&R in Thailand, where I'd fucked everything that moved. I picked up the woman and dragged her to the next room. "Sarge?" Terry called after me, but the blood pounded in my head and I barely heard him.

Hell, I don't know why I'm remembering this sordid shit right now.

Because the story I want to tell is about how an unlucky man became the luckiest man in the world today.

I never had a serious girlfriend until I met Ali. Maybe that's part of the problem. Ali's been dating women since she was fourteen, first keeping them a secret from her conservative Indian Muslim family, and then being openly defiant. But those early years of hiding from her father and then battling him have left their mark on her. If Ali is about any one thing, she's about freedom—total, absolute, uncompromising freedom. She won't tolerate any restrictions on who she will love, who she will be friendly with, who she will flirt with. Not even from me.

Thing is, I don't doubt for a second that she loves me. That she'd fight anything and anybody for me. Nobody has made me feel more secure than Ali has. But here's where my own shitty family history does battle with hers. I'm the daughter of a raging, abusive alcoholic and his timid, cowering wife. Not exactly a great formula for raising a confident, secure daughter.

I pick up my pace involuntarily, as if merely thinking of my parents makes me want to run faster, as if I'm still trying to get away from my childhood. Which, I suppose, I am. Which, I suppose, we all are.

Ali too. She just won't acknowledge it as freely as I do. It's as if she has no awareness that her childhood has left her as damaged and reactive as mine has. She's one of those outspoken, confident women who believe that they can bend reality to their will. She thinks that because she is estranged from her family, she has left all of her puritanical upbringing behind. The art of forgetting is a dangerous one—once you start, maybe you can't stop. Ali is beginning to forget those early years in grad school, when we clung to each other like refugees who had found a home. If she ever thinks of those days, when we were magic around each other, she seldom mentions them.

Most of the time, I tell myself it doesn't matter. Ali was always the more pragmatic one. I am the airy-fairy, head-in-the-clouds type.

But then, I'm the writer in the family. It is my job to understand, to piece together Ali's backstory, to connect the dots from the scraps of information about her early life that she sometimes tosses my way. Once, just once, she'd told me that when she was growing up, as the only brown kid on her street, the white kids used to tease her and call her ugly. Nobody in their right minds would call Ali ugly now. She's radiant—petite, with short black hair, big dark, searching eyes, a mouth made for kissing. But maybe this explains her inveterate need to flirt, as if she was still trying to prove those white kids wrong. I try to remind myself of this every time we're together with our friends. Sometimes I succeed. Sometimes, like last night, I want to slap her silly.

A movement to my left catches my eye and I turn my head. I gasp and stumble on a raised sidewalk before I regain my balance. I'm running fast enough now that I'm already past the house, but my brain is still trying to comprehend and make sense of what I just saw: a naked man, bald as the Buddha, sitting cross-legged on a couch on his front porch, his pale skin gleaming in the early morning light. As I replay the image, I realize that it was probably just a neighbor in his underwear, but still, the sight of all that naked flesh is unnerving and unexpected. I shake my head. Probably some oddball—nobody I recognize—doing yoga out on his porch. White male privilege on display, in the flesh.

I turn left on Stratford, heading for the lower Shaker Lakes. I trace my path in my head as I run—in a moment, the houses on Stratford will give way to the large mansions with the huge front lawns and then I'll cross Fairmount and maybe jog in place at the traffic light at North Park. Then it's down the beautiful mulched path that circles the lake. If I'm winded, I'll stop for a minute to look at the white clouds floating on top of the placid water, look for the egret that normally sits on one submerged branch, and listen to the honks of the wild geese. This is my happy place, this small but beautiful park, and it centers me. The next ten days while Mo and Sally visit will be a blur—trips to Amish country and to Niagara Falls. Cookouts on the back porch and al fresco dining in Little Italy. Sally's requisite trip to the Cleveland Museum of Art. A Cleveland Orchestra concert at Blossom tomorrow night, on July 3. The four of us lying on our blankets on that green lawn, looking up at the fireworks that will follow. Today is my final chance for some solitude, to be alone among the trees and the summer sky coming down upon the lake.

I peer down the block as far as the eye can see. Not another soul out on the suburban streets, not even a moving car. This is my favorite time of the day, early morning, when the streets are solitary and the only sound is that of the gossiping birds. Just two years ago, when we first moved to Cleveland Heights, we were renting on the wrong side of the tracks, so to speak—the houses are smaller and more modest on the other side of Lee Road, the neighborhood more Black and poor. But one year later, Ali landed her tenure-track job at Cleveland State and we bought our first home together, a beautiful Arts and Crafts bungalow on Corydon. There's not a day goes by that I don't feel deliriously lucky when I walk across the finished hardwood floors or look up at the exquisite crown molding. I am also in love with our new neighborhood, although I sometimes suspect that Ali would've preferred to stay on Silsby because it fits in better with her conception of herself as an underdog, a permanent outsider, even though she makes far more money than I do. I have run this route so many times that some of the older dogs don't even bark as I go past their homes. Ali and I used to listen to music as we ran, but three months ago we decided to leave our earbuds and phones at home. Now, for an hour, we run unencumbered by the dings and whistles that announce the incoming encroachments of our real lives.

I look up and notice the gray SUV coming down the street, the first moving vehicle I've seen this morning. The driver must've spotted me too, because the SUV suddenly swerves, as if avoiding an invisible dog crossing the street. And even though I'm safely on the sidewalk, the movement distracts me and I remember the edge of raised sidewalk only when my toe stubs against it and I trip, and the sudden, sharp pain electrifies its way up my shin and I lose my balance.

I was driving in my SUV to Home Depot to buy gardening supplies when I saw her. Tall, lean body. Red hair that flamed in the morning sun. Flushed skin against a white T-shirt and blue shorts. White socks and running shoes. She looked like something beautiful and rare that the morning had delivered.

I saw her notice my vehicle and then watched as she lost her balance and tripped and fell. She did this little twist as she fell, so that by the time I pulled up to her, she was lying on her left side. I knelt down and gently rolled her over. She was awake but stunned from where her head had hit the slate sidewalk. She tried to speak but couldn't and her eyes were vacant enough that I wondered if she had a concussion. Her face was bruised on one side. She bit her lower lip in pain and I saw that her left ankle was already beginning to swell.

I looked around quickly. There was not a single person nearby. I was less than half a mile from my house on North Park. The day burned warm and quiet. Nothing stirred—the glory of a Sunday morning in suburban Cleveland Heights. The big brick houses sat deep into their lots, away from the sidewalk, their front lawns lush and manicured. As far as I could tell, no one had seen her fall. No one had heard me pull up.

I scooped her in my arms, staggered to my feet, and carried her to my car. I struggled to open the passenger-side door while holding on to her. Sweat gathered on my face. Quickly, quickly, I thought. Before anyone notices. Before someone steps out of their home to walk their dog. Before she shakes off this stupor and pain makes her scream. *I got her into the seat and reclined it as far back as it would go. I rolled up the tinted window before I got in behind the wheel and made a U-turn.*

Halfway home, I made a snap decision, turned onto Monmouth, and pulled into the driveway of the empty yellow house with the For Sale *sign. Ann Warren's old home. I'd run into her at Anatolia Cafe just before she'd left to move in with her daughter in Seattle. It has been sitting on the market for at least three months. A problem with the wet basement, I'd heard. I reached into my messenger bag and took out the pillbox and the bottled water.* "Here," I said, "take this. It'll help with the pain."

She looked at me with incomprehension.

Fear made me angry. Stopping here was a risk and I couldn't afford to prolong the moment. I'd pulled all the way back into Ann's driveway, but someone could still see the SUV from the street. At any minute, a car could drive by. Because already I knew what I was going to do, sure as if I'd already done it. A slow burning excitement snaked its way up my limbs and into my chest. The woman in Afghanistan. The schoolgirl in Wyoming. Each time, it was the same uncontrollable feeling of inevitability. Of destiny. Like starring in a film that someone else was directing. It was a feeling like no other in the world—fear, yes, but also the exhilaration of breaking free of that fear. Explosive. Powerful.

She was still staring at me, but a sliver of cognition was fighting its way through the opaqueness of her gaze. "Take it," I said. "It's Advil. It'll help with the pain."

If she hadn't reached for the ketamine just then, I don't know what I would've done. I'd like to believe that I would've driven her to the ER.

But, destiny. She reached for the water and then for the pill. Swallowed. For one awful moment, it looked like she was going to choke and throw up the tablet. But down the hatch it went. Ten minutes, tops, and she'd be out like a light.

A feeling of tenderness swept over me, as the shiver of anger from a moment ago dissipated. She was mine, this beautiful girl. Forever mine.

This girl was a beautiful feather that had dropped at my feet. What choice but to pick it up?

I did not wish to defile, mutilate, or despoil this feather.

This was not the woman in Afghanistan, coming at me with her talons.

This was not the prostitute in Thailand who told me she was thirteen only after I'd had sex with her and then tried to rob me blind.

This was not the schoolgirl in Lamire, only two months shy of turning eighteen, who flirted shamelessly with me and then turned me in.

This was purity.

This was a second chance.

This was destiny.

This was something that I claimed for myself.

This was something to keep, away from the prying eyes of the army or the police or the neighbors.

This is where my story would begin.

I put the car into drive. I was no longer afraid of someone noticing us. There was a righteousness in how this had gone down, the universe righting itself at last. I hummed "Sunday Morning Coming Down" under my breath as I drove, not stopping until I had pulled into the garage attached to my house and lowered the automatic doors that separated us from the world.

* * *

In the eternity it takes me to fall, a rush of images—Ali flashing Janice a smile across the table, the slight tremble in her hand when she beseeched me to join her in bed last night, the look on her face when I turned away from her. And through it all, improbably but incessantly, a phrase clanging like a bell in my head—*A house divided cannot stand.*

Then, the world folds into itself and the mercury-blue sky tumbles onto the hard sidewalk and I join the ranks of the fallen.

THE ULTIMATE CURE

BY MICHAEL RUHLMAN

Shaker Square

The restaurant, Fire, a short walk in high heels from my apartment, bustled as usual. I nodded to Catherine, the hostess to the left of the door, then turned right toward the bar and saw I was in luck. At the dogleg end sat a woman against the wall, reading with a glass of wine, and beside her, a single open stool. The only potential drawback sat in the next seat over, on the long side of the bar. A bit of a schlub in a blue blazer, the top of his head buffed to a bright shine and below, a horseshoe of ginger hair. But hell, who was I to be choosy?

"Is this seat taken?" I asked both the woman with the wine and the blue blazer. The woman didn't seem to hear, too deep in her book, or the Chardonnay, but the guy looked up from his phone, smiled, and said, "Be my guest."

I hung my purse over the back of the bar chair and said, "Is that an offer?" I sat.

He chuckled nervously and said, "*No.* I mean . . . I don't know."

"The decisive type," I said, with a little more contempt than I'd meant.

Jason appeared, in classic bartender fashion, polishing a glass with a white cloth. "Usual, Roxanne?"

"Double," I said.

Jason looked to the man beside me, who'd returned to his BlackBerry, and said, "Warren? Another?"

Warren looked at his martini glass, said, "Sure," then threw back the remainder of his drink. He picked out the lemon twist and ate it.

I waited till I'd had a fortifying slug of my Manhattan before trying to show Warren here I wasn't a bitch: "I didn't know they still made those things."

"What?" he said. "Oh, this. I tried an iPhone, but I just can't give up the feel of the keypad."

Jason set down a martini so full Warren had to lower his head to it, holding its base against the bar, for a big slurp. He lifted the glass, took another deep drink, then let out a long sigh-moan.

"I can't tell if that was good or bad," I said.

"Both," he said. "The good part is the bedrock reliability of a martini to loosen the knot at the base of my neck."

"And the bad part?"

"It doesn't touch sorrow."

That was a pile I didn't want to step in, so I said, "You're new around here."

"Not really. Been here every night for the past two weeks."

"I've been gone for a bit, otherwise I'd have seen you."

"Been anyplace fun?"

My turn to sigh. "Ten days in North Carolina, getting my mom into assisted living the day after cops found her wandering the streets of Raleigh in a terry-cloth robe. She's only seventy-five, but the dementia requires more help than a live-in can provide. Plus she's running out of cash. And who knows what the fuck I'll do when that happens."

"What do you do that you can take off ten days at the last minute?"

"My agency doesn't have a problem with that kind of leave. Ad agency, account side. Or was until they included me in the latest wave of layoffs." I didn't offer that this had happened more than a year ago now, and I'd had to take work cleaning houses to make ends meet, a cycle I couldn't seem to get out of, now that I'd been effectively unemployed so long.

"Sorry."

"Yeah, well, all part of a rather bleak financial picture, I'm afraid."

He grimaced, but there was something he liked about it too, I could see, from the way the corners of his mouth curled. Misery, company.

"Hey, listen," he said, brightening. "They have a great burger here."

"I *know*."

"I don't really need a whole one though." He patted his pudgy belly. "I don't suppose you'd like to split one. On me, of course."

This was turning out to be something of a mini windfall. I sensed this guy was going to pick up my entire tab. I was so tired of worrying about money. If he expected me to sleep with him, well, let's have that burger and some wine and decide later.

"One question," I said. "You married?"

"No, you?"

"Married for thirteen happy-until-they-weren't years, divorced five years ago. So what's with the ring?"

He stared at his ring finger so long I was almost sorry I asked.

"Separated. Can't bear to take it off." He had another swallow of his martini, then turned his very blue eyes to mine, looked right through me. "Amazing that you can still love someone you hate."

* * *

Maybe he was a schlub, but he had a lot going for him. Gin martinis. Burger medium rare. He dipped his fries in the aioli rather than the ketchup. And he ordered a ninety-five-dollar bottle of wine.

Turns out we both lived in Moreland Courts, a collection of condos from the twenties, redbrick, Georgian, with gothic windows and arches. The buildings ran one long, long block from Shaker Square to Coventry. On the national register of historic places. A hundred and forty residences, some of them quite grand. I had one of the smaller units, paid for in the divorce settlement by my ex, a one-bedroom one flight up, with a den and a dining/living room area, a kitchen with linoleum tiles and ancient appliances, a back fire escape where I could smoke.

Warren and *his* soon-to-be-ex lived in one of the grandest apartments in the entire complex—the penthouse in the Point Building, the central main building. Nowadays only she lived there—though she'd fallen in love, so the new man was likely to move in, he said. Which was going to be awkward since Warren still lived in the building.

She, Elizabeth, was from old Cleveland money, old like Severance and Rockefeller money, and her parents had never approved because Warren was from Fairview Park—a *west* sider. Two kids, one just out of college living in Manhattan, the other a sophomore at Loyola in Chicago.

They'd separated a month and a half ago, after she announced she'd been having an affair and was in love with someone else. "Named Rod," he said.

"*Rod.* Ouch."

"And I've known him for ages. Not bosom pals but cock-tail-party buddies."

We'd both finished our burger and were done picking at the fries. The wine was gone.

"Dessert?" he asked.

"Definitely," I said. "Jack on the rocks."

"Whiskey drinker. After my own heart." He motioned for Jason. "Two Blanton's, ice on the side."

I could only assume that this bourbon was a step up from Jack Daniel's.

"Coming right up."

"Would you mind terribly if I stepped outside for a smoke?" he asked.

Say what you will about my decision-making processes, but the fancy whiskey and the postmeal cigarette were the nail in my coffin. That's what did it. Whiskey and cigarettes. There are so few smokers anymore, we who partake are a kind of private club. He pulled a box of American Spirit light-blues from his jacket pocket once we were outside.

"Of course you do," I said.

"Of course I do what? Is it a good thing?"

"It's a good thing," I said, accepting his light. This was my brand as well.

And so there, just outside the restaurant in the patio area, empty because of the stormy August weather, he told me the hate part regarding Elizabeth Mordecai. Money, natch.

Affairs of the heart are one thing—you simply can't control them. And the urge for sex is not something you can turn off. He got that. Money was another matter. Because Elizabeth's money was all tied up in family trusts, with sharp penalties for withdrawals where they were even available. For this reason he'd paid for most of their twenty-three years together. Private schools, two college tuitions, family vacations, with the agreement that he could retire when they both turned fifty, in two years, and a huge chunk of her trust became available. And the Moreland Courts penthouse was another bone of contention. It had been given to her by her parents on the eve of their wedding.

"I'm guessing the savvy skeptical parents put it in her name alone? And pre-wedding so it wouldn't be a marital asset when the marriage inevitably failed."

"Which is why she's living there and I'm not."

"Not quite fair, after so many years of marriage."

"She didn't work, so I basically paid for *everything* for twenty years."

"What do you do?"

"Attorney. Estate planning, ironically."

"Oof," I said.

A downtown-bound Rapid Transit car clanged by in the humid night. He took a long drag and blew the smoke at the sky in a slow stream.

"The divorce started out mediated and friendly. I loved her, I didn't wish her harm. Hurt as I was—no, devastated as I was. But then her lawyer showed me her personal assets and the marital assets . . ." He ground out his cigarette beneath his tasseled loafer. "She has virtually zero marital assets, though she lives like a fucking queen. And . . . and . . . it's likely that I will end up paying *her* spousal support because she doesn't work."

"Fuck."

"I can't believe I'm going to be paying *her*. I'll be lucky if it's less than ten grand."

"A *month?*"

He sighed again, stared at his feet, and shook his head, then to me said, "How about that bourbon?"

"You bet," I said.

Before we reentered Fire, he stopped and cupped my elbow. "I'm bald," he said.

"I noticed."

"I think I'm slightly shorter than you."

"Not if I take off my shoes."

"Is that going to be a problem?"

"No."

Shoot me for judging a book by its cover. This guy was a charmer.

Even the sex was great. He was completely confident, something I didn't manage well myself. Forty-seven and carrying thirty pounds I didn't exactly need. "I didn't think you were a natural blonde," he said, undressing me. He even asked if I preferred he use a condom (yes, thank you).

We hadn't gone to my place because I didn't know who this guy was. I had no reason to suspect anything, but I still waited for him to use his key fob to enter the building—you never know. He apologized and explained that he'd been renting the guest suite on the ground floor—kitchenette, living room, bedroom with two double beds, and all the impermanence of a hotel room.

I'd finished a postsex cigarette and had curled around his cute pudgy body while he lit a second.

"Roxanne," he said.

The way he said it made my stomach cramp. Something was coming and I didn't want to hear it.

"Will you tell me this is not a one-night stand?" he said.

My whole body exhaled. I kissed him. "This is definitely not a one-night stand."

And he could cook! The following morning, he woke me with a kiss, said he'd be back in thirty, and that coffee was brewing. He returned with fresh eggs and spinach from the North

Union Farmers Market in the Square, a fresh loaf of On the Rise bread. And he made shirred eggs Florentine. *Shirred eggs Florentine*, for godsake. With toasted, buttered baguette.

He reached across the table and squeezed my hand. "*You are like a gift from the gods.*"

"Fuck you," I said, and gave him a coy smile.

We talked more about the divorce but I could see he was starting to get worked up.

"I mean it's funny. In a kind of cosmic way."

"What?" he asked.

"The guy's name is *Rod*. The guy who's fucking your wife."

He shook his head at me and said, "Roxanne, I haven't laughed in six weeks."

I guess this is the power of great sex: by the following weekend, he was all but moved in to my place.

It was weirdly easy—we got along so well. I was a little suspicious that he might just be doing this to show Elizabeth he was over her, that he might be using me. But I pushed these thoughts away. It was such a pleasure having a companion after so many years of ending the night by myself, making myself dizzy with one last nightcap and an equally unnecessary cigarette. But he seemed genuinely happy as well.

September in Cleveland is my favorite month—the abundant trees turn and the air dries out, leaving just low golden sun, chilly mornings, and warm afternoons.

It didn't take long to establish a fall routine. Warren took the Rapid to work and returned around six. I had his gin and a martini glass chilling in the freezer. I'd mix my Manhattan and his martini, one capful of vermouth and a twist (which he always ate). We'd watch the news and have a snack. Then he'd make dinner—he was a fabulous cook, and I certainly didn't mind shopping for groceries, or doing laundry, or any of the mundane chores that had been a weekend headache, but were a breeze midweek since I was now a happily kept woman and could shop when stores weren't busy.

Of course I snooped a little but the most revealing thing I found was a well-stocked supply of Viagra in his Dopp kit— but hell, sex like that? I'll make that errand to Rite Aid for him myself.

We were into October when it dawned on me that I was living the kind of provincial suburban life I'd always dreamed of. I'd graduated from Kent State in 1992 with a useless bachelor's degree in anthropology. After a couple years of scraping by on little freelance pieces for *Cleveland Magazine* and the *Plain Dealer* and waiting tables at Yours Truly, I got a job in sales at the magazine I contributed to. I moved into advertising for a bigger paycheck. Danny, my ex, and I had an okay life, but we were always struggling. Eventually, Danny got bored selling cars and went back to school to study architecture, which I helped pay for, of course. By the time he'd learned enough to get a decent job in the field, he'd had enough of me, and this went on for two unhappy years until we divorced and he moved to Atlanta.

That was five years ago, and my life had gone downhill fast. My sister died three years ago in a carjacking (buying drugs in Woodland Hills, we suspect)—that happened about the same time as my divorce. I started drinking too much, and my life tanked. My dad died of a heart attack ten years ago, and now my mom was on her way out. So it's just been me and my cat, a tabby named Wilifred, for a long, long time.

And suddenly, a chance encounter at Fire and I was magically living the kind of boring bougie life I'd once coveted.

No more cleaning rich people's toilets. Being taken care of, even loved. This was heaven.

On Saturdays we'd shop at the farmers market at Shaker Square. He bought squash and apples, Tea Hill Farm's chicken, even a slab of pork belly that he himself intended to cure into bacon. I hadn't eaten so well in my life. Maybe we'd see a show at the Cedar-Lee. Sunday mornings were special. We'd lounge in bed with the *Times*, then around eleven he would open a bottle of Perrier-Jouët, and set out a tin of caviar, a bowl of crème fraiche, and potato chips—and we'd watch an old movie, *Bringing Up Baby*, *My Man Godfrey*, *Dark Victory*. We'd spend the rest of Sunday watching the Browns lose. Warren would get so mad it was almost scary. If the Browns fumbled on the goal line, a specialty of theirs, he would shout so loud I was afraid he'd give himself a coronary. But that was the only time I saw him angry. Otherwise, at least when he wasn't speaking of Elizabeth, he was gentle and as cuddly as twelve-year-old Wilifred the cat.

The worst you could say about him was that he had expensive tastes—especially given what would soon be a reversal of fortune. He owned a red Mercedes and an expensive Cartier watch. He overspent on wines when we went out. The weekly champagne and caviar.

We'd cross paths with Elizabeth not infrequently. I'd officially met her at the front desk when I had some business with Mary, the desk attendant there. Elizabeth wore tight jeans and espadrilles, an almost masculine pink shirt, diamond earrings, gold bracelets and necklace. Casual but impeccable.

Elizabeth had wavy brown hair, very dark-brown, beautiful eyes, and the kind of natural good looks that didn't require makeup. I had to spend thirty minutes in front of the mirror before I felt presentable at one of Warren's events.

When she'd finished her business and started to leave, I stopped her.

"Excuse me, Elizabeth?" She turned. "I've been wanting to introduce myself. I'm Roxanne DeFranco.

It took only a couple seconds before she knew who I was. "Ah, we meet."

"How do you do?" I said, already feeling uncomfortable.

We shook hands.

"I hope this is going to be okay," I said.

"Hell, it's okay with *me*. I'm thrilled he found you—he's been so much nicer. My *God*. I'm sure he told you we're back into a civil mediation. I just want everyone to be kind to each other."

"I'm hoping we can all be friends."

"Nothing would make me happier. I'm skeptical but open." She looked at her watch. "And I'm twenty minutes late for my hair appoint—must dash."

Later that week, Warren and I headed downtown for barbecue at Mabel's and passed Elizabeth in the garage. When Warren saw her approaching, he put his arm around me.

"Hi, you two," she said, easy but chilly.

"Elizabeth," he said warmly. And that was all. Until we got to the car. He had his hand on the start button but paused and said, almost to himself, "Wouldn't it be grand if she were gone?"

"What do you mean?"

He started the car, then leaned back. "No spousal support!" he chirped, smiling easily.

"That would be nice."

We exited the garage, and almost as an afterthought he said, "And the twelve-million-dollar trust."

"The what?"

"Oh, she's got a zillion family trusts but one of the trusts is in both our names, for the kids. We can't take distributions without heavy penalties, but we both have access to it for the kids."

"Really," I said. "You never told me that."

Every time I thought about twelve million dollars, and perhaps living in a penthouse, I pinched myself to stanch the thought. I mean, life was pretty good—what more did I want? Happy for the first time in God knows how long. But whenever Warren came back from a meeting with the divorce attorneys, he sounded obsessed with what she was getting away with to the point that he flushed with pent-up resentment. He always referred to her as "that bitch."

Once he said, "If that bitch were gone, my problems"—he put his hand on my knee—"*our* problems, would be gone. Our life would be grand."

Oh, I knew. I must have thought about it once a day. "Maybe she'll get hit by a bus," I said hopefully.

"Or we could facilitate something a little less random."

I chalked this up to his third martini, which was unlike him. I let it go, and he went to baste the duck roasting in the oven. It was eating at him, and all I knew was that I loved him and couldn't bear to lose him, or this new life, the first genuine happiness and ease I'd ever known.

So when he returned from work and said, "I've got an idea"—I remember it was Halloween, smack in the middle of the week, he'd had another divorce meeting—my stomach turned. I'd been hoping this idea would go away. I brought him his nightly martini and some Marcona almonds. "She's going down and Rod is going to take the fall for it. *Somehow.*"

My mouth hung open, and I shook my head slowly. This time he hadn't had three martinis. Or maybe he had.

"I just had drinks with him," Warren said.

"What? Where?"

"Nighttown, why?"

"I just . . . I . . . I didn't know you were even cordial, let alone drinking pals."

"I've talked about this. I'm trying to make nice. We have to be seen as friends if this is going to work."

"If *what's* going to work?" I paused. "You're not . . . Why?"

"I'll give you twelve million reasons," he said, with something close to anger. "And throw in a penthouse for good measure." Then he smiled. "Think of it, my love."

And I did, I couldn't help it. I went to the kitchen to prepare the salad—he'd taught me how and this was my contribution to dinner.

I'd never actually met Rod Collinsworth, but I'd seen him in the lobby and at a couple of charity events Warren had to attend. I knew from Warren that Rod was a realtor for Howard Hanna. He wore his dark hair long on top but brushed back with some sturdy gel, shaved close along the sides. He wore his cranberry corduroy trousers to fit in with the hunt club ethos, a sport coat each time I'd caught sight of him, brass-buckled loafers, and probably no socks. To me he looked, I don't know, precious and exacting.

But it hadn't been the drinks. Over duck à l'orange, roasted potatoes with rosemary, and my fennel, orange, and arugula salad, Warren mapped out his plan at the kitchen table, or as much as he'd figured out so far. And I listened.

"Welcome," I said to Elizabeth and Rod as they entered my place, *our* place. "Thank you so much for coming,"

I brought out olives, Marcona almonds, and Cowgirl Creamery Mt. Tam cheese, as Warren had instructed. He delivered a tray with four drinks: two martinis, a La Crema Chardonnay ("the only chard she drinks," he'd explained when he gave me the shopping list), and a Manhattan for me. Elizabeth and Rod sat on the loveseat, Warren in the adjacent leather chair, I opposite him.

I felt confused by it all, and scarcely followed the niceties of the conversation until Warren said, "I know! Not even divorced and already thinking ahead!" He smiled at me and shook his head before turning back to Elizabeth. "So. Elizabeth. Let's show them how this is done. We don't want to give our money to lawyers. Let's just do this thing."

This was part of the plan. His new love had given him a change of heart. He was the soul of magnanimity toward her. She had to believe it, as did Rod, and the whole gossipy building.

Elizabeth looked at him kind of google-eyed and said, "Okay."

"But it's almost Thanksgiving, then there's Christmas. Can we wait till just after?"

"Um, okay," she said, glancing at Rod, who only lifted his eyebrows.

"Let's plan to sign on December 31—make it a clean break tax-wise and a hopeful start to the new year!" Warren exclaimed.

My stomach was in knots—he seemed like a different person. He was really planning this.

Elizabeth polished off the La Crema, and Warren and Rod had more drinks, but I didn't—I just didn't feel a part of it. They were all from the same social world. I didn't really follow their small talk. And I was relieved when Rod made a show of looking at his watch and said, "It's almost eight," whereupon Elizabeth said, "We'd better be off then."

* * *

A week before Thanksgiving, it was decided that I would go to North Carolina to be with my mother. This hadn't been the plan until Warren said that his kids were coming home for Thanksgiving and that Elizabeth had asked him to be a part of their dinner. To show the kids this new arrangement was civil. They were young adults and were accustomed to unusual relationships, as long as everyone was happy. But he thought it best if I didn't join them. That might be a bit too much.

I swallowed my hurt and said, "Of course, love. Whatever you think is best."

"That's my girl," he said, and kissed my forehead.

"I'll go down to North Carolina and spend it with my mom. I should do that anyway—it may be the last Thanksgiving I have with her."

And that's how I spent the most depressing Thanksgiving of my life. Mom could barely remember who I was. Her retirement facility did its own turkey dinner, on plastic trays. Even the ribs on the cranberry "sauce" now made me wince. I suppose I have Warren to thank for that.

I was supposed to fly home Sunday morning, but the thought of two more days with my mom was too depressing. So I caught a Friday flight out of Raleigh-Durham that got me into Cleveland at three p.m. The night before, I'd spoken with Warren when he'd gotten home. He said the evening went perfectly fine: "Everyone was very civil. I even managed to enjoy myself!"

Which of course made me fret that he'd start having feelings for her, that he'd go back to her, and to her money, and I'd be left high and dry. That was another reason for wanting to get back home.

He was asleep when my flight took off, and by the time I landed at Hopkins, I'd decided to surprise him.

"Hello? I'm home!" I called out. As I jiggled the key to remove it from the lock, I heard some light fumbling commotion, before Warren called out, "We're in the den, hon." And when I entered I found Rod Collinsworth there as well.

Warren said, "What a surprise! Welcome home!" He hugged and kissed me. "What happened? You were supposed to stay till Sunday!"

"Rod," I said.

"Roxanne, hi."

"Rod was returning your hors d'oeuvres platter I'd brought over last night. I insisted he stay for a drink."

"I was just leaving," he said. And he was gone before I could hang up my coat.

"How about a cocktail, hon? I made us Negronis."

"It's a little early, isn't it?"

"It's a holiday weekend. Join me."

"How many have you had?"

"Just one," he said, but I knew from the way the corners of his mouth curled slightly, like an embarrassed boy, that he'd had more. He was a terrible liar.

"What are Negronis?" I asked.

"Rod's cocktail of choice. Give one a try?" He stepped toward me in a kind of dance, kissed my neck, and squeezed my ass with both hands, pulled my hips into his. I tried to wiggle away, saying, "I probably smell like an airplane."

"Mmm, you smell sexy," he whispered. "Let me make you a Negroni while you get into something more comfortable? Such as a bed, perhaps?"

This just wasn't getting old—to be wanted. Nothing more sexy than that. I kissed him back, squeezed him through his chinos. "My, you are ready," I said. "Make me that cocktail and I'll see you in there."

Sex had tapered off since the white-heat beginning, as I suppose isn't unusual. I could have gone for more but mainly because I loved the way he fucked me, which I would say was aggressive but thoughtful—he could really last and always made sure I was satisfied, even if he didn't finish. I'd never met a guy who did that. When we'd cooled off a bit, I asked, "What's with having Rod for a drink? Isn't that odd?"

"Why? Just establishing our friendship."

"You know, Warren, I used to think my gaydar was pretty good."

"Don't be silly. He's just a bit of a fop."

I emptied my glass. "This was delicious. What was in it again?"

"Gin, Campari, and sweet vermouth. I'll make us another?"

"What the hell," I said. We could order out and make an early night of it.

"That's my girl," he said, kissing my cheek. Then he whispered in my ear, "Rod gave me what I needed. I've got the plan."

Again my stomach knotted. But Warren was in control. He was so capable—I loved his certainty. It felt like protection. I couldn't lose him.

December 21 would be the night, Warren said, returning to bed with two more cocktails, ice rattling in the glasses. Elizabeth and Rod were having a big Christmas party, and they'd invited us. A lot of Cleveland socialites and bankers and McKinsey types, but also artists she patronized (apparently she had access to money for the art) and other literary types. None of them *my* types.

It was here that he would do it—where Rod or any number of people could be suspected—she had good friends and better enemies, both invited, Warren said. There would be too many suspects to keep track of.

He made the plan sound simple. He'd dose her wine with Rohypnol, which he could buy online. After she'd been put to bed, he'd sneak in and help her to swallow a teaspoon of sodium nitrite.

I'd watched Warren cure his own bacon and corn his own beef. "This is the magic," he'd said, holding a bag of pink crystals. "Sodium nitrite. Curing salt. This is what gives bacon its flavor and keeps the meat pink."

"Is that why it's pink?"

"No. They color it pink so people don't mistake it for ordinary salt, or sugar. It's poisonous if ingested directly. The nitrite binds to oxygen in the blood so the body can't access it, and you basically suffocate."

A teaspoon of sodium nitrite would be about seven grams, seven times a lethal dose for her weight. She wouldn't be able to breathe, would likely have a heart attack, and no one would be the wiser. The nitrite dissipates, he explained. They wouldn't even know what happened. It would look like she died in her sleep.

"Are you sure?"

"Google it."

"Warren," I said, "what will keep you from being the suspect right off the bat?"

"Nothing, I'm afraid. That's why I'll have to be careful and make sure the evidence is well placed in their apartment."

"But someone's going to see you leave her bedroom, or something. There are too many ways you could get caught."

He turned to me and stroked my hair, stared into my eyes.

"My love. It's a risk I'm going to have to take." He kissed me and lay back on the pillows.

If he got caught . . . If he got caught, he'd go to prison, and I'd lose him. And I'd go back to cleaning toilets. We'd both basically lose everything. That's when I knew. My stomach rolled and I almost felt like I would throw up.

"You can't be there," I said to the ceiling. "You can't do it."

"Why?"

"Why? You're going to be the main suspect, the jilted husband. Who has more of a motive than you? Too many ways to get you."

"That's why we've been palling up for the past months— everyone in this building has seen us. That, plus there will be too many people at the party. I know how these Christmas parties go. They are tipsy affairs. Anyone who's not drinking tends to slip out early. And Elizabeth always gets so nervous when she entertains that she starts drinking early, and after a few hours she's well in her cups." He smoothed my hair, petting it. "And again, no one's even going to know she's been—"

"Murdered." I breathed out heavily but with conviction. My stomach rolled over again. I said, "I've gotta do it."

"My love, no."

This was going to happen one way or another. And I couldn't bear to lose him. "I just see bad things."

"You're not going to lose me," he said, reading my mind.

"I know. That's why *I'm* going to do it."

"Roxanne."

"It's the safest way. And like you said, no one will know what happened. And why would *I* do it—risk my life? For what?"

He leaned back, stared at the ceiling, exhaled. "I don't know, Roxanne."

"You're going to be suspect number one. You need a rock-solid alibi. You can't be there. You need to be at work—you'll work late that night."

We were in this together.

I wore a black glittery jacket over a red dress—a jacket I'd bought because it had pockets. I heard lively conversations through the door to 8G—the party was in full swing. I felt for the goods, the roofies ground to powder in capsules, several, though we should only need one. In my left pocket a small prescription bottle Warren had filled with the pink salt, twenty grams. I'd done obsessive Google searches and knew this was triple what I'd need, but Warren told me to bring extra in case.

"Welcome, Roxanne," Rod said as he opened the door. He wore a burgundy velvet jacket over a green shirt, with a paisley ascot. He had festive house shoes with reindeer on them and red-and-white-striped socks. I felt hyperalert. "But where's Warren?" he asked.

"Stuck at the office, I'm afraid. He'll try to be here, he said."

"What a shame. Well, welcome. I don't need to tell you where to put your coat since you don't have one!"

"You're just an elevator ride away."

"Well if it isn't the Stubens," Rod said, to a couple who'd arrived at the open door. "Welcome." As they were removing their coats, Rod said, "Jim, Gina, this is Roxanne."

Both raised their eyebrows. "So *you're* the new girl," said Gina.

"I guess you could say that."

Rod said, "Jim, just toss those on the bed in the guest room down the hall to the left."

Gina threaded her arm through mine and said, "I want to hear everything about you," directing us toward the bar.

The penthouse was huge and gorgeous, vast living room with a marble fireplace. *I* could see living here. One of the guests, I think it was a guest, sat at a baby grand piano, playing carols. Or perhaps he'd been hired. There seemed to be a fleet of women in black dresses with white aprons passing hors d'oeuvres. Two bartenders stood behind a bar set up in the den.

"Scotch and soda and a glass of white," Gina said.

"I'll have a glass of white," I said, glad for something to calm my nerves.

Gina said, "I went to high school with Warren forever ago." She spotted her husband. "Don't move, let me give this to Jim and I'll be right back."

When she wasn't right back, I did a little exploring. The place was huge. I counted four bedrooms, one a huge master bedroom with a king-size bed facing the biggest flat-screen TV I'd seen. A bay window. A huge bath with his-and-hers sinks. The kitchen was small but packed with people along with kitchen staff. The whole place and the people, it all smelled like money to me. The kind of money people had had forever and took for granted as their due.

I'd arrived at six thirty, an hour after the invitation time. I planned to wait for forty-five minutes. I'd already said hello to Elizabeth, who wore a svelte black dress, a rope of pearls around her neck, diamonds dangling from her ears. We had exchanged air kisses, the way I imagined wealthy people do. I didn't speak much to her as a number of people introduced themselves to me—the curiosity in a room filled with people who all knew Warren.

At seven fifteen I slipped into a bathroom to collect myself before I latched onto Elizabeth. I would tell her I'm shy. I'd ask to get us both a glass of wine. All evening she'd had a glass of wine in her hand.

"You're a dear," she said, when I asked if I could get her a fresh glass. "But I'm ready for a cocktail. Something festive!" This was going to be easy, I thought immediately. I'd been worried whether the Rohypnol would be visible in white wine.

"A Negroni?" I asked.

"Per-fect," she said.

I ordered two Negronis, took them to a bay window, and pretended to look out at the snow while I emptied a capsule of crushed Rohypnol into one glass. "Left is right and right is wrong," I whispered, worried I'd hand off the wrong one. Just to make sure I didn't, I left my Negroni there.

"You're a love, Roxy. But where's yours?"

"Silly me, I must have left it at the bar."

"I thought you'd never get here," I said, throwing my arms around Warren when he entered the apartment a little after nine p.m that night. He kissed me and went straight to the window in the dining room that looked out on the semicircular drive and entryway to the building.

"Any activity?" I asked.

"No," he said.

He made us both Manhattans and we sat in our den. We whispered, even though no one could be listening. I'd done it and I gave him the blow-by-blow. How I'd got her the drink, how it took about thirty minutes to take effect.

"I could see her wobbling," I said, remembering every second clearly. "When she dropped a bacon-wrapped water chestnut on the floor and couldn't focus on it to pick it up, I moved in. Rod had seen it too, and rushed to help. I panicked a bit—what if he stayed with her?—but there was nothing I could do. He took the glass out of her hand and set it on a nearby table. This was happening fast. I held her other arm. He said, 'Goddamnit, Elizabeth.' Rod was clearly angry. But not surprised. Does this happen often, Warren?"

Warren shook his head and said, "More than I can count."

"We got her to the bedroom," I went on. "No one seemed to take much notice. Rod said, 'Just throw her on the goddamn bed.' He was disgusted. So I said, 'I'll get her into bed and sit with her a minute. I want to make sure she doesn't throw up.' And Rod said, 'More than she deserves.' She was dead weight by now, but I got her shoes off and put her under the covers on her back. I found a glass in the bathroom for water. And I just opened her mouth and poured in half the pink salt, more than half. She gagged a bit but I poured a little water into her mouth a few times to make sure it all went down. Then I turned her on her side, facing away from the door so it would look like she was just asleep. And I left."

"And?"

"Just like you told me: I put the bag of pink salt and the baggie of roofies in the spice cupboard to the left of the stove."

"Good girl," he said. "Let me fix you another."

"Please," I said, finally beginning to calm down. Finally feeling the full weight of what had happened.

I remember taking a big gulp of the drink he brought me, and thinking, *This is really going to work.*

And that's the last thing I remember. Because those roofies work incredibly quickly.

I've had a long, long time to think about this, with only dim memories of the police pounding on the apartment door with a warrant. My throbbing head and confusion.

Warren had given me a roofie or two because he needed me out cold so that Rod could collect the roofies and extra pink salt, where he knew to find them, and bring them to Warren. Warren left them out on my bedside table in plain view. The police also confiscated my laptop, and a Google search history, along with the poison, did me in.

The coroner had suspected nitrite poisoning because the body had turned a light shade of blue. Rohypnol was in her blood. Obviously, I'd googled this as well.

They'd tried and tried to find evidence of Warren being an accomplice because of the story I told, but he was well-oiled and nothing stuck. I was a fucking gold-digging house cleaner. Now he and Rod had the life they wanted—they had just needed someone to take care of the one last obstacle—the wife. And I did exactly that.

There are only two of us, women on death row here in Marysville, Ohio. We have our own little compound, a drafty old shithouse, and not a whole lot to do. When I'm not angry, I even find a little perverse admiration for those two and their plan.

What a fool I was. I'd been the mark all along.

Warren didn't even smoke.

LENNY, BUT NOT CORKY

BY DANIEL STASHOWER

Coventry

Are you Rachel? Yes, it's me. Anders. Please, sit down. Watch out for the guitar. I—no, that's fine. Sure, I get that a lot. I look different. But seriously, what were you expecting? I'm seventy-three. You thought I'd still have the long hair? The Grateful Dead vibe? No, don't apologize. That's why I brought the guitar—so you'd recognize me. Yeah, I know. Those were different times.

It's fine, I'm glad to do it. Actually, no. *Glad* is the wrong word. I really don't talk to reporters about Alex. About what happened. Not anymore. I've been burned too many times. And with the big anniversary rolling around, well, I have reporters jumping out at me from all sides.

Yes, I understand, of course. It's a sad occasion, the anniversary. Somber. Fifty years this month. But this whole thing, boiling up to the surface again after all this time. It's uncomfortable for me. Seriously uncomfortable. Yeah, you mentioned that—sure. A chance to clear up some misconceptions. I get that. But if you'll forgive me, reporters always say that. *A chance to tell my side of the story*—but somehow it never comes out that way. So I said no to the *Plain Dealer*. I said no to *Cleveland Magazine*. But when you called? From *Scene*? Cleveland's answer to *Rolling Stone*? Couldn't say no. I admit, I was surprised to get your message. I didn't think anyone remembered me over there.

But I used to have a following, especially when I was with the Buckeye Biscuit Band. I opened for Todd Rundgren once. Before you were born, of course. I still have the clippings. But nobody ever wants to talk about that. They just want to talk about Alex. About his disappearance. About Smitty Eagleton. I get that, of course. Hell, I'm the guy who *wrote* the song. I'm the "Turtle Park Troubadour," right? I wrote "The Ballad of Alex Berger"! But nobody remembers anymore. I was huge. Well, in this town, at least. I was going places—opening for Todd Rundgren! At the Agora! So, this—talking to *Scene*—it's like coming home. Finally getting my due, you know? Finally. Sorry. I'm rambling. Reelin' in the years.

Doobie Brothers? Never mind.

Do you want to order something first? I'm getting the Uncle Russ—falafel and veggies, mostly. It's my wife's favorite. Was. Was my wife's favorite. Sorry, I think I'm a little nervous. No, you're right, we should get started.

I'll tell you everything I remember, but don't expect too much. Like I said to you on the phone, after all this time I can't even be sure—I'm not sure what's real and what's just stuck in my head. Hammered in there by repetition. And my memory isn't all that great. Actually, no. My memory is pretty sharp for things that happened fifty years ago. Like, this place—just for instance. This place is a Coventry landmark. I remember it before it was Tommy's. It was just a drugstore with a lunch counter—Ace Drug. Then it was the Fine Arts Confectionary for a while. *Best Milkshake East of the Mississippi*. That's what they said. Useless information. My head is like a weird carnival claw machine grabbing for useless information. I remember every detail about Dennis Kucinich, for all the good that does me. I remember the glory days of WIXY 1260 and WMMS: Home of the Buzzard. Just don't ask me the title of the book I'm reading. Sorry, yes. What? Dennis Kucinich. He used to be the *mayor*? He ran for president. His wife had hair like Farrah.

Farrah Fawcett. You don't—? She was this—forget it. It doesn't matter. So, where do you—

Oh, come on. Do we have to go straight to that? Somehow it always comes back to that *goddamn book and it never*— sorry! Oh, hell, I'm sorry. I didn't mean to—I didn't mean to knock that over. Did any of it get on you? The water? Let me get you—you're okay?

Okay. If we must. Yes, of course, I've read the book. *A Vanishing at Turtle Park* by the great and all-knowing Julian Story. I mean, seriously. It came out almost forty years ago, and we're still talking about it? It was a terrific piece of writing, I'll give you that. But he—a lot of it wasn't fair. It felt—what's the word for it? Reductive, yes. It felt reductive. Heavily biased, anyway. I spent hours talking to that guy. Right where you're sitting now, in fact. And when the book comes out, he's turned me into a clueless pothead who could have prevented the tragedy! *The human equivalent of stale bong water*—that's what he called me. *How disagreeably ironic that Anders Mack chose that afternoon for his tiff with the lovely Clara. If, as usual, our feckless stoner had been slumped in his beanbag chair, wreathed in mellow vapor, the boy might have been saved.* That's a crock of shit. Like there would have been anything at all unusual about seeing Alex get into that van. Assuming that's even what happened! We don't even know—not for sure. And Clara and I didn't have beanbag chairs. Shit, we didn't even have a bed. We slept on a mattress on the floor. Please don't write that down. Please take that out—stale bong water. That's been hanging over me all this time. This is supposed to be a chance to clear up misconceptions, right? To correct the record? I want that cleared up.

Okay, yes. Thank you. *Thank* you. Here's my side, because I actually knew Alex. I really knew him. I used to see him every day. Every afternoon at about half past three, starting his paper route. The *Press*. The afternoon paper. Out of business now. Alex would ride up on his Sting-Ray bike, with his canvas carrier bag strung across the handlebars. At the corner of Lancashire and Euclid Heights, alongside the park. He usually got there right as the van pulled up. Big blue van with *Cleveland Press* painted on the side. You couldn't miss it. With the glowing lighthouse, you know? Scripps Howard. You've seen photos. The driver was Smitty Eagleton, of course. I mean, I didn't know his name at the time. We all know it now, but nobody knew it then. He was just the guy in the van. He always wore this long, baggy sweater, like Starsky and Hutch. He looked a little like Starsky. You'd see the van parked at that corner all the time, while Smitty popped into Arabica for a coffee.

They had a sort of rhythm. Alex usually got to the corner just as the van pulled up. Smitty would throw out the bundle of newspapers, and Alex would cut the twine with his knife, a big blue Boy Scout knife, and then he'd start folding the papers into bundles. I liked to watch him do it. He took pride in it. Sometimes he'd shoot the breeze with Smitty, especially during baseball season. There was nothing sinister in it, just baseball talk. At least from what I could hear. Which wasn't much. I'd catch a name every once in a while. Frank Robinson. Boog Powell. Just baseball players, you know?

In the book, it all sounded dark and foreboding. Like somehow we were all too blissed out to register this tragedy unfolding under our noses. But it wasn't like that. People got the wrong idea about Coventry—about Coventry Village. Julian Story called it the sad, redheaded stepchild of Haight-Ashbury. Clinging to the fading ghost of sixties counterculture, while calamity waited in the wings. That's what he said. That guy couldn't blow his nose without a sneer. Look, you're a very young woman. You wouldn't know how special Coventry was back then. Hippies and flower children standing in line at the Dobama Theater. Hell's Angels helping old ladies across the street. Harvey Pekar sitting on a stoop, scowling. It was a nice place then. A community. It still is, to me.

And Clara and I were right at the center of it. Because we lived in the building on the corner, right alongside Turtle Park. When we were out front, we could see everybody coming and going. Clara and I were there in the afternoons, most of the time. Wreathed in mellow vapor. I worked an early shift at Pick-N-Pay, stocking shelves before they opened. Clara had a counter job at High Tide Rock Bottom, part time, so sometimes I'd be alone, just noodling on my guitar, watching Alex fold his newspapers. But then Clara started working nights at Winking Lizard—no, Turkey Ridge, or Pepper Ridge, whatever it was called then—and she'd be there with me. We loved that building. You've probably seen it. Dark brick? We were on the ground floor. The place had these great stone balconies at the front, they looked like ramparts on a castle, where you shoot arrows. Crenellations? We'd sit out there for hours. I'd play the old Gibson, Clara would sing. We had big dreams, we were going to be the Ian and Sylvia of Cleveland.

You haven't? Seriously? Well, you should look them up when you get back to the office. Anyway, we loved that balcony. Clara used to say that you could set a clock by when Alex started folding his papers. By the whistling at three thirty in the afternoon. Always whistling. He was a sweet kid. Young man, actually. That's another misconception we ought to clear up. Everyone thinks of him as a kid, because of that Boy Scout picture on the cover of the book. He was a young man when we knew him. Nineteen, I think. He was still into the whole scouting thing, though. What do they call the older ones? Eagle Scout? Or Assistant Scout Master or something? Whatever, they could barely find a uniform to fit him anymore. His legs stuck out of the shorts like—

Yes, okay. The fire. Not my favorite part, but okay. Yes, that's how Clara and I really got to know him. That damn fire. Julian Story called it Alex's "fiery baptism" or some such. The truth is, it wasn't that big a deal. We had this mangy terrier, Rufus. He knocked one of Clara's macramé shawls onto an incense burner. She always had some macramé project going, she kept trying to sell them at Glass Llama. Anyway, this shawl fell onto the burner and it gave off a terrible stench. It never felt right to say this, especially after what happened, but it wasn't a fire at all, just some oily smoke. Clara wasn't there, and I'd fallen asleep in the back room—yeah, I know, it plays into the whole stoner-slacker thing, but I'm telling you, that's really not fair. My shift started at six a.m. in those days, and we'd been at the C-Saw the night before, for an open-mic night. I was tired. Sue me.

Anyway, before you know it, there's this big, honking cloud of macramé smoke and incense wafting out through the open windows, just as Alex pedals up on his Sting-Ray. In his scout uniform, as fate would have it. Merit badges everywhere. Anyway, Alex smells the smoke, and he hears Rufus barking. He bangs on the door but I don't hear him, so he climbs in through a window and wakes me up. Shakes me by the shoulder, as if there were flames nipping at his heels. Urgent. "Get up, sir!" *Sir*, he calls me. I was only four years older than him. "There's a fire, sir!" Again, there was no fire, but he was caught up in the drama of the thing. Had his neck-erchief wrapped around his nose, like he got a merit badge in fire rescue or something. And he drags me out of bed and out onto the sidewalk. By this time some of the neighbors are milling around outside and one of them has a camera. I'm sure you've seen the picture—it made the papers. It's in the book. Alex looks all shiny and resolute in his scout uniform, with the dog in his arms, licking his face. And I'm off to the side, rumpled and bleary, just out of bed at three thirty in the afternoon. That's how it all started. The origin story. Clean-cut American boy on one side. Stale bong water on the other. The caption on the photo said it all: *Goofus and Gallant*.

No, please, don't use that. Goofus and Gallant. Please, take that out. If you have to drag all this up again, at least let me tell it my way, like you said. No, I'm not bitter, but seriously, there was no fiery baptism. It was just smoke. Not to take anything away from Alex. But I kind of feel, you know, people ought to know. Clara's macramé got scorched. That's about it. Not to speak ill of—you know. Not to take anything away from Alex. He was a great kid.

And that's where it started. Alex Berger, the hero of Tur-tle Park. Everybody called him that. Which is pretty funny, if you think about it. After the book came out, people seemed to imagine that Turtle Park was this big, sprawling animal preserve, crawling with happy turtles. Frolicking turtles. It's just a little corner playpark with a concrete climbing turtle. I guess it's a plastic turtle now.

But Alex was prince of Coventry after that. People called out his name wherever he went. The hippies flashed peace signs, the bikers raised the old power fist salute. Every day it was like a parade when he biked down the street. Mrs. Mitchell gave him free popsicles, Pee Wee tuned up his bike. He took it in stride, always tried to look bashful and play it off. But you could tell he loved it. Who could blame him?

And Clara and I, that's how we all got to be close. Alex got to be like a kid brother. Every day he'd pull up at the corner and Clara would sort of call out to him. Like it was the start of a song: "Hey, hero! Who are you gonna save today?" And he'd make a joke out of it. He'd do, like, a Carnac routine. You remember Carnac the Magnificent? Johnny Carson?

It doesn't matter. The point is he made a little comedy thing out of it. He'd close his eyes and hold up a folded newspaper to his forehead, like he was using his psychic powers to read a hidden message. He'd say, "Cher. But not Sonny." Or he'd say, "Garfunkel. But not Simon." It didn't really make sense, you know? But we loved it. It was funny, pretending to be Carnac. Clara ate it up. So it became our thing, every day. "Hey, hero! Who are you gonna save today?" "Tennille. But not the Captain. Marie. But not Donny." He'd have one for us every day.

Clever, yes. A clever guy. And Clara just melted. She'd swing herself over the balcony rail and give him a big hug. "Oh, Alex," she'd say, "what am I going to do with you?" She'd ruffle his hair or kiss his cheek, and Alex, man, he'd go beet red. Vibrant red. Eyes like saucers. He was nuts about her, so he wouldn't let it drop. "Big Chuck. But not Hoolihan. Lenny. But not Corky." Afterward, his mother found a whole notebook full of them, in his desk at home—these little quips. He must have spent hours thinking them up. Just to impress Clara. That broke my heart.

Take your time. Uh-huh. Yes, Lenny. But not Corky. Because of the deli—Corky & Lenny's. The other one? Hooli-han and Big Chuck, they showed movies on Friday nights. You're too young. Horror movies on Channel 61. Or maybe Channel 5. No, wait, I was right the first time, it was Chan-nel 61. It's funny how your mind—

Puppy love? No, I wouldn't say that. It wasn't puppy love. He wasn't a puppy. He was a young man and he had it bad. I get it—I absolutely do. Every day, the same thing. "Oh, Alex, what am I going to do with you?" She had that effect on every man she met. Even the vampire, Julian Story. He was under her thrall. "An ethereal goddess," he called her. "Cloaked in regrets."

Me? Do I have regrets, you mean? Yeah. Of course. I re-gret everything about that terrible day. I know what they say. What everybody says. If I'd seen him get into Smitty's van, it might have changed things. We might have started looking sooner. Or maybe it wouldn't have happened at all. What if. I know. You think I haven't been over that a thousand times? In my head? A million times. But we don't *know* that. We don't know that it would have made any difference. Not for sure.

You probably know how it played out as well as I do. Clara and I were fighting, yes. No, I don't remember what it was about. Money, probably. You'd have to ask her. I was at Turkey Ridge, cooling off. But we were right out in front with the search parties. The whole neighborhood came together, looking for Alex. The whole city, really. The police, the fire department—everybody. There was a candlelight vigil, and Clara and I were out front with his parents. We handed out leaflets for hours and hours. We put up posters. Trying to bring him home safe through the power of positive thinking. Naive, maybe, but sincere.

And then, well, you know. They found Alex's cap in the back of the van. Covered with blood. Alex's blood. It was—it got dark. The newspapers, the local TV crews—they just went after that guy. No, I'm not defending him—of course not—but I've never seen a media lynch mob like that, before or since. The names they called him. The Press Pervert. The Pain Dealer. The Scripps Coward. The *Press* came down harder than anyone, because Smitty worked for them. I guess they were worried about guilt by association.

Me? Do I think he did it? I wouldn't have said so at first. He just didn't—I wouldn't have thought he had it in him. But now? You know that Smitty died in Lucasville, right? In prison? There was a lot of talk at the time that he confessed, but they couldn't get him to say where he'd buried the body. So what do I know? Your guess is as good as mine.

No. Look, we've been over this. I didn't see either of them that day. I didn't see Alex, I didn't see Smitty. Everyone always asks me that. The answer hasn't changed in fifty years. I didn't see him get into the van. I wish I had, but I just wasn't there.

Nope. Haven't spoken to Clara in years. Decades.

Did she blame me? No, absolutely not. And neither did his parents, which says a lot. They used to invite me over to the house for Thanksgiving, for years afterward. So, no. They didn't blame me for anything. They knew. That meant a lot to me. Good people, Geoff and Helen.

Look, I don't know what else to tell you. I'm amazed I remember even that much after fifty years. Yes. Uh-huh. I know, half a century. I can't believe it. But listen. Rachel? Aren't we going to talk about the song?

My song. I mean, I don't want to seem disrespectful or anything—that's the last thing I'd want—but on the phone,

I kind of had the impression . . . you know. We agreed that the point here was to tell my side. My perspective. The song is my side of the story. The Turtle Park Troubadour, right?

It just sort of happened by chance, you know? It was about three weeks afterward, and I was sitting out on the balcony. It was three thirty in the afternoon. That was the time when Alex always showed up, regular as clockwork, and I was feeling pretty blue. So I picked up my guitar and I started strumming. And it just came to me. *"He was our hero, our bright, shining youth, with a baseball cap and a beautiful truth."* Just like that. And it kept flowing out of me. *"Our city is weeping, 'neath a lighthouse of blue, missing our brother, so noble and true . . ."*

Sometimes it just happens like that. I played it at Arabica that night, and this girl, she started crying. Just sobbing. That's how it started. The Turtle Park Troubadour, singing "The Ballad of Alex Berger." They played it on WMMS for a while. There's a YouTube of me performing at the C-Saw. When I opened for Todd Rundgren, I added a special verse. The crowd loved it. *"Something was lost, something deep inside, but we'll always remember, that sad, sad day—the day the turtle cried."*

I mean, there's your title. For your article. "The Day the Turtle Cried." It's perfect. You know what? I brought my guitar— let me play it for you. No, nobody will mind, this place has always catered to free spirits.

I'm sure—what do you mean? Of course it's *relevant!* Of course it's *germane!* Why have we been talking this whole time otherwise? You told me—look, the song *is* my story, like I said. And you don't even want to hear it? Would you have even mentioned it if I hadn't brought it up?

Sure, Rachel. Fine. I understand entirely. No, I'm not

sulking. Don't be ridiculous. That's fine. If you have what you need, sure. No, don't bother—I can pay for my own sandwich, but thank you. All right, if you insist, but—sure. Thank you. No, anyway, yep. Good meeting you too.

Uh-huh. Yes.

Actually, no. No, fuck this.

Listen, just listen to me for a minute. Just listen to me. Sit. Sit back down. I don't—this is what I want to tell you. It's important. This is what I want to tell you.

Please don't tell me to calm down. I'm perfectly calm. I'm wreathed in mellow, that's what I am. Uh-huh. Listen, I'm sorry to tell you this, but Alex was a piece of shit. Okay? Once and for all. Let's clear up some misconceptions, once and for all. You want to know about Alex Berger, the hero of Turtle Park? I will fucking tell you all about the precious, sainted Alex Berger. No, I'm calm. I'm perfectly calm. But I can't do the genial-stoner thing anymore. I can't do stale bong water. I'm seventy-three years old. Screw it. Screw it all.

So you know where I was that day? That disagreeably ironic day when I wasn't slumped in my beanbag chair or whatever? I was with Alex Berger, the walking monkey-turd. He said he needed to talk to me. Man to man, he said. He insisted on taking a nature hike. Way the fuck out in the woods. Middle of nowhere, as it turns out.

And you know what he says to me? When he finally spits it out? He says, *She's a grown woman, and a free spirit. She can make her own choices.* You believe that? And then he just stares at me. Clara, she wasn't there. Just him and me. The Boy Scout and the clueless stoner. Miles from nowhere. And he's just staring at me. Like, what do you have to say to that, Goofus?

You know what I said? *Oh, Alex, I said, what am I going to do with you?*

What am I going to do with you? Yes. You can. You absolutely can.

Leave that in.

Acknowledgments

The literary community of Greater Cleveland made this anthology possible. We are especially grateful to Sarah Willis for putting the two of us in touch and helping us to pull together a diverse group of writers from this storied city. We would also like to thank Harriett Logan, the owner of the independent bookstore Loganberry Books, for being a patron of local writers and an advocate for *Cleveland Noir*. Her decades-long passion for promoting local writers through weekly programming and summer festivals provided an easy network for finding the writers within this anthology.

We are grateful to Johnny Temple, publisher of Akashic Books, for recognizing the dark power of Cleveland. Thank you for adding this city to the Noir Series family.

Miesha thanks Raymond Headen, her husband of twenty years who always answers attentively when she asks, "Hey, what do you think of this?" And Michael thanks his wife, Ann Hood, who was the first to say to him several years ago, "You've got to do a *Cleveland Noir*!" We're glad she did.

ABOUT THE CONTRIBUTORS

Dunia Hantucb

J.D. BELCHER is an author, screenwriter, and journalist. He serves as editor for the online news publication the *Yellow Party News* and the daily devotional website Ephod and Breastplate. His debut memoir, *Hades' Melody*, was long-listed for the 2019 Sante Fe Writers Project literary awards. *The Inescapable Consequence*, his first novel, was released by Yorkshire Publishing in the spring of 2021.

Beowulf Sheehan

JILL BIALOSKY is the author of five volumes of poetry, including *Asylum: A Personal, Historical, Natural Inquiry in 103 Lyric Sections*, a finalist for the National Jewish Book Award; four novels including *The Deceptions*; and two memoirs, including the *New York Times* best-selling *History of a Suicide: My Sister's Unfinished Life*. Her poems and essays have appeared in the *New Yorker*, the *Atlantic Monthly*, *Harper's*, the *Kenyon Review*, the *Paris Review*, and *Best American Poetry*.

Gerry Conrad

SAM CONRAD is a Native American writer who launched his professional journalism career in 1994 as a student at Cuyahoga Community College in Parma, Ohio. After Tri-C's public safety targeted him for hanging around Black women, Sam founded the *Naked-I*, one of the first web-based underground student newspapers exposing institutional racism, corruption, and homophobia. At Tri-C, Sam met and later married Gerry, artist, novelist, and woman of his dreams. The couple lives in Cleveland's historic backwoods whitopia of Berea.

Mary Rynes

ANGELA CROOK is the author of three novels: *Fat Chance*, *Chasing Navah*, and *Maria's Song*. She is a mother from Cleveland who loves writing dark thrillers that often involve the exploration of the inner workings of family relationships.

Christina Ramirez

ALEX DiFRANCESCO is the author of *Psychopomps*, *All City*, and *Transmutation*. They are a 2022 recipient of the Ohio Arts Council Individual Excellence Award, and the first transgender award finalist in over eighty years of the Ohioana Book Awards.

Joel Hauserman

MARY GRIMM has had two books published, *Left to Themselves* and *Stealing Time*. Her stories have appeared in the *New Yorker*, *Antioch Review*, and *Mississippi Review*, and her flash fiction in places like *Helen*, *Berlin Fiction Kitchen*, and *Tiferet*. Currently, she is working on a historical novel set in 1930s Cleveland.

Raymond Headen

MIESHA WILSON HEADEN is a writer and bookseller who has been awarded the Best Minority Issues Reporting from the Society of Professional Journalists, a BINC Bookseller Activist Award, and a CLE AKR Informed Communities Award from the Cleveland Foundation. She is the former mayor of Richmond Heights, Ohio, where she lives with her husband and two sons. She graduated from Columbia University and Ursuline College. She is a preacher's kid.

Amber Ford

PAULA MCLAIN is the *New York Times* best-selling author of five novels, including *The Paris Wife*, *Circling the Sun*, and *When the Stars Go Dark*. Her work has appeared in *Town & Country*, *Real Simple*, *O, the Oprah Magazine*, the *Guardian*, the *New York Times*, and elsewhere. McLain is also the author of the memoir *Like Family: Growing Up in Other People's Houses* and two collections of poetry. She lives in Cleveland with her family.

Winston McSwain

DANA MCSWAIN is the author of *Roseneath*, winner of four national independent press awards. Her previous books include *Winter's Gambit* and *Winter's Roulette*, a cult-favorite action-adventure series set in the Rust Belt. Her essays have been published in *Belt Magazine* and the *Atherton Review*. A native of Cleveland and a graduate of Kent State University, she divides her time between the Midwest and New England.

Paul Simon

SUSAN PETRONE is the author of the forthcoming *The Swinging Santoros*, as well as *The Heebie-Jeebie Girl*, *The Super Ladies*, *Throw Like a Woman*, and *A Body at Rest*. She received an Ohio Arts Council Individual Excellence Award, and her writing has appeared in such diverse publications as *Glimmer Train*, ESPN.com, *Belt Magazine*, and *Whiskey Island*. She is also one of the cofounders and former president of Literary Cleveland.

D.M. PULLEY is a best-selling author who previously worked as a professional engineer rehabbing historic structures and conducting forensic investigations of building failures. Her survey of a vacant building in Cleveland inspired her debut novel *The Dead Key*, winner of the 2014 Amazon Breakthrough Novel Award. Pulley has published three more novels inspired by true crime in the Rust Belt, including *No One's Home*, named Best of Horror 2019 by *Suspense Magazine*.

MICHAEL RUHLMAN has written or coauthored more than twenty-five books of nonfiction, fiction, memoir, and cookbooks, including *Boys Themselves* and *Walk on Water*, both set in Cleveland. A native of Shaker Heights, he lives in Providence, Rhode Island, and New York City with his wife, the writer Ann Hood.

DANIEL STASHOWER, who was born and raised in Cleveland Heights, is a *New York Times* best-selling author and a three-time Edgar Award winner. His most recent books are *American Demon: Eliot Ness and the Hunt for America's Jack the Ripper* and *The Hour of Peril: The Secret Plot to Murder Lincoln Before the Civil War*. He still roots for the Browns and the Guardians.

THRITY UMRIGAR is the author of nine novels, including the best sellers *The Space Between Us* and *Honor*, a Reese Book Club pick. Her books have been published in over fifteen countries. She is the recipient of a Nieman Fellowship to Harvard, the winner of the Cleveland Arts Prize, and was a finalist for the PEN Beyond Margins Award. She is a Distinguished University Professor of English at Case Western Reserve University and lives in Cleveland Heights.

ABBY L. VANDIVER, also writing as Abby Collette and Cade Bentley, is a hybrid author who has penned more than thirty books and short stories. She has hit both the *Wall Street Journal* and *USA Today* best seller lists. Vandiver spends her time writing cozy mysteries and women's fiction, as well as facilitating writing workshops at local libraries and hanging out with her grandchildren, each of whom are her favorite.